WINTERS IN THE SOUTH

ALSO BY NORBERT GSTREIN IN ENGLISH TRANSLATION

The English Years (2002)

Norbert Gstrein

WINTERS IN THE SOUTH

Translated from the German by
Anthea Bell and Julian Evans

MACLEHOSE PRESS
QUERCUS · LONDON

First published in the German language as *Die Winter im Süden*
by Carl Hanser Verlag, Munich, 2008

First published in Great Britain in 2012 by MacLehose Press

This paperback edition published in 2013 by

MacLehose Press
an imprint of Quercus
55 Baker Street
7th Floor, South Block
London W1U 8EW

This translation was supported by the
Austrian Federal Ministry of Education, Arts and Culture.

A CIP catalogue record for this book is available
from the British Library.

ISBN (MMP) 978 1 84916 404 7
ISBN (Ebook) 978 1 84916 984 4

2 4 6 8 10 9 7 5 3

Designed and typeset in Roos by Patty Rennie
Printed and bound in Great Britain by Clays Ltd, St Ives plc

it's war, baby, it's war

ONE

IT WAS IN HER SECOND MONTH IN ZAGREB, IN THE AUTUMN the war began, that the news reached Marija that made her life foreign to her for ever. She had not set eyes on her father for more than forty-five years, and had thought he was dead for almost as long, so at first she did not react at all to the advertisement that the neighbours had left outside her door and that couldn't possibly have been from him. There had to be some misunderstanding, even though when the same thing happened again a few days later she hurried down the street, bought a copy of the paper at a kiosk, unfolded it in the teeth of the wind and, with a feeling that objects around her were losing their outlines and blurring shapelessly together, stared at the not especially large boxed ad in the middle of the "Miscellaneous" section. A week went by in which she did nothing but felt constantly uneasy, and then, when she finally came across a further advertisement as she sat one day at a café table, tears immediately welled in her eyes and she looked around to see if people at the other tables were watching her and had noticed what was happening.

In December the previous year she had had her fiftieth birthday, she and her husband had spent a week on Elba, and his clumsy attentions there had made her suspect that, once again, he had a lover. In the middle of the day she sat with him, swaddled in a rug in the sun, and looking out at the sea didn't know whether she could smell it in the damp air, or see it far away, at the line of the horizon, or hear it, but as hard as she tried not to give in to gloomy calculations about her birthday, it was at that exact moment, as time stood still, that she realised how fast it was flying by. Although at home they had slept separately for a long time, for these few days they took a double room, and in the end she decided to reward his efforts to show her how much he still desired her, bent over him, with quick motions of her hand brought to life the dormant worm she had once summoned, like a snake charmer, by the tenderest nicknames and only stopped working on him when, twitching limply, he came heedlessly in her mouth. Then that was behind her, accompanied by the lengthy apologies he always made when he didn't manage to come out of her in time, and the next morning he didn't know how to face her, surreptitiously casting her the despairing glances of the boarding-school boy he had once been and joking with the young Englishwomen who shared the breakfast room at their hotel, while she sat beside him in silence and thought, how does his longing compare with mine, I could be just like those overdressed ladies and set out to explore the island in a large and completely unseasonable hat too, I could be a girl again for a day.

Back in Vienna she let a few months go by before she finally asked him, more in flattery than because she really wanted to know, why he was out so often in the evenings. It would not have been a catastrophe for her to hear the truth, and she observed him as he went round and round in circles, until he had gone so far in his evasions that he was ready to hear anything she might say in reply. Then she asked him if he had anything against her going to Zagreb for a while, and was annoyed with herself for weakening as soon as she had said it.

"It would only be for the summer."

This made it sound as though she herself had significant reservations, so that when he asked her to explain why she wanted to go and all she could do was hold out both hands, it was easy for him to disconcert her.

"All these years you haven't given the place a thought and now, of all times, when it looks as though everything is going to go up in flames at any moment, you suddenly have to go back there," he said. "Why don't you go and stand in front of a loaded cannon and hope it won't go off instead?"

He could hardly have been clearer in his dismissal, but, as was his way, as soon as he had worked himself up he started to backtrack.

"It's such a crazy idea, you must know that."

And thereafter he confined himself to repeating what he had said in the weeks before she asked her question, whenever she bent his ear about what the papers were saying about the "powder keg" that the Balkans were again turning out to be, and got carried away into predicting that it wouldn't stop at the few bodies there had been already.

"You're not starting on that again."

More than two decades before, their first night together, she had told him she had been born in Yugoslavia, and she remained sensitive to his remarks about it. Back then, down in his basement room in Vienna's Second District, he had bombarded her with questions, and all she had managed to do was either invent answers or counter his assault with the most trivial things she could think of, to cut short his rapture at the thought that she came from a country where Communism had won the day, to cut short his fiery speeches, between kisses, in praise of the Great Leader and of the true comrades in the struggle. In those days he had seen her as a trophy, as someone he could boast about to the friends he met each day in a rehearsal room, hired for the purpose, that they filled with smoke as they planned worldwide revolution, and he had given her the sense of being a precious ornament in a double sense, both as a Mediterranean beauty (in the connoisseurs' sense) and as a splendid political example, and perhaps it had been the beginning of all their misunderstandings that she had been reluctant to tell him that none of it was as simple as that and afraid of losing him instantly by confiding any more details about herself and her origins and thereby shattering his dreams.

In the event she had only taken her protest as far as his bed, in fact strictly speaking not to his bed but to the bare floor of his hideaway behind the Praterstern, which had no bed, and she was still full of shame when she remembered how it had come about, at the end of an evening when he had angrily told her off for being a reactionary goose because she had been incautious enough to laugh at one of his slogans. Little as she liked to admit it, she knew she had only gone home with him that evening because he had humiliated her and because she wanted to make everything right again, to crawl to him on her hands and knees if she had to, to erase everything in the world that spoke against her and to show that she could be a good and teachable student. As was fitting for a real revolutionary, all he had possessed was a hammock, which under their combined weight had detached itself from its brackets and collapsed, and she still remembered how grazed her back had been from falling onto the floorboards – a fall that had left weals as though she had been whipped till the skin had broken – and the total darkness in which it had all happened because he didn't pay his bills and so the power had been cut off weeks before, a darkness like one of those nights in wartime.

She also remembered how, the morning after, he had walked over to a pair of cabin trunks stacked one on top of the other, his only pieces of furniture, and from the lower one had taken out a copy of a pamphlet he had written, a leaflet entitled "The Partisan Disease as Opportunity", of which he had had a few hundred copies printed and which, after a half-hearted attempt to hand them out on the street, he had given away individually to his friends. She was probably the only friend far and wide who did not yet possess a copy, but as he took out his pen to sign it for her she knew before he started writing what the inscription would say, having so often seen his two variants on the bookshelves of other students. To the men he always wrote "Comrade", to the women a macho "For that night", as if they had all somehow passed indiscriminately through the darkness and mustiness of his little room and only then qualified for the higher form of dedication, and then what an honour, she had got both, there was a "*compañera*" because he happened to be in his South American phase, with an added exclamation mark that could only be described as phallic, and then "*para esta noche*", authenticated with name and date and only lacking an official stamp, a five-pointed star, a clenched fist or some other menacing-looking symbol.

In the excitement of those days he hadn't been able to get enough of her Yugoslavia stories, and the mixture of weariness and irritability with which he now tried to silence her had not developed in him until later.

"You're going to have to break free from all this eventually," he said. "Your childhood dreamland doesn't exist any more and probably never did."

The same old story.

"Your life is here."

She felt like prompting him.

"I've never said it wasn't," she said instead, wishing she possessed as little doubt as he did. "That would be something else, wouldn't it?"

The summer semester was over, and with it the Serbo-Croat course that Marija taught at the university, and until the autumn she was free and could treat it all as a kind of holiday, despite the fact that those who were in their right minds and could afford it were getting out of Zagreb rather than going there. She had no specific ideas about the trip, but her decision had become so fixed in her mind that any expressed reason as to why she should expose herself to its risks would have struck her as a pretext behind which lay some other quite different motive. It was her homeland, and the news reports of the first confrontations had pitched her straight back into faraway thoughts, to what would have happened if she had not had to go away as a child, back during the war, with her mother to Vienna – still apparently safe – because the fighting between partisans had the whole country in tumult and they could no longer stay at home on the Croatian coast. She had always asked herself whether, if she had not left then, life would still have felt so contingent or whether it would have seemed more essential, more difficult perhaps than in the paradise she had preserved in her memory but more essential, and now she was making up for lost time.

When, a few days before leaving, she saw two of her girlfriends at their regular weekly meeting at the Hotel Regina, she told them she had nothing to complain about because she neither wanted to make it too easy for herself nor to let it look as if they might be right when they asked if it had anything to do with her husband. It would have been far too easy for her to explain her restlessness that way, and she did her best to disappoint their expectations, until they too became uncertain of what was required of them, whether they were supposed to sympathise with her or envy her, so instead they resorted to enthusiastic promises to come and visit her, after all, they could do with a little adventure too, and it couldn't all be as bad there as people said. And the artificiality of their forced humour, the gaiety with which they ordered a bottle of champagne in the middle of the afternoon and drank it with the little *Punsch* cakes they had brought, grated on Marija so much that for the first time, considering them both with irritation, she herself began to have qualms. Their kisses as they parted, their hugs no longer just a formality, their promises to write, all too clearly demonstrated that she was not simply getting ready to travel a few hundred kilometres, a few hours in the car, but was setting off to go far further than she had imagined until that moment.

After her first announcement her husband said nothing more, as though he hoped the whole thing would blow over if he didn't make a fuss about it. In the morning he hurried to the editorial offices of his paper and in the evening came back maybe a little earlier than usual, and if there was anything striking or unusual about that it was how quiet he was, as though he had told all the colleagues and friends who were otherwise used to calling him up at all hours, to give him a bit of air. He went to the cinema with her, something he hadn't done for years, and when he took her out for a meal avoided his usual watering holes, the city-centre restaurants where he was well known, and at home for the first time in a long time she found him lying reading on the sofa that had moved with them every time they moved house and on which, when occasionally she came home late from work, she had used to lie down beside him without a word, nestling close to him, hardly daring to breathe, just wanting him to put his arm round her and go on reading. She had often grumbled that there were too many people around them, yet none of them was really close, and quite suddenly he seemed to take her yearning to heart and to notice her desire not just to sail on into the apparently inevitable, not to confuse his closed journalistic world for the one they had once dreamed of, while he turned into a bar-room celebrity increasingly fawned-on from all sides, complacent and hectoring in his articles in a way that he would have found contemptible earlier on in his career.

Their daughter had spent a year studying in Philadelphia and shortly before the start of her summer vacation had said that she wanted to stay on another few weeks and look for a job there, and it was a conversation about her, or more precisely its opening question, that showed Marija that her husband was not, after all, simply accepting everything.

"Do you miss the child?"

She had hardly nodded before she regretted it, realising simultaneously that it had been an eternity since he had last called Lorena that.

"The child?"

Incredulously she repeated it.

Their daughter was twenty-three, and of course something had changed since she had left home, but this was going too far.

"You surely don't think that has something to do with it, do you?"

The same evening Marija walked into the living room just as he was putting the phone down, and although she hadn't caught any of the conversation she knew that he had been talking to Lorena. In the last few months she had always been the one who stayed in contact with their daughter, he had either asked her to send his love or exchanged a few words with Lorena at the end of their conversation, more out of a sense of duty than because he really seemed to need to, and now he looked as if he had been caught out. So, as he hovered around her, Marija could have told him to his face that she knew exactly why he was showing this sudden interest, and in fact confirmation came almost immediately when Lorena called back and came straight to the point.

"Is everything alright?"

She and Marija had spoken only a few days before, but perhaps that was indeed the question. To Marija it sounded oddly like a phrase translated from another language, and she had to take care not to answer in English. Instead she laughed, which sounded a bit forced in its cheerfulness, and the moment passed.

"Of course."

It was her own fault that she said nothing more and didn't even attempt to hide her displeasure, but she did not expect her daughter's directness.

"Are you going to leave Father?"

The pause started to seem significant before she could even hesitate over her answer, and she glanced at her husband as though he himself had confronted her with it, and waited. He stood still, with an expression on his face that told her neither whether he guessed what they were talking about nor whether the question had, perhaps, originally come from him. As long as she had known him, he had always been the one who had everything under control, and she would have given a great deal not to have this sudden glimpse of his vulnerability, of a look in his eyes with something submissive about it, an abjectness in his posture as, without a word, she handed him the receiver and watched him try to extricate himself with a few meaningless remarks.

"Don't worry," he said finally, though he had stopped speaking into the phone. "The world won't end without you."

The following day he took Marija into the city and did some shopping for her, as if she were a schoolgirl going to camp, and although he seemed both wound up and obsessive she made no objection to being fitted out from head to toe. It was his way of dealing with the situation, of making it all into a game, and as she watched him accumulating one item after another she gave up pointing out that she was not off on an expedition to the desert or one of the polar regions and, realising that his only concern was that he had to have a hand in everything, let his bizarre offensive wash over her. Starting with a fountain pen that was chosen to match a leather-bound notebook and letter-paper on which she knew she would never write a line, progressing via the reversible raincoat (camouflage colours, turquoise on the inside) and stout boots to the gas stove that he took carefully down from the shelf, by the end all she lacked was a sola topi and a machete to turn her into a caricature of a traveller, and unfortunately that wasn't the end of it, for her laughter at his insistence on deciding everything for her died away in the chemist's when she saw him about to place a ten-pack of condoms on the belt at the checkout.

"You never know," he said, and simultaneously appeared to realise how inappropriate his remark was. "Well, better to be safe than sorry, anyway."

She recognised his sometimes contrived way of making jokes and took the pack from him, as if he were a child who had grabbed the sort of toy he ought not to play with.

"No-one's going to rape me."

She replaced the pack casually on the shelf.

"Anyhow, if it did come to that," she added, "the person is hardly likely to be a gentleman with exquisite manners. At least I really rather doubt that he would take such niceties into consideration."

She pressed home her point by following it with her dirtiest laugh, at which he looked at her so imploringly that she instantly regretted it, and even two days later when they were in the car on their way to Zagreb she had to restrain herself from apologising. Despite her strenuous objections he had insisted on driving her all the way there, and so she sat beside him in silence, looked out at the landscape rolling past, and waited for everything to be different on the other side of the border, but apart from a military convoy that they overtook at one point and the fact that besides them hardly anyone else was on the road, the land spread out motionless ahead of them, quivering at the horizon in the flickering heat of August. If it hadn't been for the newspapers she bought the first time they stopped, everything might have been the same as it had been in previous years, they might even have been going on holiday to the south together, although, after their first visit to Yugoslavia, when he had jealously watched her talking to the local boys on the beach in their own language, he had never gone there with her again.

"There's nothing happening," she said, as if trying to stiffen her resolve in the face of the threatening reports she had read, but it just came out sounding forlorn. "I mean, look."

She gestured at the countryside with both hands.

"Can *you* see anything?"

Her gesture took in their field of vision.

"Does it look like a country in a state of war?"

Although she knew the answer, she asked him then why he had never written about it himself, when he didn't avoid any other subjects in his work. A few weeks earlier she had discovered that he was also selling pieces under a pseudonym to his paper's nearest rival, writing there in a polemical and inflammatory style about subjects that under his own name he sometimes considered at such length they threatened to dissolve into thin air, and now he was afraid of her sarcastic comments. She no longer commented on his articles themselves, as she had always done in his early days of working at the paper, and these days she either didn't read his column, which appeared three times a week, or she forgot what it was about almost as soon as she had finished reading. It was a defence mechanism she had gradually built up, and she couldn't help making him aware of it.

"You don't know which side's the right one, do you?" she said scornfully. "Does it matter anyway if you're going to end up on both sides?"

She thought she had come to terms with that side of his character a long time ago, yet she now felt furious at his eternal indecision, his striving to please as many people as possible.

"So long as what you write is brilliantly phrased."

She had never said so much before today.

"So long as it's always for, against, and you having your clever say," she said, feeling uncomfortable herself. "So long as it's you, you, you."

He ducked as if she had tried to hit him and then slowly raised his head, as if emerging cautiously from cover but expecting a worse assault at any moment.

"You still haven't forgiven me."

He had slipped back into his tone of weary resignation, after having at first energetically parried her questions with protests, as though he had only let himself in for this double game for her sake. She remembered how he had tried to justify himself and could still only wonder at his self-righteousness. It had been pitiful, each sentence more oppressive than the last, particularly as he had given her the impression of having fallen for his own trick and not noticed that he was deceiving himself.

"Where do you think the money comes from?"

He had said it again and again, interrupting himself repeatedly in his enumeration of their expenses, and those being only the ones he could immediately think of, starting with the two city apartments, the house in the Waldviertel, the annual skiing holiday at Lech, and Lorena's escapades, as he put it, her stay in America and the car she had been given for passing her final school exams, not to mention the small change a lady such as their daughter required for her everyday needs.

"We get it all for free, I suppose."

Mean and contemptible as this was, it was still preferable to the way he was talking now, as if she were imminently about to pass judgement on him, to be followed by his penance, after which everything would be alright again. At heart she couldn't even say if she really was repelled by his ability to say one thing here, another there, for the longer she contemplated it, the more his manoeuvring seemed justified to her. She only had to think back to how, sometimes, as soon as the evening edition came out, the phone would start ringing and at home in his easy chair, which with his penchant for obvious plays on words he called his "cheesy air", and with closed eyes he accepted his callers' tributes, addressing them as "my dear chap" or "my dear girl" in a voice she never heard at any other time, and she had had enough of his cosy world once and for all. Then she was glad that he could deal with the whole story in a few paragraphs a couple of days later by assuming his other role and pouring out a full-blown saloon-bar diatribe aimed at those same sycophants and their obsequiousness, supposedly protected by his *nom de guerre*, a name that had a Jewish ring to it, for the shady business at hand he couldn't have chosen one that was more offensive.

They had never set out to be like this, but now was not the moment to say so, and she stopped herself, took the hand he had laid on the gear lever in both of hers and pressed and kneaded his fingers to suppress her own unease, her urge to go on driving him into a corner, the rising desperation that overcame her whenever she thought how pointless it all was, until she finally shook her head.

"It's O.K.," she said. "It's O.K."

It was her usual absolution.

"There's nothing to forgive."

Of course it had once been different, and she could have reminded him of the time when he spent his days in discussions with his friends that lasted for hours and his nights out on the streets, she could have told him how often she had waited for him until he finally came to her in bed in the grey light of dawn, snuggling up to her wordlessly, as if he were glad to have a day's delay and then one more, no need to put any of his grandly announced plans into practice, instead to go on waiting for the right moment in the hope that it would never come. It now seemed utterly impossible to her that then she had actually believed his commando unit to be more than a fantasy, that some day they would strike, he and the few crazies he had gathered around him, that his "unit" was more than the sum of the few pranks that they dressed up in undigested rubbish from the books they read, that every public urination was an act of resistance, a gesture of solidarity with the oppressed of the earth, a protest against poverty and exploitation, a silent howl against that empire of evil, America. Very little of it had got further than the warm-up stage, at most there had been a few slogans painted on walls, shop windows broken here and there, with belligerently worded warnings or flyers that prematurely claimed responsibility for actions they had yet to be accused of, all of it belonging, more or less, to the folklore of those years and no big deal, and she reminded herself that whatever heroic acts he had made up later, the only action they really had to their credit was when they had gone around the city plucking the tri-pointed stars from the bonnets of Mercedes and replanting them in the flowerbeds on the Karlsplatz, an act that had at least got them onto the front pages. But it was in the distant past now, like his tight-lipped answers each time she had wanted more details when he stayed out late, fobbing her off with a kiss and telling her that criticism and self-criticism were the same thing, then from one moment to the next behaving so affectionately that he seemed to have suddenly become aware of what he stood to lose if things got serious, and on one occasion distancing himself to the point of dismissing his group's agenda as total nonsense and on another attacking it repeatedly by mocking its jargon, repeating the same phrase over and over again until he ran out of steam and had to stop.

"I fuck you because I'm a chauvinist, imperialist pig, and I'm an imperialist, chauvinist pig because I fuck you."

All of this occurred to her again as she suddenly wished that he would call her his girl, the way he sometimes did when he wanted to cut short a conversation with her. She had asked him a thousand times to spare her such drivel, but right now she would have liked to be able to slip back into the childish ritual he expected after his words, to lean her head on his shoulder, close her eyes and think of nothing, and it disappointed her that this time he said nothing. She pretended to be asleep, and from time to time he put his hand on her thigh, and she felt how the imprint of his fingers, damp and warm, spread across her bare skin beneath her dress. Each time she waited to see if he was going to say something, a hint, the slightest movement, even some last-ditch attempt to stop her leaving, but he stared fixedly ahead and seemed to have forgotten her, in spite of his touch.

If he had had his way, they would have gone to the best hotel in the city, but she insisted and they checked into a modest boarding house near Britanski Square. Although he was annoyed he tried not to let it show, but he couldn't help himself and as soon as he had put their cases down he started to turn over the bed sheets with ostentatious distaste. She knew he thought it was childish of her to choose to do without comforts, and left him alone to sulk until he had finally calmed down. He showered at length as she sat on the room's only chair and leafed through her guidebook, and later, when he was getting ready to go out, she couldn't tell whether she felt queasy because she was moved, or whether it was the slight nausea she had been prone to for some time whenever she saw how after each irritation he went on just as before, a capacity she had loved so much in him at first and that over the years had increasingly given her the creeps. Then there he was there in front of her in his best suit, and she had to laugh, because among the room's basic furnishings his distinguished exterior made him look like a gangster oblivious to his crooked appearance or a businessman who hadn't wandered into such a sleazy place inadvertently but was deliberately there for the purpose of transacting some not totally legal business.

It was getting dark when they went out, but the air was no cooler, and there was hardly any life on the streets, a few men in uniform, otherwise nothing remarkable, apart from the many flags on the buildings and perhaps the greater number of beggars, and when she thought about it later she did wonder whether it was because of him that she had seen so little that evening. The mere fact of his presence seemed to rule out the worst evils as unthinkable, for now, with his stately manner, his way of walking that of a gentleman on his way to the opera or the theatre, or rather of such a gentleman at other times and probably other places, he radiated a certainty that his rank protected him, and that was something she could never have pictured about him in his youth. However uncertain he had been as a young man, for a long time now he had seemed confident of his ability to show the devil the door, of having a voice at the moment of death that would preserve him one last time from all ills, never mind whether it was confidence in his own merit or just an arrogance that had become second nature to him over the years, while her idea of herself had been that anything might happen to her, at any time, and she would have no right even to complain. It upset her to think how completely helpless that made him in any situation where his authority didn't count, where he couldn't even run away but would just stand there, the way he did at home in their apartment when other people had monopolised the lift and he had had to walk up three floors, a well-fed, pampered, giant baby with rosy pink cheeks gasping incredulously for air as he leaned against the wall, until she took his case from him and he was able to light himself a cigarette and smoke it greedily there in the hall. With all his airs and graces he had never seemed stranger to her than he did in this city, as it awaited catastrophe but for now still spread intact in every direction, and it made his presence there seem intolerably temporary, like that of a sea creature thrown onto the shore by an unexpected wave and not yet realising that the water had already receded.

Most restaurants were already closed, but they finally found one still open, and he sat down and ate with such demonstrative relish that she could hardly touch anything herself and simply watched him. They hadn't walked around for more than an hour looking for somewhere to eat, but to judge by the way he was tucking in it might have been half the night in pitch blackness, and it took Marija some time to forget how bad-temperedly he had let her drag him from street to street. He seemed to take everything personally, to see the locked doors and darkened windows as just as much a lack of respect as the super-attentive manner of the waiters now was the correct way to receive him, and it made her look around her to see whether all eyes were fixed on him, but no-one was taking any notice of them. He was a well-known figure only in Vienna, in specific and familiar conditions, and although that was to be expected she enjoyed recalling how at home even his former fellow students and activists would sometimes greet him with a little bow which to her was recognisably ironic, and on every other occasion went out of their way to demonstrate their respect and deference.

As she thought about this Marija noticed a woman at the next table, who reminded her of a T.V. evening news presenter whose bed he had shared for a few weeks in the passionate days of the past, and she remembered the absurd fuss he still made about her. For instance, she had thought for a long time that he must be joking, but no, he would claim in all seriousness that his ex-lover was winking at him personally from the T.V. screen whenever, in interviewing a politician, she would savage them so thoroughly that they ended up entangled in their own tautologies, contradictions and awkwardness, and yet his admiration of her had nothing to do with real life but was simply his way of continuing to devour her with gourmet relish even after all these years, Marija suddenly realised, watching his pitiful drooling as he sprawled on the sofa with a second bottle of his favourite wine, glued to the on-screen drama and wallowing in a moral approval that reached its highest expression with an encouraging "It's war, baby, it's war" every minute or so before he finally slumped in exhaustion.

Whenever she observed this, she had the feeling that something had gone wrong not just with her life but with the world, and that it had gone wrong long ago, and she felt the same way when they found themselves out in the street after midnight and he suddenly behaved as if he were being mugged, although nothing had happened except that two men had approached them to ask the time. He immediately took out his wallet and offered it to them, but they were already retreating with their hands in the air, and Marija saw that he was finding it hard to regain his composure, shifting from foot to foot, running fingers through his hair, repeatedly patting down his jacket and seemingly slow to comprehend what was happening. Baffled he watched the men walk away, and when he had recovered enough to start cursing the inadequate street lighting for making it impossible to see their faces she knew he felt embarrassed, and that it would be better not to say a word.

Back at the boarding house she finally realised how drunk he was. Despite the late hour he rang for the owner and demanded a second room, and as she was to keep the car also asked for the time of the early train to Vienna, as if he had forgotten that he hadn't intended to leave until the afternoon. Key in hand, he climbed the stairs, and although he didn't once look to see if she was following him, outside his door he turned abruptly to her and hugged her.

"We have a good life," he said, after clearing his throat a couple of times. "We're happy, aren't we?"

With that all the strength seemed to go out of him, and as he let himself slump suddenly she stood there, his whole weight leaning on her shoulders, and watched her hands making empty movements above his head. Finally she ran her fingers mechanically through his hair and peered into the half-darkness of the corridor, as if rescue must come from that quarter. This lasted no more than a few seconds, but she started to be afraid that he had fallen asleep standing up because his breathing close to her ear was so peaceful and he took his time before he spoke again.

"Were you ever sorry you married me?"

That was all she needed now, for him to launch into one of his melancholy moods, demanding protestations of fidelity from her in the middle of the night, and here of all places, so she spoke to him as if she were speaking to a child.

"Albert, oh Albert."

She could hardly get the words out.

"Why are you doing it?"

She hadn't thought he would answer her, but when he did, and repeated what she had said parrot fashion, she didn't know if he was babbling drunkenly or not.

"I'm not doing anything," he then said, taking care to speak clearly and not to sound whiny. "You're the one who's doing it."

He stepped away from her, as if he were ready to engage in a new battle, unlocked the door of his room and disappeared. For a while she carried on standing outside the door. At any other time she would have been sure that he was just waiting for her to knock, and she would have gone in and asked humbly if she could sleep with him, and would have done it whether she felt she was in the wrong or not, but this time she walked away and did not have to force herself to go. She was just getting undressed when he came to collect his things, and as he picked up the shirt and trousers he had dropped on the floor that evening and stuffed them into his bag, went into the bathroom and threw his toilet things into his sponge-bag with a clatter, she did not move from where she stood. Then he came back, walked around the bed and looked at her, and she thought that if he had been in any fit state to do it he would have hit her.

"I know, you're expecting an apology from me," she said, surprised to hear the derision in her voice. "But I'm not going to apologise."

It followed the same pattern each time, and although he suddenly seemed perfectly sober, not just his cold gaze but the scornfully turned-down corners of his mouth made her remember how quarrels with him had ended all these years. The attitude he was now assuming was one he took refuge in whenever he felt driven into a corner or had run out of arguments, and it was meant to show her how, above and beyond every difference of opinion they might have, there was a much deeper reason for everything, and that reason was her and where she came from. Whether he openly said so or not, after his aggressiveness towards her in the first weeks of their relationship she knew that whenever he treated her so dismissively it was because in his eyes nothing better could be expected from her, and now, as he still stared at her as if he were about to attack her, she remembered how her girlfriends had said more than once that beside him she didn't look like his wife but like a much younger lover, and in a sudden change of mood she decided to make the most of the situation.

"What can a poor little Yugoslavian girl do to make the great master forgive her one last time and stop being so sad?"

His expression did not change, and she laughed, but he remained deadly serious, looking at her even more stonily for showing how pathetically he was behaving.

"If you're trying to say I made you into that poor Yugoslavian girl," he said, "there's something important you've forgotten. Do you remember what you once said to me, right at the beginning?"

She didn't know what he meant.

"I said a lot of things."

He nodded almost imperceptibly.

"You said a lot of things."

He seemed unable to decide whether to say what he had been thinking, but his hesitation only lasted a moment, in reality he had no choice any longer.

"'If one day you don't love me anymore, then kill me,'" he said. "What kind of an impression of you do you think that gave me?"

He had her where he wanted her again and yet, with everything now said between them, he couldn't help wanting to have the last cutting word.

"Perhaps there wasn't ever very much there for me to conquer, and you're kidding yourself if you think there was."

He had already gone by the time she found herself sobbing on the bed, and when she stopped she spent a sleepless night and in the morning stood at the window and watched him as, bag in hand, he walked out of the house, strode round the nearest corner and disappeared without a backward glance. She had hoped that he would come to say goodbye but, seeing him leave like that, she realised that he had made his decision and that, if he still thought of her at all, it was probably with exactly the same feeling as in Vienna, as if she were an object to be taken for granted, something not really worth thinking about very much. There was no sign from his appearance that he had gone through any kind of crisis in the night, he was wearing black jeans and a loose black polo shirt that covered his hips, a baseball cap on his head – she didn't know where he had got that from – and from having been a person alarmingly close to collapse he had reverted to being a composed middle-aged man whom she would have found difficult to place at first glance, if he happened to cross her path unexpectedly. In any case he seemed to have sorted everything out for himself, and she could not shrug off the impression that once again she had under-estimated his capacity for survival, for the world in which he would soon find himself was undoubtedly his world, in which he had long ago stopped responding with a self-deprecatory joke and instead shrugged his shoulders in feigned resignation whenever he was described as the figure of the century in Austrian journalism, the nation's conscience, a flower among the great and good in the land, and heaven knows what else.

TWO

THE BUSINESS WITH THE DAUGHTER CAME AS A SURPRISE TO Ludwig, and when months earlier he had entered the old man's service at the end of a two-week stay in Argentina, it had been the decision of a moment and there had been nothing to suggest that it would finish with an assignment that under normal circumstances he would have refused. He had spent the Christmas break in Buenos Aires, sweating and immobile in the damp heat, in a hotel in the Avenida Callao, not far from the congress building, and was already on his way to the airport and intending to be back at home in Vienna the next day, when he suddenly told the taxi driver to turn around, asked the hotel reception to store his bags, and caught the first train from Retiro out to San Isidro. He had met the old man's wife the previous week at Villa Gesell, a seaside resort north of Mar del Plata, but when she had urged him to call in and see them at the end of his holiday, because her husband was looking for someone like him, he hadn't pursued the invitation seriously, feeling that Claudia would remain what she had been, a chance encounter on the beach whom he had spent a pleasant evening with.

In fact the young woman in her sari-like dress and gold bangles; and what she had told him about her apparently much older husband as they sat behind the glass windbreak looking out to sea, had been a strange combination, her painted lips in their glossy red lipstick jarring with the melancholy black and white of a story whose origins lay half a century in the past. Despite the way she made herself up, everything about Claudia had seemed girlish, her bare shoulders white and vulnerable against the falling dusk, and it had seemed odd for her to be talking about a time when she had not even been born, so Ludwig had paid less attention to what she said than to how she sucked her lemonade through a straw in one go, apparently lost in thought, then went on sucking noisily around the bottom of the glass before ordering another one. The way she drank lemonade had riveted him, but her husband's destiny had aroused no interest at all, all that Yugoslavian stuff she had wanted to explain about where he came from, whether he was a Serb or, as it turned out, a Croat, and all that Ludwig had really remembered was that since the old man's emigration at the end of the war nearly fifty years before, which in reality had been more of a flight than an emigration, he had not seen his country again because he would instantly have been put on trial and either executed or spent the rest of his life behind bars.

"Now the situation there has got him planning a visit, for the first time," Claudia had said. "But if he's right, it means there's also going to be fighting."

Ludwig had failed to see what the connection was, but he thought of Claudia's precise manner as he headed for the address she had given him, close to the cathedral, where the land sloped down to the river mouth and he could sense the presence of the huge expanse of water, even though he couldn't see it. She had appeared to have simple explanations for everything, and as he walked up to the house he remembered the mixture of hostility and derision in her voice when she uttered the word "Communists", and remembered it again as he tried in vain to peer over the two-metre wall around the property and could see only its roof and the crown of a lemon tree, laden with fruit. There was a surveillance camera over the entrance, but by the time he realised it was there he had already rung the bell and his thoughts about what he might be letting himself in for came too late, there were already dogs barking inside the house and he had probably been under observation for some time too from the neighbouring houses in the otherwise apparently deserted cobbled street.

The old man was alone, Claudia and their twin daughters had gone into town with the nanny, and few words were exchanged. He dismissed Ludwig's attempt to introduce himself, as if he already knew all about him, turned his back as soon as he had opened the gate, and walked ahead of him back into the house, a cold cigar stub at the corner of his mouth and the two German shepherd dogs Claudia had mentioned held fast by their collars. His face was browned by the sun, contrasting sharply with his razor-cut white hair, his eyes were a clear blue, his gaze penetrating with a trace of irony, and Ludwig could not have said why, but he had not expected a man of such stature, muscled and sturdy despite his height, looking as though he were lying in wait, ready to pounce at any moment, had not expected this undiminished charisma in a man of seventy, this aura of superior but reticent self-confidence, this startling mental clarity of a man of principle who from time to time might have had to deal with the forces of the law, from both sides. He was barefoot, and his feet briefly left damp footprints on the stone flags of the hall floor, their soft padding covered by the slow smacking slaps of the German shepherds' paws. He wore a black shirt loose over a pair of light trousers, so far unbuttoned that its collar had slipped and Ludwig saw, just beneath where the hairline met the back of his neck, the tattoo, four letters that blurred together on the scarred skin. They formed the word "*križ*", and as he was still wondering whether he could ask about it the old man seemed to guess that his eyes were fixed on the letters.

"Don't let that cattle brand bother you," he said, without turning to face him. "You don't need to know, but if it sets your mind at rest it means 'cross'."

This little performance, on top of his mannered first appearance, spelt out how aware he was of the impression he made, and as the dogs pranced lightly around his legs he carried on with the self-conscious reception by placing Ludwig carefully in an armchair in the living room, in which there stood a Christmas tree sagging with tinsel, angel's-hair decorations and electric candles, before sitting down opposite him. He put a bottle of beer in front of him without asking, took another for himself, and when he spoke softly to his dogs, calling them Capitán and Teniente, names that could hardly have been more telling, it struck Ludwig that his intention was to show him that he didn't care what Ludwig thought of him, and that he did it with a sly glance of satisfaction, a perverse pleasure at arousing suspicion, and possibly a desire to mock him too in the process. After all these years his Spanish still had a distinct Slavic accent, and for Ludwig who had studied the language for a few semesters it was not hard to follow, each word clearly separated from the one before, very different from the usual Argentinian singsong in which he seemed to catch only the recurrent *che* at the beginning of every fourth or fifth phrase, or when there was a pause.

Plainly Claudia had prepared her husband for Ludwig's visit, and he ran through only the most important details, his questions more like confirmations that sought to establish the facts once and for all.

"I hear you're a police officer."

It was a predictable beginning, and he returned to it at the interview's end, though it left Ludwig, being used to quite different reactions to his profession, at a slight loss. Claudia had shown the same keenness: he remembered her joking that he must be able to drive then, and fire a gun, which was all he really needed for this job, and while he had laughed too, he now felt her remark had been rehearsed, for the old man repeated it word for word, this time in all seriousness.

"At least it means you're somebody one can have a sensible conversation with," he said. "That's a rare event among the kind of Austrians who usually come here."

Ludwig had only to see the probing quality of his look, the need to see how far he could go, to know what the old man meant, but he shrugged off the comment.

"You think so?"

He hadn't finished speaking before the old man was waving his arms, looking at him like a man insulted.

"Do I think so?"

Turning to an imaginary audience at his back and shaking his head, he seemed to want the world to agree with him.

"You try telling one of your countrymen that you came here from Europe right after the war," he said. "Then watch his expression, and you'll know what I'm talking about."

He didn't look like a man who needed sympathy, but when Ludwig offered no comment he could not conceal his displeasure. The corners of his mouth turned up in a derogatory expression, a twitch he didn't have entirely under control, as he reached for his beer bottle and threw his head back, letting the liquid flow down his throat without any apparent need to swallow. Then he wiped his lips on the back of his hand and, dropping into a consciously easy, conversational tone to cover up his forceful manner, said, "Did you know that in the Second World War the Argentine military formally appointed the Virgin Mary as a general to their combat forces?"

It was an anecdote he probably repeated to all visitors, though he seemed to enjoy it as if telling it for the first time.

"No, you didn't know," he said, not waiting for an answer. "But if you want to understand anything about the customs here, you need to know that."

This seemed to settle the awkwardness for him. He crossed himself, as a taxi driver might when he passes a church, a sketchy, diffident gesture that might have done as well for Satan as for the Almighty. He had straightened for a moment to do it, and he let himself sink back again, burying his hands in the dogs' coats as they lay right and left of his armchair and slumping as if exhausted, but still relishing his grotesque story, murmuring that the officers responsible for it were damn fine fellows.

"Our heavenly Mother as commander-in-chief."

His mockery was mingled with growing admiration.

"Something the gentlemen in Europe might do well to imitate," he said. "But they'd shit their pants at the mere idea."

He got to his feet and went to the kitchen to fetch more beer, although the smallest sound was enough to make the two dogs, who had got up with their master, come straight back to stare watchfully at Ludwig, who hardly dared move. He had time now to look more closely at two photographs on the mantelpiece that he had asked the old man about when they entered the room. They were of his daughters and, despite the obvious difference, the deckle edge and yellowing black-and-white print of one and the high-gloss colour of the other, Ludwig would not immediately have guessed that half a lifetime had passed between the two pictures, the first of a girl standing alone in the last or penultimate year of the war, the second showing her two half-sisters, also apparently alone, and probably taken some time in the last few months. All three girls had something doll-like about them, he felt, but the truly uncanny thing was how alike they looked, as if in a pair of puzzle pictures, wearing the same white dresses, the same white patent leather shoes, the same white slides in their hair, gravely watchful creatures of a type doomed to extinction, he thought, and imprisoned in a time warp.

He was so immersed in studying the photos that he hardly noticed the old man come back and went on staring at them.

"I see the girls appeal to you," Ludwig heard him say casually behind him. "Do you have children yourself?"

He nodded.

"Why?"

He realised how brusque he sounded.

"I have a daughter."

He would have preferred not to think about her, but straightaway he was forced to remember again how he had called Graz on Christmas Eve and his ex-wife had rebuffed him, saying that his daughter couldn't speak to him and using the word "unscheduled" several times, which he hated most of all. Meanwhile he heard her talking without interruption in her clear voice in the background, and said nothing in answer to his ex-wife's reproaches, concentrating on the child's unselfconscious chatter, oblivious of the situation, that came to his ear now louder, now more softly. He saw his daughter every two weeks, though perhaps less in the last few months, and when the old man asked why he wasn't at home with her during the holidays and couldn't resist, simultaneously, turning on the Christmas tree lights for a few moments, the winking electric candles that hardly glowed at all in the bright noon light seemed to reflect back through the summer heat all the sadness of a life in exile, and Ludwig yearned for the first snow of winter, which had probably fallen at home by now, and for the darkness of winter nights and bright-lit dusk of the weeks around Christmas.

He knew that the question must come of what had brought him to Argentina, but he felt so defenceless that he said nothing, merely nodded as the old man went on with his assumptions.

"You don't look like a tourist."

Since he had arrived in the country, he had waited vainly for a sense of strangeness to descend, a sense of being away from home, but now he found he was no longer ready for it to take hold. He had walked all over Buenos Aires, and might as well have been walking all over any south or east European city, so little out of the ordinary had it seemed to him, but now he suddenly found himself back in the uneasy state of mind he had been in as the plane came in over the wide, milky-brown mouth of the Río de la Plata and the housing blocks that spread for kilometre after kilometre, the flat unpopulated plain visible beyond them, full of expectation, full of anticipation and anxiety, no past and yet perhaps a future. In the face of that immeasurable space and immeasurable time he had felt an undefined pain, and he knew that he was not armed, not armed against longing nor against the dread that the right answer might not find him.

"Does one need a reason to come here?"

The old man seemed to acknowledge this calmly.

"Except that you're unlikely to have decided to do so voluntarily," he said, laughing. "If you did, you'd probably be the first, apart from a few fools who all lived to regret it."

He was still standing next to him, holding the two beer bottles he had opened with his lighter and staring at him with narrowed eyes, as if the bright daylight had dazzled him.

"So what have you run away from?"

He gave the impression that he had a precise idea of the answer and nevertheless wanted to hear it from Ludwig himself, but simultaneously shrank from hearing, because it was always the same sad, the same stale stories.

"Just don't say that it was an unhappy love affair."

Up till this point it had been a game from which Ludwig could easily have extracted himself with a joke, but since he was so far from home he thought he might just as easily try to tell the truth, and he nodded.

"She was a colleague of mine."

Though it was true, it sounded so wrong to him that he hesitated. Then he took the bottle the old man held out to him and waited until he had sat down. He knew that he ran no risk telling him, though when he looked at his shaking hands he doubted that it would all be as simple as he had imagined.

"That's only one half of the story," he said. "The other half is that she died while we were on a joint operation together."

However strictly he tried to confine himself to the facts, in his head the same tangle of images came back, none of them connecting, Nina, the way she abruptly pulled away from him when the call came, in the hotel bedroom, rented by the hour, near the Westbahnhof, the room they had visited repeatedly in those last few weeks when they were on patrol together, the haste with which she flung on her clothes and buckled on her holster, and then only a couple of minutes later lying on the bare asphalt, a pool of blood beneath her body that spread as slowly as it did inexorably. She had once been a sprinter, and not only for that reason had she reached the crime scene before him, but also because he had hung back in order to watch her, had found her so irresistibly beautiful in those moments, her fleet figure in headlong pursuit, the figure who had been lying in his arms moments before and trembling through her whole body, her flying footsteps, her hair bouncing in the light of the street lamps, her effortlessness. He would never forgive himself for those fractions of a second, for delaying, and then it was too late, there was only the silence after the first shot, white and filling the space in a soundless explosion, and he was condemned, for all time, to stand there, helplessly holding in his hand the knickers she had left behind while the other hand raised his pistol and fired it blind.

"I didn't find out till later that he wasn't much more than a boy," he said. "I just saw a blurred figure and didn't have time to think."

He noticed that the old man had moved forward in his armchair, and was perched on the very edge of it. His jaw clenched, he strained in every muscle, as though it were the hardest thing for him not to whisper the words to Ludwig, and without apparently being aware of it, he was nodding, trying to coax him to the point of his story, and then he couldn't restrain himself any longer.

"Do you mean to say you liquidated him?"

He was on his feet again, standing so close that a smell of mothballs and aftershave, of that iron cleanliness of cold showers and laundry soap, rose to Ludwig's nostrils. Liquidated: it was an unusual, ugly word, and he couldn't mistake the relish with which the old man had uttered it, or his avid look, a raw and naked look that Ludwig had not seen in his face before, and he knew it would be difficult to stand up to this man.

"I had no choice," he said, wishing as he spoke that he sounded more self-confident. "I had to shoot."

The old man looked at him sceptically.

"Self-defence?"

There was a crude undertone to his chuckle.

"Tell that to the marines!"

There was something camp in the way he flung one hand up in the air and then clapped it to his mouth in an extravagant gesture, as if stifling something inappropriate that was on the tip of his tongue.

"Did they suspend you from duty?"

Said with an even more triumphant note.

"Say it! Say you shot the boy because you wanted to shoot him, and stop acting as if you were in court," he said, his voice cutting now. "Didn't you love the woman?"

Ludwig did not answer him. He just looked at him and wished himself back at Villa Gesell, where from his hotel room on the eleventh floor he had had a panoramic view up and down the sandy beach that, blurred by the sea spray, for long hours of the day gave him the mounting feeling that nothing in the world existed outside of what he saw, and that even that was in the process of disintegrating when the wind rose just before dusk and everything around him became more and more porous in the swirling sand, eventually including, irresistibly, himself. He had come to Argentina to forget, to get as far away from home as he could, and because it was warm there and he spoke the language moderately, but the old man had only had to ask that one question and it all came back to him, everything that had been more like a bad dream when he had jogged the dunes to the point of exhaustion and afterwards sat for hours on his balcony, looking out to sea until the view made him dizzy. It only needed the smallest thing to bring back Nina's whimpering, the same barely audible rising and falling sound that his daughter had uttered as soon as she was born, notes like the sound of a violin apparently undecided between life and death, sounds that in the days by the Atlantic still plagued him at night when he lay on his bed, staring through the plate glass at the black expanse of water and its crests of foam whipping across the surface like will-o'-the-wisps.

He said finally, helplessly and desperately, that she had still been

alive, and he avoided looking at the old man as he spoke, because
as he said the words he knew they were only words and was
ashamed of them. She had lain unnaturally crumpled, face down on
the ground, her legs stretched out at what looked to him like an
improbable angle to her knees, and he had not uttered a word,
although this time she wouldn't have contradicted him, wouldn't
have called him a pathetic idiot or made fun of him as she so often
had when he couldn't stop talking, with the usual mocking comment that he'd grown to long for, her sometimes lightly spoken,
sometimes merciless "Forget it, Ludwig, give it up, or go and write
a poem!" that always stopped him in his tracks. But her face had
worn exactly the same expression that had so often captivated him,
had had the same childlike softness as in the eternal half-light of
those sanctuaries they had hurriedly found in the last few weeks
and months, the fragility of an early-morning monochrome, before
the world struggled awake and colours returned and yet another
day in the light was assured. The memory hit him hard, and as he
sensed the old man's gaze on him his words got carried away and
he blurted out that he would have preferred to lie down on the
asphalt with her and die by her side.

Then he took out his wallet, and showed the old man the photo
of Nina he had talked her into giving him and carried with him ever
since. He had never liked people who did that kind of thing, but
now he was one of them himself, and he held it out to the old man
as an explanation for everything. It was an unspectacular portrait
that he liked because it showed her with the beginnings of a smile,
and that once after a quarrel he had torn up and then so labori-
ously stuck back together that you could hardly see the fine rips
that criss-crossed her face.

The old man took it in both hands, like a gift, and Ludwig
couldn't say what disturbed him about that, though it was partly

the way he then said that she looked like an angel, an old man's dusty gallantry that was intended to rule out all suggestive meaning and for exactly that reason had something clammy about it. As he gave the photo back the old man told him that his first wife and their daughter had been killed at the end of the war by the Communists, and he not only loaded the word (as Claudia had done) with all his contempt, but in doing so made it clear that he was trying to create a connection, a complicity between them on the basis of similar fates, tenuous as the comparison might be. That was all he said, and Ludwig had no time to question him because immediately afterwards came his offer: five hundred a week, in cash every Saturday, Sundays off, an apartment in the city at his disposal. He offered no clarification as to his duties, except to say that he was planning a return to Croatia and when he went he would very much like to have someone like Ludwig around, which he emphasised by clapping him on the shoulder.

Then he said, as Claudia had done already, and as he would repeat at every opportunity from now on, "There'll be war."

When he saw Ludwig looking at him in bafflement, he urged him not to let it bother him and just to take things as they came.

"It may be a while yet, but it will be enough if you can learn a few words of Croatian by then, and be patient with me," he said. "Insofar as I've understood you correctly, you're under no obligation to go home tomorrow either."

The deal was sealed with a handshake, followed by a sort of initiation, as the old man let the dogs out into the garden and took him around the house. He led him from room to room, and Ludwig could not say why his sense of displacement kept increasing, whether it was because of the unsophisticated pictures on the walls, Argentine and Croatian subjects side by side, enlarged and unframed photographs like those in a travel agency, or the Christmas tree in the summer heat that they kept passing, or whether it was because the old man listed even the simplest items of furniture, like the television set in the living room, not out of pride of ownership, it seemed, but to reassure himself that they existed. In the toilet, conspicuous because it was in German, a hand-embroidered verse hung in which "the gentle rains of May" rhymed with "oh, how fair is our world today", and "the nightingale doth sweetly sing" with "borne on the Soviet Union's wing", and when the old man opened the door and read this doggerel aloud, almost without accent, he hastened to add, unnecessarily, that it was meant to be a joke.

Ludwig followed, sticking like glue. Each time the old man fell silent he had the feeling that he was waiting for him, Ludwig, to confirm that all this was real, that it was a genuine life he led here and not merely a dream, however much ingenuity and imagination it might require to do so, that it was not a poor imitation of life that could dissolve into thin air, a pale, upside-down mirror-image of a world he had fled half a century before. It was the first time the old man had asked Ludwig for anything, let alone absolution, but whenever it was repeated it happened in the same wordless way, with him standing dumbly beside Ludwig, trembling with bated breath for a word of release, and it always brought to mind how, on this first occasion, they had climbed a spiral staircase together to the little girls' room, which had a view of the river's mouth, and how he had looked out for a long time over the broad expanse of water, shimmering today in an iridescent blue, where dozens of sailing boats could be seen and far out a convoy of freighters making their way upstream and beyond that, lost in the vibrating haze, no more than a faint outline suggestion of the Uruguayan shore opposite.

The shooting range in the cellar, which they visited next, struck Ludwig as a complete contrast, pure factuality, as he thought to himself, a long windowless tunnel of a room fitted with a small lockable gun cupboard, three targets on winches, and on one of the side walls a huge picture of a condor, with outspread wings and a wing span of at least two metres. The moment the old man closed the padded door behind them, he heard a subterranean silence take over, and had the sensation of being in an enclosed space that was not just soundproofed but airtight. He had not held a pistol since firing those shots at the Westbahnhof in Vienna, yet each gesture came naturally to him when the old man slipped an Army-issue Ballester-Molina from its soft leather case and held it out to him along with a pair of ear protectors. He unclipped the magazine, replaced it after checking that it was full, and the small click with which it snapped home gave him the same satisfaction it had always done. He ran his forefinger lightly over the oiled metal, gleaming dirty blue in the neon lights, and despite the heat that permeated even down here, it felt as cold as he liked it. He raised the barrel experimentally and, when the old man nodded, started the count-down exactly as he was used to, an automatic voice in his head slowing down, inhaling and exhaling slower and slower until his breathing came almost to a standstill and he had no choice but to squeeze the trigger, or his heart would burst.

What surprised him, however, was not that after all the weeks when he hadn't touched a pistol his concentration, the deadly calm for which his colleagues had envied him, had come straight back, but that the old man acted as if it were the most natural thing in the world to have a shooting range in his cellar, and said not a word about it, indeed said nothing at all until they climbed back up the stairs.

"The way a man handles a gun tells you everything about

him," he said at last. "It's no different from horses and women."

A few moments before, he had winched Ludwig's target towards him, removed it from its clamp and looked at it with an appreciative nod, and now he delivered another of his hackneyed maxims. "Not too forceful, not too hesitant, that's the motto."

Ludwig obliged him by laughing.

"There speaks an expert."

He felt at his waistband the pistol that the old man had positively pressed upon him, and the memory of Nina's look of fragility with her service weapon, despite her height, overcame him so strongly that this conversation seemed even more repellent. The mere thought of the thrill that had gone down his spine each time they unbuckled each other's holsters, for that half-hour or so in their hotel room, instantly gave him goosebumps all over again. It had always felt that they were freeing one another not only of their guns but of everything else that could bring death to them, as though they stood facing each other as immortal and naked as Adam and Eve before the Fall, but he could not and would not tell the old man anything about that.

"You sound like a dancing master," he said instead, to disguise the conversation's uncomfortable effect on him. "It wouldn't get you far with women today."

The old man let this pass, leading him wordlessly back to the living room, and only as Claudia arrived back with the two little girls did he start speaking again.

"You should see the way he shoots," he said, almost as soon as she came into the room. "If he does everything else as well, you'd better watch him."

Judging by the speed of her retort and the withering glance she gave her husband, she was used to this sort of remark.

"Didn't I tell you he had good qualities?"

She looked at Ludwig as if she might devour him whole, and the old man hastily agreed with her.

"Don't worry, I'm not going to steal him from you," he said, and his laughter didn't succeed in concealing his irritation. "After all, you were the one who found him."

A string of similarly insinuating comments followed as Ludwig sat talking to the couple that day. Not only did they discuss him without inhibition in his presence, they also persisted in wanting to compete for him in a game that felt as though it could turn serious at any time, taking turns telling stories about each other so laden with irony that they sometimes sounded deliberately incriminating. He didn't notice it as long as the two little girls were still with them, but as soon as the nanny had taken them up to their room he became aware that the old man and his wife had almost nothing in common, or at least that there seemed to be a his-and-hers version of everything, and from the impression they gave they might easily have been in this house together by accident, a couple who were nervous of strangers and just happened to be visiting themselves.

It began with their telling him how they had met in Bariloche, more than fifteen years before. Usually such private myths bored him, but with these two something else was going on, something about the way they spoke about that city at the foot of the Andes, and for all their derisive remarks the story had charm, the old man camping out right next to the famous Llao Llao hotel with the management's permission, in a one-man bivouac specially imported from Austria and put up in a grassy meadow that was part of the golf course, and in the evenings after he came back from walking in the mountains and swimming in the icy lake, paying court to Claudia in the hotel bar, already well past fifty and married to his second wife while she had just turned twenty-one and started her first proper job as a waitress in that exclusive establishment. Yet it had not taken much to bring them together, he the generous gentle-man, maybe with a touch of the straight-backed military manner but with thoroughly civilian ideas about love, she the Patagonian girl who had no idea about her future except that she wanted to get away, to Buenos Aires if possible or even further afield; and Ludwig could imagine the rest, their walks in the grounds, the little presents, the excursions by car out to the inhospitable pampas, and once on her free weekend, or with time off to keep a hotel guest of such long standing company, right over the Chilean border as far as the Pacific.

Whenever there was a danger of the story getting too romantic it immediately seemed to make them uncomfortable, and they switched back to practicalities and to discussing Ludwig himself with as little inhibition as before. Then the old man launched into one of his utterly unfunny stories, running down his wife as if it were the most natural thing in the world, and it ended in a heated exchange.

"Without me, at the end of the season she'd have had to go back to that slum on the outskirts of the small town she came from," he said. "I took pity on her, rescued her from an incredible mess."

"There are all kinds of slums in this world," she retorted with contempt, and then seemed to think about it for a moment and added that in fact he had been the barbarian and she had civilised him, he had been the laughing stock of the hotel's entire staff for the way he held his knife and fork, took snuff in front of ladies, was simultaneously generous and mean in his provincial fashion, his rounds of drinks always laughably tight-fisted and then suddenly so liberal when only the last lonely ghosts were left lingering at the bar.

"Everyone except me saw what a skirt-chaser he was," she said. "It took me a bit longer, and I ended up learning the hard way."

They sat in silence, glowering at each other from their respective corners like boxers after the first flurry of punches, while Ludwig tried to turn the conversation in a harmless direction.

"I know about that resort," he said. "A friend of mine from the Tyrol was a ski instructor there in the summer months for several years."

He meant it as small talk, the usual nonsense, it's a small world, but then Claudia interrupted saying that she wasn't in the least surprised, and his remark turned into the bell for round two.

"There have always been lots of Germans around there," she went on. "Some came before the war, the rest after it."

She looked at Ludwig.

"Do you understand what I mean?"

He duly nodded, and as she turned to her husband he saw she wouldn't be content until she had landed a few more blows.

"That's why he went there so often," she said, real aggression in her voice. "It was where he felt closest to the good old days."

She suddenly fell silent as the old man called loudly to the dogs and held them by their collar, as he had before. There was no real threat in his gesture, far from it, there was even something absurd about its obvious theatricality, but he succeeded in stemming her flow of words completely. Patting and stroking the two animals, he looked like the leader who had gathered his last loyal supporters around him, and it seemed perfectly in keeping that he should ignore Claudia and talk only to the dogs.

"There now," he repeated to them again and again. "Down, good boys, down."

It was not a real quarrel, the way it had first struck Ludwig, just their forthright manner with one another. He could read in it the whole story of their marriage, the old man's incredulity when faced with Claudia's rebelliousness, her certainty, increasing with the years, that he had gone too far for too long and must now pay for it or keep his mouth shut, and her pride at the fact that that he no longer had power over her or at least wouldn't very soon. The difference in their ages could not have been more visible than in this stand-off, and Ludwig registered that that, if nothing else, was her triumph over her husband, that she would still be alive long after he was dead, and he might perhaps keep trying to fight her, one more time and then again, but there was no avoiding the fact that one day it would all be over.

This impression was emphasised by the way he kept feeling that some unspoken agreement existed between Claudia and himself. On that one evening by the Atlantic he had not really seen what kind of woman she was, the clichéd southern woman with dark complexion and dyed blonde hair, and now he could not fend off the thought that but for her plunging neckline and the unblinking look with which she hid her defeats, she could shed her femininity any time she liked, just as, before going to bed at night, she probably removed her rings and the gold bangles she was wearing on her upper arms again, and at that moment her lipstick and eye shadow, as thick as they were plastered on, would once again seem, like a miracle, a schoolgirl's first stumbling efforts to put on make-up at home. She was very well aware of the effect she had on men, and he wasn't fooling himself, none of it was an accident, it was all part of the image she presented, even the crackling and tinkling of the ice cubes in her lemonade as she stirred it absently with her straw, even her breath coming warmly and huskily the moment she opened her mouth to talk, the fine film of sweat on her upper lip, trembling imperceptibly in the sunlight, the same film of sweat on her arms and calves.

Ludwig was relieved when the old man gave up needling his wife and decided to talk about himself instead until it was time for

Ludwig to go. The facts were few, starting with his arrival at the port of Buenos Aires early in 1948 on the *Cabo Buena Esperanza*, and he didn't seem to know whether to turn it into a success story or just a way of justifying his life. The stages that followed were not spectacular, his first jobs on the two major building sites of the time, the Ezeiza International Airport and the new Buenos Aires district of Evita City, both just going up, followed by his few weeks as a reservist in the president's bodyguard, from which he was dismissed as a result of his affair with a secretary in his office before his first real operation, or the subsequent years in the slaughter-houses; and while he listed them all he showed not the least emotion. That changed, finally, when he talked about starting his own transport company (his shares in which he had long since sold to his partners), and he became positively lively as he talked about the trucks that were like his own children, pointing out several times over that they had all been Mercedes, though made in Argentina and not Germany, and telling Ludwig how he had personally collected each one from the works in Gonzáles Catán and kept it strictly under his own wing for the first thousand kilometres, letting no-one else near it.

There was suddenly no end to his garrulousness, but if he had intended to conceal some emptiness in his account he failed, merely making it all the more visible, as Ludwig could not resist pointing out when he left.

"Now I know almost everything about you," he said. "But you haven't said a word about why you came here."

It was late afternoon now, still hot, and the two of them had come out of the house together. In the silence Ludwig heard a window open above them, and when he looked up he saw the two little girls put their heads out, trying to hear what they were saying. He waved to them, and the old man shooed them away with a sharp gesture and folded his arms dismissively across his chest.

"You can hardly be waiting for some big story from me," he said. "If you want to play detective, I'm afraid I can't help you."

His face bore the wounded expression that Ludwig had noticed in the girls' bedroom. His watery eyes were looking past Ludwig, first to one side of him, then the other. He scrutinised him, as if he had found a way out.

"Why does a man leave home?"

He raised his index finger.

"What does the poet say?"

It was clear from his face how very pleased he was with his inspiration. Now he could not be criticised anymore, and his wholehearted laughter confirmed it. The right tone came naturally.

"To the steadfast only death or exile remains," he said, with a peculiar mixture of pathos and humour. "Shall we leave it at that?"

It was a pointless conversation, and Ludwig wondered whether the old man was playing some mischievous game to neutralise him and keep his mouth shut. If so he succeeded, for Ludwig said nothing more, and by the end of the day, when he had moved into his apartment in the Calle Juncal, not far from the Hospital Alemán, he thought that both alternatives were possible: maybe the old man really had something to hide, or maybe he was just toying with the idea of concealment, to test Ludwig in some way. He had already decided to stay and get a closer look at the situation, but less because the prospect intrigued him than because it was a way for him not to go home for the foreseeable future. Now that Nina was dead, there was nothing waiting for him in Vienna, and he preferred the uncertainty of whatever it was the old man had in mind, and would miss very little back in Austria, except for the visits to Graz every fortnight when he had his daughter and could go with her to the city park or the Schlossberg or, painfully aware that he had nothing to reward her expectant glances, do something else with her and then, late at night, back in Vienna, occasionally pick up a prostitute on the Gürtel in his car, hand her five hundred schillings and hope she would know what to do for him without having to be told.

THREE

IT ONLY TOOK ONE PHONE CALL, AND IN REALITY EVEN THAT wasn't necessary, more a courtesy than anything else, to let his ex-wife know he wouldn't be coming back in the next few weeks, one short conversation, no more, and Ludwig had a new life when he began work at San Isidro the following day, even though at the outset he had no very clear idea of what the work involved. If he had imagined that his employer would give him instructions, he was mistaken, the old man did come out to meet him but just said that he should hold himself in readiness, that was all, not even for what, so it took him some time to develop a sense that it was his presence that was important, some time too to establish a daily routine, beginning with instruction in Croatian alongside the two little girls from a student whose parents were from Yugoslavia and who came to the house specifically for that. Afterwards, despite the midsummer heat in the kitchen, there was the inevitable *dulce de leche* with a cup of cocoa for everyone, which the girls' nanny made so thick that you could stand a spoon up in it, and then the waiting started, till either the old man or Claudia called for him and he accompanied one on his outings on his Vespa, or drove the other to the golf course or tennis court or her appointments with the psychiatrist on Tuesdays and Fridays, near the Plaza Italia next to the Botanical Gardens.

His impressions of his initiation into the household aside, over the first few days there was nothing to suggest that it was not a completely normal family. He might have been a chauffeur, a body-guard, or just someone kept by the family because it was the chic thing to do, and both the existence of a shooting range in the cellar and the old man's insistence on Ludwig's carrying a gun even in the house might have been considered the quirks of an elderly gentle-man, clinging to the image of an incorrigible old warhorse. At least, it was as easy for Ludwig to accept those quirks as it was to accept his other antics, the way he would issue a password in the morning without which no-one could leave or enter the house, some non-sense like "The Angel of the Lord", to which of course one had to respond by adding "Brought glad tidings unto Mary", or the way he called Claudia Caudillo, putting her in the same category as the dogs Capitán and Teniente, or his suggesting lunch at the Café Edelweiss in the Calle Libertad and waiting for a reaction to the name, and when none came pointing to the sign above the door that announced its founding in 1933, as though that alone should shame anyone who harboured suspicious thoughts. They were all childish games, and it visibly pleased the old man when Ludwig went along with them, like the time he told him to wait in the car outside the Café Tortoni and a few moments later suddenly stormed out and ordered him to drive away at once, crouched in his seat, pistol in hand, and looking repeatedly over his shoulder as if they were being pursued, until finally, way out of town on the northbound Panamericana with San Isidro well behind them, he straightened and burst out laughing, asking Ludwig where he thought he was going, it was all a joke, of course there was no-one following them.

Ludwig was bound to build up a picture of an oddball, maybe a bit crazy, a man of wild fancies, extravagant and all too dogmatic in his opinions about Yugoslavia, but harmless, despite his evident state of agitation whenever he repeated that there would be war. He had his own newspapers from which he collected information, yet even though he liked talking about the situation, it seemed to Ludwig very far away and therefore futile to speculate about it in earnest, and he classed it as the leisured occupation of a man with no responsibilities who had little else to think about. If it had not been for his time in the police, Ludwig would have judged his employer a fraud, a man crediting himself with a more interesting life than he really had, and for lack of real experiences keeping everything vague, dropping a hint now and then but immediately denying it if he feared being pinned down to any definite statement.

The way he told his story reminded Ludwig of interrogations he had conducted, for instance, the old man's decision (if it was a conscious decision) to leave out crucial facts while sometimes going into such detail about minor points that his account could equally easily have been either the truth or a lie constructed with excessive precision. He also had a habit of associating his own good or bad fortune with great historical moments or public events, and from them extracting abstruse connections that verged on the outright nonsensical, oracular pronouncements about what Argentina's defeat by Italy on home ground in the first round of the 1978 World Cup, or the sinking of the *General Belgrano* in the 1982 Malvinas War, had meant for his own life. This particular quirk meant that he could say exactly when it had snowed in Buenos Aires in the 1950s, apparently for only the second time in the century, because it was a week later that he had met Violeta, his first Argentinian wife, or that he knew the country's greatest writer, by name at least, because they shared a liking for the Bengal tigers in the zoo, and so, as the old man saw it, he couldn't have been such a bad fellow as some people assumed from the photographs that showed him affecting the attitude of an English gentleman. (Bound up with this was a quotation that he sometimes recited, for no apparent reason, in his poor English, *"Tyger, tyger, burning bright, in the forests of the night,"* though he had no idea where he had found the few lines, yet felt them as a sort of dark invocation that clearly soothed him.)

Ludwig gradually became accustomed to his own role as adjutant. He drove the old man into the city and accompanied him on his weekly visit to the barber, waiting outside and watching him sitting in the chair to be shaved. Afterwards he went on to his appointment with his shoe-shine man, whom he had patronised for more than twenty years and for all that time had probably asked regularly and without much interest about the man's family, and then, when he was in a good mood, either to the Turkish baths in the Hotel Castelar and a concluding Pernod at the bar, or Ludwig followed him around the cafés in the Avenida de Mayo, where he liked to stay in the shade of the plane trees. On Saturday afternoons he always had a special errand, to buy flowers or a box of chocolates, then drove the old man to the Calle Maipú, where his lady friend lived, dropped him outside the house with the tiny red heart above the bell push, and picked him up again when he came out exactly an hour later, looking either like a small boy, eyes shining with pleasure, or morose and silent. Dressing up as he did for these excursions, in a dark suit whose jacket he never took off even on the hottest days, a silk neckscarf that was probably a concession to the gaucho fashion of earlier times, and his inevitable hat, he looked like a caricature of himself and made Ludwig feel that he had been transported back decades and at the same time, unable to decide whether the sight reminded him more of his father or of his grandfather, in some inexplicable way safe and secure in the past.

It was a life full of ritual, that took Ludwig a while to assimilate and some time before he realised that the old man was acting out a role, the role of someone to whom nothing mattered more than the cultivation of his own tragic isolation. He was capable of denying his entire existence in order to do so, of abruptly dismissing Ludwig and propping himself up at a bar on his own as if there were no house at San Isidro, no wife and children, and he would be going back later to a wretched sub-let somewhere in the suburbs. He conducted himself rather like someone dancing a tango, though he fled whenever he caught, from however far away, the sugary notes of a bandoneon and once told Ludwig that he hated nothing so much as that music and the way it made you want to weep, and that he was still ashamed of his addiction to it in his first few years in the country.

He did not, however, mention a song that had apparently been dedicated to him, which Ludwig learnt about only because Claudia told him the story. By her account it was a mawkish piece ironically entitled "The Cold One", written by an acquaintance of his at the time, and she described it as an unbearably pompous tribute, the self-pitying lament of an immigrant bewailing the loss of his happiness, believing that he has lost all that a man with a heart and no brain can lose. Whenever Claudia wanted to annoy her husband all she had to do was hum a few bars of it around the house, or sing the refrain, two lines in English that drove him crazy: *"No more years of hurt, no more need for dreaming."* She had also found that she could go one better just by throwing in, also in English, the casual comment that "Only gringos dance tango for fun," and then, with him in a towering rage, add mischievously that there was no sadder sight in the world than a European stranded in Buenos Aires (although she herself had a grandfather from Sicily, who must have immigrated with his fiancée straight after the First World War) and that she felt nothing but scorn for all those little men with dreams too big for them, as she put it, all those have-nots with their ridiculous pride and laughable honour, who tried ineffectually to stretch up to their full height beneath a canopy of fresh, empty sky and ended up doing nothing their whole life long but kissing the dust beneath their feet.

Just once, the old man himself told Ludwig about the mood of desolation he had succumbed to back then. It had been triggered by an airline advertisement he had seen in a newspaper, one that solicited passengers not by offering them the whole world, but by a short, simple slogan, "Going home, every day", which had so shaken him that his usual reserve had deserted him. Ludwig listened in some astonishment as he talked about the longing that had almost choked him at the weekends after he had seen the advertisement, about how he had felt capable of any crime in that state, he could have murdered a man, it might have been his final way of communicating his grief if nothing else had worked, not the walking and walking till he was numb with fatigue, or the spending time in the saddest bars or buying a woman or just studying the notices of ships' movements in and out of the harbour and imagining how quickly he might be on his way, a rapid stopover in Montevideo, another in Rio de Janeiro, then out on the Atlantic, Europe-bound.

For a long time Ludwig could only guess at the Yugoslavian part of the old man's story, assembling it from hints rather than actually hearing it from him. That the Communists were to blame for everything was the first thing he grasped, and that anyone in the family might fling the word at anyone else as an insult, it was what the old man called Claudia when he wanted to needle her, and even the two little girls used it too readily, in every imaginable situation. Yet there was something folkloric about its usage, and Ludwig took little notice whenever the old man launched into yet another political rant, dividing the world into powers of light and powers of darkness or bellowing his favourite saying to the effect that straight after the war there should have been a general and thorough cleansing, so that you could see where your real enemies stood and at least avoid having anything to do with the sinister comrades, and sometimes getting carried away enough to declare what a blessing it would have been, what a gift from heaven if the atom bombs had been dropped not on Hiroshima and Nagasaki but on Belgrade and Moscow instead.

Extreme as this sounded, it would have remained mostly bar-room talk to Ludwig if Claudia hadn't happened to mention one day that her husband had been on a Yugoslavian secret service hit list all his life, and probably still was. It was the same thing she had told him on the Atlantic beach, but he had been too preoccupied with himself to listen to her properly there. Now he did, but when he tried to make light of it, asking mockingly who in the world might feel threatened by her husband, she did not rise to the bait.

"You can make of it what you want, as far as I'm concerned," she said. "I just want you to know so that you understand why he gets so worked up about it."

It explained, at least, a good deal about the old man's semi-clandestine behaviour, and Ludwig was unsurprised to learn that it had been even more marked in his first years in Argentina: that he had explained his Slavic accent by claiming to be a Pole or a Czech, strictly avoided meeting with any compatriots, and moved on the moment he had the faintest suspicion that someone might have picked up his trail. He had been so possessed by his fear of being tracked down by an agent and shot in the street that he had even suspected her, Claudia, when they had first got to know each other, had engaged a private detective to poke around in her past and on their wedding night slept with a loaded pistol under his pillow. In her eyes that was the reason why he still lived like a soldier, a reservist officer who might be mobilised at any time and have to report for duty, and when she reminded Ludwig of how he had kept himself in readiness all these years, with his unvarying routine of fitness training first thing in the morning and shooting practice twice a week, she left him in little doubt that she admired him for it.

But when he wanted to know how the old man came to be in such a situation in the first place, she became evasive, saying that he would have to ask him himself. The one thing she was prepared to tell him was that straight after the war he had let himself be recruited to carry out sabotage in Yugoslavia, and it was connected with that. These acts of disruption had probably been conducted from Austria with little or no chance of success, a handful of men crossing the border, every time encountering resistance long before they could organise anything, and she made no secret of her opinion, calling it a naïve flirtation with danger whose only real impact lay in him having been declared an enemy of the state in his absence.

Her account was pretty vague, but when Ludwig took the opportunity to talk to the old man himself his employer only said, morosely, the hell with their accusations of attacks on railway lines, the hell with blowing up pylons, the whole thing had just been a bunch of superannuated layabouts playing cowboys and Indians. On later occasions he let one or two other details drop, usually prompted by some sentimental moment, like the time he showed Ludwig photos of his family home in Dalmatia, or when they drove out to a friend's estancia and he searched the night sky restlessly for the Southern Cross, grumbling in a melancholy voice that in the Middle Ages you could still see it from Europe, or when they both had the same idea of looking in on the children late one evening, and they stood side by side leaning over the little girls' beds for a few moments in the darkness of their attic room. These sudden outbursts were never very revealing, however, and he became really loquacious only once, on the day they went to Liniers for the cattle market, the Mercado de Hacienda where he had once worked, and he showed Ludwig the animals crowded together in the corrals, ready to be auctioned, and said that it always reminded him of the end of the war, which had happened for him in the open air amidst a huge crowd of people in southern Carinthia.

"That's how I felt then," he said, more careless than usual about giving too much away. "Like an animal going to the slaughter."

It was the first time he had mentioned the end of the war, and the first time he mentioned Bleiburg, the town close to where he and his unit of paratroopers had surrendered to the British columns that were just arriving. As Ludwig understood it, in the wake of the Germans' retreat from Zagreb a large part of the allied Croatian Army, with tens of thousands of civilians following it, had tried to flee from the vengeance of the advancing partisans by escaping to safety over the Austrian border, and he knew what that meant, and what the old man was implying as he emphasised that more than half of them were women and children. There was no mistaking the bitterness in the old man's voice as he related how in the tented camp put up by the British near Bleiburg the Croatians had had no idea what would happen to them for days on end, as they waited for a decision on whether they were to be taken further into Austria or moved out of the country altogether, having agreed unanimously that they would accept any decision, let themselves be moved anywhere, even if it were to the ends of the earth, only not back to Yugoslavia.

"But that was exactly what happened."

After all these years he still seemed unable to grasp it, and spoke of his own guardian angel who must have been watching over him as he slipped away from the column on the night of the transfer and disappeared into the forest.

"If you believe what the textbooks say, the war had been over for a week and I had the devil's own luck," he said. "Or the same fate would probably have befallen me that befell so many others, killed the moment they crossed the border and buried on the spot."

Thousands must have perished that way, and the numbers were even higher if you included those who were not killed immediately but driven halfway across the country, through villages where they had to run the gauntlet of the villagers, as far as Slavonia or Vojvodina, and if they survived that then they perished in the camps a year or two after the war ended. Ludwig guessed, from the way he was talking himself into extreme agitation one minute and then lapsing into an icy calm again, that he had reached the watershed of his life story. The British had known what would happen, he said, and had handed them over to the partisans in that full knowledge; his voice hovered between abhorrence and grief. Then he fell silent, and when he raised his eyes to look at the sun, standing low on the horizon in a barely visible haze that hung in the early light, he blinked repeatedly, a nervous flicker of the eyelids that had an existence of its own, until he began to speak again.

"Whatever happens, I'll never forgive those fish-and-chips-eaters for that, not if I burn in hell for it."

As if to check that he could trust him he looked at Ludwig sharply, and from one second to the next there was a hardening in his eyes that vanished again as soon as he fixed his gaze on the distance once more.

"It makes matters no better that we thought, in all seriousness, they would regard us as allies," he added. "Of course it was naïve, but we had persuaded ourselves that they would need us and wouldn't spend too long trying to find out which side we'd been fighting on a few days earlier, now that the real enemy was involved."

Compared to the kind of things he had come out with before it sounded harmless enough, but Ludwig was baffled.

"The real enemy?"

It was absurd.

"Maybe some people just had a different idea of where the real enemy was to be found," the old man said. "They can hardly be blamed, in the circumstances."

Ludwig looked at him, and the old man looked back, and though he was no longer looking into the sun he went on blinking.

"That's exactly it."

For a moment he hesitated, but then he could no longer contain himself and began to rant the way he had before, declaring that a few weeks of determined action with all available forces would have finished the job, if only the British and Americans had seen the omens.

"Then we would have been spared the last fifty years, stacked in a holding pattern," he said. "We really could have done what, if all goes well, we may be able to do now."

Ludwig could not say where his sudden feeling of nausea came from: the conversation, with its increasingly unpleasant aftertaste, or the smell of the stockyards rising more strongly to his nostrils, a smell of cows and calves and grassy meadows in the middle of the city that might have had a touch of paradise, but instead reminded him of death and decay. He saw that the old man was relishing the occasion but he himself could hardly stand the solemn silence that spread over the corrals, broken only occasionally by shouts from buyers who moved on horseback along the fenced paths between the pens or surveyed the cattle from the footbridges above them. The animals' resignation and helplessness in the white pens oppressed him, and when he thought that only the day before they had still been grazing somewhere on the pampas and that evening would end up at the abattoir, his throat tightened and he would rather have been anywhere else, anywhere he didn't have anything to do with the old man and his grim story.

He dismissed his forebodings and let himself be distracted from his silence as they returned to the main gate and, without a word, up the Lisandro de la Torre to the ramps, where the old man wanted to show him the trucks being loaded up.

"They almost all once belonged to me," he said, as if the sight were enough to put him in a state of reverie. "Aren't they magnificent brutes?"

He had laid a hand on the hood of a truck, and was indeed patting it like a living creature.

"If only you could drive one of them."

They were claret-coloured, and the old man told him that his partner had changed their colour when he took them over fully, and before that they had been white with blue lettering, like the Adriatic ships of his childhood and youth. Ludwig, having expected another lecture, was surprised at how easily he changed the subject and apparently forgot his tirade. Hearing the trampling and scraping of the cattle's hooves on the metal surface of the loading areas, he felt that nothing the old man could say next would surprise him as he observed him running his fingertips lovingly over the inscription *Mar del Sur*, still visible under the new colour.

"Magnificent brutes," he repeated. "Magnificent brutes."

The more Ludwig thought about it, the more mysterious the whole excursion was, but the picture fell into place for him a few days later when Don Filip came to visit, a Franciscan priest who was originally from the Mostar area and was introduced to Ludwig as someone who had known the old man in his earlier life and arrived from Europe on the same ship as he had. Ludwig heard how he had spent the first two days at sea almost uninterruptedly hanging over the ship's rail, heaving up his guts and the last of his belief in goodness, and then spent the rest of the three-week crossing below decks, playing cards and seeing to the thorough decimation of the ship's alcohol stocks. As if to foster the worst suspicions of him, the pin on Don Filip's chest, which might have been taken for a cross at first glance, turned out on closer inspection to be an upside-down sword, and as if that were not enough he dressed in a soutane, at whose hem showed the toes of his Western boots. The whole outfit was faintly ridiculous, but he was devoutly attached to it, as a great admirer of Butch Cassidy and the Sundance Kid, and could not only talk forever about their bank robberies and train hold-ups in Wyoming and Nevada, but once a year showed practical devotion by travelling to Cholila, the gangsters' Patagonian refuge after their flight from the Wild West, and reading a mass for their poor souls.

His martial trappings aside, he was a small, wiry man who widened and narrowed his eyes incredulously at his own stories. He cut his hair in the same style as the old man, shaved aggressively short at the nape of his neck and around his ears, and his face had something of the feigned innocence of a perpetual altar boy. He had cultivated the gentle, almost unearthly smile that accorded with his station in life to such a high degree that it was capable of appearing spontaneously on his lips at any time, and he cast his eyes down and even managed a faint blush when the old man described him as a saint and jokingly backed up his description by adding that in the '50s and '60s he had climbed several six-thousand-metre peaks in the Andes just to get closer to God. With the same slightly ostentatious gesture of inner humility Don

Filip accepted the information that he held the record for the cellar shooting range, twelve bullseyes out of twelve, and was also the sort of pistol-packing hero who could hit a coin tossed in the air and perform heaven knows what other stunts with a handgun, as though the only explanation for any of it was the operation of heavenly forces.

Ludwig felt ill at ease in his company, not because of his inclination frequently to stop what he was doing, fold his hands and let his gaze dwell on the infinite, but more to do with the joviality he displayed whenever he spoke to the old man.

"It's a disgrace you're still here," he said, as soon as he had embraced him, kissing him on both cheeks then pushing him as far away as possible, only to clasp him close again. "If you don't get a move on, I'll get home before you."

As it turned out, he had an arrangement with an undertaker's firm in Vicente López, and it was to this he was alluding. At his embarkation in Genoa he had vowed never to set foot on European soil again as long as he lived, and since then had paid absurd sums to ensure that at the earliest opportunity his mortal remains would be carried back to Bosnia and laid to rest in the cemetery of his Franciscan brothers at Široki Brijeg. When he told this story, he rapidly crossed himself, which in his case looked little more than a superstitious gesture, and glanced at the old man as he did so.

"Perhaps you can explain to me what's holding you back?"

He mentioned his own conviction that it would come to war in Yugoslavia and objected that others in the exile community had been far less hesitant than he had, setting out months ago, grasping the opportunity to fly back to Zagreb and a hero's welcome. He made it sound as though he were talking about crusaders who had been resurrected after centuries, bestowing on the mission of these weary and homesick warriors a special seal of approval. He had just returned from a tour up the Paraná river soliciting funds, where he had met people everywhere who would have given the last shirt they owned for the common cause, and adopting an unctuous tone as he glanced at the two little girls, he mentioned all the children who had pressed their small savings into his hand, peso by peso, an act that was sure to secure them a place in heaven for ever and a day. Here he could no longer conceal his love of bombast and sentiment, and presented the star character on his agenda, a little boy from Santa Fe suffering from cancer who, with his parents, had been to Bosnia the previous year to pray for a cure at Međugorje, the scene of the apparitions of Our Lady, and who had also asked him, Don Filip, to spend the money he was giving not on a candle to pray for his own swift recovery, but on a gun and a thousand rounds of ammunition, bless them in his name, and send them to Croatia as soon as possible.

Highly impressed with himself, Don Filip continued to bluster, and when Ludwig asked him how long the Church had dabbled in such matters, he looked put out.

"Do you not believe me?"

The idea seemed to amuse him, but he hesitated for only a moment, then went on bragging unabashed.

"Any time you are troubled by doubt you are welcome to accompany me to the Plaza de Miserere, and there you will meet people who are willing to obtain anything that the heart may desire, for cash, and just so long as it's to be had somewhere in this world."

He pretended that his pride had been wounded, and there was something of the market-trader about his enumeration of goods that followed, despite his precaution of whispering almost inaudibly.

"It depends what sort of things you like," he said. "You can have weapons, drugs, women or a relic of the True Cross of Our Lord."

Claudia disapproved of his performance so much that when Don Filip gave the girls little holy pictures to keep, she immediately took them away from them, and when he again tried to talk to them, she sent them out of the room. Then she had to watch the old man withdraw with the priest to the living room, which put her in a furious temper. For as long as their tête-à-tête lasted she kept glancing at the time and regularly knocking on the door to ask if they had everything they needed, and when she had taken them another bottle of wine or simply returned from the living room, she sat in the kitchen with Ludwig, whose job was to stay in the house and wait in case he was called, and let rip about Don Filip, her highly strung state suggesting that she was worried about her husband and trying to soothe her fears with a constant flow of words, not noticing that she was doing exactly the opposite.

"He's going to put all sorts of fancy ideas in his head, the way he's egging him on," she said. "He can hardly expect him to fight with a gun in his hand at his age."

This sounded melodramatic, and Ludwig failed to grasp her anxiety until she told him that it had been Don Filip and another brother from his order who had recruited her husband immediately after the war to an insurgent unit to continue the struggle in Yugoslavia. After his escape, and saving himself from being handed over to the partisans, the old man had been picked up in the Austrian mountains and taken to a camp near Villach, where he had met the priest. Months and months of living underground had followed, of which she knew only the barest outline: the hiding out in the forests, the waiting for the right opportunity to cross the border, and finally the road to Rome with Don Filip after all hope of a swift coup had been dashed, going from monastery to monastery, until at last they reached the Vatican and safety.

The journey had made them lifelong friends, and Claudia

seemed to know perfectly well what she was talking about when she saw in the visitor a danger to the old man.

"He only has to appeal to his honour, and my husband will be fool enough to let himself be taken in again, forgetting that he's not twenty anymore."

Ludwig insisted she drink something, and after he had poured her a glass of wine, which she drank and immediately refilled without letting go of the bottle, he suddenly knew why, as they had sat beside the sea, and later too, she had sucked so obsessively at her lemonade, like a teenager addicted to it. He had never seen her so agitated before, and tried to soothe her by stroking her hair, pointing out that Don Filip was a man of the Church, but even before she picked up the word he heard how useless it sounded.

"Man of the Church?"

She regarded him with astonishment.

"Well, he has a good story, that suits him very well," she retorted. "There are also rumours that during the war he was a camp guard in Croatia."

If true, such rumours could only have furthered his career in Argentina, she added. At the very least it was no coincidence at all that during the time of the generals his sphere of influence, as she put it, had been in the Rawson state prison in Patagonia, whose inmates were almost all opponents of the regime. She had heard him boast more than once of being assigned to them as an expert in difficult cases and special tasks.

"If you can believe his version, he was their father confessor and spiritual comforter for many years."

She said it with an emphasis that caught Ludwig's attention.

"What's so bad about that?"

He had been waiting for a chance to make a harmless remark,

to try to calm her, and as she lifted her eyebrows and looked straight past him her derision seemed all the more dismissive.

"You really don't know?"

She shook her head.

"In his case father confessor doesn't exactly mean father confessor," she said. "It means he was responsible for interrogations."

Don Filip was guilty, it seemed, of an endless list of misdeeds, and all Ludwig could think of was to laugh it off and ask if the priest had any other skeletons in his cupboard he should know about. She had carried on rapidly drinking wine and was occasionally slurring a syllable, while the look in her eyes could have come from an old film as she nodded, her Rita Hayworth look, the old man had once called it, that radiated a certainty that he knew nothing about her and, precisely because he was a man and she was a woman, never could know anything. Ludwig saw the bright red of her lipstick on her incisor teeth as she smiled, then she burst into a hard, husky fit of laughter that had a touch of hysteria to it.

"What would you say if you heard him claim that he helped my husband to disappear his wife?"

Ludwig shrugged his shoulders.

"His wife," he said. "What do you mean?"

Only then did he understand.

"Violeta."

She nodded, and he remembered the photo she had once shown him, a photo of the old man looking youthfully slim in a pinstriped suit and a woman beside him, who wore a dress like a petticoat. It was a photograph from their honeymoon in Montevideo, and with her headscarf and sunglasses she had looked to Ludwig as if she were not so much anxious to shield herself from the brightness of the day as to protect an observer from the radiance of her eyes. The memory struck him again at once, and the way she stood in front of a picture-postcard background with the sea glittering in the sun where the Rambla ran along the waterfront, her knees slightly bent, one arm in front of her body, as though she were naked and wanted to cover her bust and sex, the other, a handbag in her hand, raised as if to ward off the camera, though at the same time she was looking at it both shyly and provocatively.

"Why would he have wanted to disappear her?"

There had been no clue from the few impressions he had formed of Violeta, but when he asked the question Claudia scrutinised him like a T.V. detective whose interrogation would only be finished when everything had been spelt out for even the dimmest viewer.

"It was around the time he met me," she said. "A time came when he couldn't stand her jealousy any longer and he wanted to give her a fright, so he had Don Filip denounce her to the police."

Although she had already finished a bottle of wine, her voice sounded sober, and when she spoke again her tone alternated between indifference and horror.

"In those days it was enough to say that she was a subversive who sympathised with the guerrilleros and their opposition to the state."

Ludwig knew she had a tendency to melodrama, would often spend whole afternoons lying on the couch with a pile of photo-novels, and would probably have liked to structure her life to a similar design, but something told him that this was entirely different and that when she called it the most dreadful story she knew, she meant it. A few days earlier on the Plaza de Mayo, he had passed for the first time the demonstrators who still came out on the street there week after week, in memory of those who had been abducted during the last military dictatorship, and he knew that that was what she was referring to. Her voice dropped as she nevertheless declared that the old man hadn't reckoned on Violeta vanishing for ever when the uniformed men came to take her away that same evening, shoving her into their car and driving off without even giving her time to pack a bag.

"A night in prison was supposed to make her see reason, once and for all," she said in a whisper, and the horror of it, something she had warded off so far, seemed to have her in its grip. "He thought those monkeys knew it was a joke, he had no idea that they would go the whole way with her."

Her phrasing could not have been clearer, yet Ludwig fought against it, as though retrospectively he could somehow prevent what had happened.

"The whole way?"

He would have given a lot to be disabused, so the verdict with which she responded hit him all the harder.

"You must know what your colleagues are like."

She apologised when she saw the look in his eyes, but what is said remains said, and her smile's coldness and insincerity spoke volumes.

"I always thought methods were the same everywhere," she went on. "But of course I ought to have known that our officers are model pupils at these sorts of things and come up with particularly original ideas."

Abruptly the stillness of the house was clearly audible, and from the way her words followed, tumbling out breathlessly and at speed, Ludwig felt she wished she had never brought the subject up and now wanted to put it behind her as fast as she could.

"Their speciality was to fly out to sea a short way with their victims and then throw them out of the plane alive."

This was the image that stayed before Ludwig's eyes long after Claudia had gone to bed, when the two men finally resurfaced and he was instructed to drive Don Filip back to town. After what he had heard, they were no longer the same men who had gone into the living room only a few hours ago, and he shivered when he looked at their drink-reddened faces and thought of the two little girls sleeping in their attic room, with its view far out over the mouth of the river. It was after midnight, and they had abandoned their original plan of going down to the cellar to fire off a few rounds, but they were waiting arm in arm outside the house as he brought the car out of the garage. They took their leave of each other with the kisses, the solemn "God and the Croats" that he had heard the old man say so often over the phone, and then he was alone with Don Filip in the back of the car, who instantly started talking and wouldn't stop.

He still felt, he said, that the old man was assessing the situation in Yugoslavia correctly, but he was not so sure that he was drawing the right conclusions and he might end up sitting around and doing nothing.

"Half his life he's been doing nothing, except wait for the Third World War to break out so that he can go home at last. Now, all of a sudden, he has doubts," Don Filip said, his voice sounding in the car's dark interior as if it were coming from somewhere offstage. "He's always thought that one day he would march into Zagreb behind American tanks, and he can't get it into his skull that it's about to happen all on its own."

It was grotesque, he said, that at first the old man had believed that 1948 would be the year when everything was decided the way he wanted, and then for years afterwards had pinned his hopes on the smallest, furthest skirmishes in Africa or Asia, building up every flickering flame into the expectation that it would turn into a bush fire. Only Don Filip's habitual certitude stopped Ludwig thinking that this was an isolated case of careless talk. He would have been relieved to have some inoffensive subject of conversation occur to him to discuss with his passenger, but he found all he could do was sit silently in the driver's seat, both hands on the wheel, staring straight ahead down the road, which had never seemed as empty before, while he eavesdropped on the priest's musings as though they were dispatches from a world long gone. He was to drop Don Filip off at the Franciscan monastery in the Alsina, on the corner of Defensa, and could have followed the number 168 bus route past Chacarita cemetery, past Plaza Once and Plaza Constitución, but something made him stay on the Avenida del Libertador, and when they came level with the Naval College of Technology he tried to catch Don Filip off guard by commenting casually that the generals had once had a torture centre in the college grounds. The old man had mentioned it whenever they drove past it, with an irritating matter-of-factness, as if he were talking about an institution for some general community purpose, and now Don Filip too reacted with perfect composure, looking out at the grounds that extended in the dark over several groups of buildings, where only the outlines of individual blocks could be discerned and there was no trace of the guards, muffled in camouflage gear, who patrolled back and forth behind the fence during the day, armed to the teeth.

Don Filip lit a cigarette, and in the light of the match his face flared in the rear-view mirror. He offered Ludwig one, and as he gave him a light it was like another flash in the night. He snapped his cigarette case shut and let himself sink back into the rear seat, and for a while there was just the glowing and fading of their cigarettes in the dark.

"I must say you disappoint me a little, with that wagging forefinger of yours," Don Filip finally said, falling back into his grand-seigneurial aloofness. "It seems to be a disorder of your compatriots to confuse politics with morality but, as a former police officer, you should in my opinion be above such childishness."

Ludwig was reminded of the conversation he had had with the old man at their first meeting, but this time he was under no illusions, guessing it would go much further and already regretting starting it. The darkness of the city here oppressed him, and he felt like an animal that, after a life spent in a zoo, has no instinct for the wild, no capacity to distinguish between fear and curiosity. He had never been quite clear about that distinction at home in Austria either, whenever he had passed a prison or a barracks, feeling a yearning to be shut up and guarded, even if only to enjoy the anticipation of being released and have a better idea of what being outside really meant, but now the mere idea of confinement horrified him, and he shrugged it off as quickly as he could.

Don Filip said no more, and they were already at Palermo and driving past the Parque 3 de Febrero when he started talking again, saying that visitors who came to Argentina could be divided into two groups.

"Apart from all the kitschy Evita nonsense, there's not much going on here," he said, "though more and more people fall for that. A few are interested in football and tango, and the rest aren't satisfied unless they spot a war criminal around every street corner."

He wasn't talking about the generals of the junta but the ambition of the cheapskate holidaymakers, as he called them, to track down the last Nazis in the country's deepest and remotest corners.

"You sometimes feel they're the same people who go to the theatre in Vienna, Paris or Rome, all very well-behaved, or visit museums, and then as soon as they get Argentine soil under their feet they start acting like the wildest bounty-hunters and aren't happy until they've been to the flea-market and found a Wehrmacht jacket, a tattered old paybook or some give-away Nazi decorations, or got hold of a half-senile old dodderer who'll tell them a tall story in broken German."

Ludwig knew all this folklore: he himself had been accosted by an old man in the Café 36 Billares who wanted a hundred dollars for the true story of the German U-boats that had appeared off the Patagonian coast just after the war with their cargoes of prominent passengers, as he put it, and from sheer curiosity Ludwig had split the cost with another visitor to the café of this faintly macabre guided tour of history. It began with the old man claiming to have been a sailor on the *Graf Spee*, originally from Hamburg, who these days set out his stall at the La Biela or the Richmond, gathering knots of people around him to tell the story of the Battle of the River Plate, after which, on a fine summer's day in December 1939, his beloved battlecruiser had been scuttled on her captain's orders in Montevideo harbour. When the story was finished, he took anyone who was interested out to Chacarita cemetery, to the German sector where they stood in silence over the grave of the captain who had shot himself in the wake of the catastrophe, and Ludwig remembered a small huddle, looking lost, of a few elderly, red-faced gentlemen in shorts and sad orthopaedic shoes, touchingly keen to show their cultural interest, whose wives held their hands as if they were children, and who stared at the swastika carved on the gravestone under the southern sun as if it were entirely unknown to them.

It struck him that it was absurd to be talking, at this moment of all moments, to someone like Don Filip, whose own story could probably make just as convoluted a performance and attract an equally ready audience.

"You must know that weird business pretty well," he said, seeing Don Filip in his mirror but failing to catch his eye. "You sound like you're speaking personally."

He did not expect this to provoke the priest, and sure enough Don Filip seemed to look through him as he brushed him aside. "You'd like that."

He sat forwards and put his hands on the back of the passenger seat, and Ludwig was beginning to think that he had finished with the subject when he spoke again.

"If you ask me, it's Russian manoeuvres all over again."

Outside, the silhouette of the Kavanagh building on Plaza San Martín was outlined against the night sky, which meant that it could only be a few blocks to their destination, but Don Filip wasn't giving up.

"I'm sure you know who we mean by that in Buenos Aires."

But innuendo was not enough for him.

"It's the same old Jewish game."

He fell silent again, and Ludwig listened to the hiss of the tyres on the asphalt, hoping it might be just a bad joke, an effort to extract something from him, or some other fixation that could be easily explained.

"That's nonsense," he finally said, looking around with a feeling that he and Don Filip were no longer alone in the car and someone else had joined them. "What are you talking about?"

He had always thought, when he heard similar outbursts at home, that it was just posturing, the inflated anecdotes of people trying to make themselves interesting, and so he kept his composure.

"I mean, there *are* no Jews in this story."

He had barely finished his sentence when he realised that Don Filip welcomed his remark as a pretext for further comments.

"You know perfectly well that there are *always* Jews around, don't say you don't," he said, his voice cracking with excitement. "Behind every rottenness there's a Jew somewhere, and if there isn't then it's someone acting like a Jew, which is worse."

The affair he went on to describe was intended to illustrate his claim, a bluntly factual account of the Jewish pimps' mafia that had dominated trade in the city at the turn of the century. After his first inflammatory accusations he seemed to take care to confine himself to the facts, and had he not previously revealed his feelings, he might have been displaying a passionate amateur historian's interest in the subject, in how accurately he knew its details and how well up he was on dates and figures, as if it were his job to produce a story and a proof, then broadcast it authoritatively abroad. Here, though, he gave himself away, because there was no mistaking in the telling the relish with which he described a vulgar brotherhood of men, great and small, with their own synagogues and cemeteries, who had the fresh meat for their trade brought to them from the poorest villages of Galicia: from the very heartland of their own communities. Here he suddenly fell victim to a pragmatic cynicism, speculating in a reflective way on the likelihood that life in an Argentinian brothel had been the saving of many Jewish girls lured to the country by promises of marriage, particularly if you stopped to think what had happened ten or twenty years later when the Germans marched into Poland.

That was what Claudia had meant when she said that Don Filip wasn't just anti-Communist and anti-Yankee, as two-thirds of the population probably were, but a pathological anti-Semite too. Ludwig was at a loss to know what to do, apart from maintain his inoffensive conversational tone.

"Do you tell everyone that?"

In spite of the road noise he could hear Don Filip's breathing, and when he turned to look at him he found him leaning so far forward between the two front seats that their heads almost collided.

"I'll admit that it's strong meat for most people to hear," he said, and the idea seemed to give him strength. "As soon as I start talking about it, they don't just want to wash their hands, they want to wash their eyes and ears out as well."

He laughed, and Ludwig replied that given the choice, he would have preferred not to have to hear it either, true or not.

"That's exactly it," he went on, afraid that he might be offered more proof positive of what had happened all that time ago. "It doesn't actually matter how much of it is correct."

He gave all his concentration to the road again, and heard Don Filip inhale and prepare yet again to comment, but without getting out a word.

"Ah," he said at last. "Yes, indeed."

His contempt could not have been clearer but Ludwig had decided that he was not going to be intimidated anymore and said, as firmly as he was able, "The question is where you're really going with all this."

They had arrived, and he waited for Don Filip to get out. When the priest did not move, he turned to him again, seeking his face in the dim light of a single street lamp. He saw that he was smiling, a pointed smile to which Ludwig responded by simply holding his gaze. Then he himself got out of the car, opened the rear passenger door and stood beside it without a word, until his silence alone caused Don Filip to start to move, though not without first giving him his blessing.

"Perhaps you won't see it that way, but it was a pleasure for me to talk to you," he said, and seemed to mean it seriously. "If you have no objection, I shall include you in my prayers."

He had already disappeared by the time Ludwig started the car. He drove for some time aimlessly through the city, which in the darkness seemed an even more provisional place than during the day, an assemblage of wooden shacks and huts on the edge of the pampas, hardly redeemed by the fine buildings in the city centre, which like everything else could be swept away by the first real hurricane as if they had never been. Day was breaking when he reached his apartment in the Calle Juncal, and without fully being aware of the thought, he had made up his mind to hand in his notice that morning, but when he called San Isidro it was Claudia who answered the phone, saying that she was expecting him, and it was all back to usual, despite his feeling differently now, because two hours later she let him into the house alone and led him straight down to the cellar room next to the shooting range, where he sometimes spent the night if it got too late, and without more ado pulled her dress over her head, lay down naked on the camp bed that was set up there and asked him was he gay, was he waiting for a manual, or did he just have reservations about doing his duty during working hours?

Ludwig stood staring at her like a man who had not seen a woman for half a lifetime, and at the same time absent-mindedly unholstered his pistol and put it down gently at the head of the bed.

"Your husband will kill me."

He watched as she raised her arms in a lazy slow-motion movement and clasped her hands behind her head, as though it could make her more naked than she already was.

"You'll have to give him some reason to kill you first."

She laughed, and he saw the fine beads of sweat that had formed on her smooth forehead, shimmering marble-white in the dim glow from the overhead bulb, as she pulled him down beside her.

"The rest shouldn't all be up to me," she said, closing her eyes. "I think you ought to do it yourself."

FOUR

ONE NIGHT IN THE BOARDING HOUSE WAS ENOUGH, MARIJA knew she couldn't stay there, and immediately after breakfast, as though retrospectively getting back at her husband, she booked a room at the Palace Hotel and spent the next two days in Zagreb under a spell that she only broke by deciding to drive to the seaside. In a flight of poetic fancy she wrote to her girlfriends, saying that she felt borne up by a giant wave lapping lazily back and forth, preparing to cast her up on one side or the other, and she didn't care which. She had been warned against taking the direct route by way of Karlovac and the Krajina, so she turned off towards Slovenia, driving in small stages from Rijeka along the coast until she was nearly at Split. She thought of visiting the village and the house of her childhood, but felt afraid of the memories it would bring back, she had after all revisited the place once before and was under no illusions about it, she knew that most of all she was afraid of realising all over again how few memories she had of it, and so she let herself carry on drifting aimlessly. It was a holiday, one that she would look back on at some future date like looking at the photos of a long distant time, so despite never quite shaking off a sense of threat, she gave up reading newspapers and instead spent hour after hour on the beach, dozing or immersed in a novel, not leaving until the evening when the sun was going down and people finished swimming, emerging from the water in a paradise-like backlight, as though they were the first and perhaps also the last men and women in the world.

Stunned by the heat, the land seemed to crave delay, and the same craving affected her. From the way summer lingered on in these September days you could imagine, by the sea, that everything would be alright, even though there was already fighting going on inland and one night, near Zadar, she thought she heard artillery fire, and on another occasion sat up suddenly from sleep, sure that she had been woken by the sound of shots. Because she did not talk to anyone, the first time it struck her something was wrong was when she became aware of her own mood swinging unusually between sudden excitement and equally sudden calm, and of the change from elation to resignation in the behaviour of others, in the artificial high spirits of the drinkers standing in bars, talking noisily and then going home as quiet as mice as soon as the groups began to disperse. Watching them, she felt that the noisiest were often little more than children, and though she hadn't seen anyone openly carrying a weapon since the last war, at least no civilians, she knew what was going on when one of them glanced at her from the darkness with a directness he would never otherwise have dared, sizing her up as if very soon there would be only two possibilities: either she would turn out to be under their protection, or she would be legitimate prey.

When a young man did follow her one evening, wordlessly grabbing hold of her outside her hotel, and she was able to fend him off only because he was startled to hear her speak Croatian, she phoned her husband. She could still feel the weight of hands gripping her upper arms when he picked up the receiver and said his name, a piano sonata audible in the background, its faint tinkling instantly silencing her with a longing to be at home again. She didn't like the thought, but she pictured him lighting a cigar, busying himself for a time getting it properly lit before he said anything, or whatever other leisurely task he had in mind, she would happily have accepted it all if it had put to flight the panting breath in her ear, the reek of alcohol, and the over-high, breaking voice that had asked her in a whisper whether she liked this, while she had retreated further and further until finally she bumped against the stone wall, feeling its edges and roughness through her thin dress.

From where she stood in the phone booth she gazed out over the water, on which occasionally a light flashed, just this side of the barely perceptible curve of the horizon, and as she listened to her husband making a scene, wanting to know why she hadn't called before, she watched and waited for the next flash, until at last she interrupted him.

"Where do you think I am?"

She had herself under control.

"I'm at the seaside."

She repeated it, as though she could hardly contain her excitement, and he asked her where exactly and mentioned the T.V. pictures he had seen, showing villages burning in the karst landscape.

"Isn't that close to where you are?"

She was glad to hear his voice, and wanted to ask him to come and fetch her, but as she waited for some sign that he had sensed the upset in her voice, he went on talking and the moment was gone.

"You know what I think whenever you start acting the heroine," he said. "Promise me at least to keep away from the worst areas."

This was the least of her worries.

"I promise," she said. "I promise."

Involuntarily she answered him in the same tone.

"It's all quiet here, and nothing's going to happen."

She talked and talked then, telling him that the water was still warm and she would really like to stay till the autumn winds drove her north again, yet she was no longer talking for his benefit, she didn't really care what he thought, it was just her way of holding back her tears, though she also knew she would be inviting them if she didn't stop soon because, far more than he could ever guess, it had been the summers that had kept her alive, and so many years when she had had to get somehow from one summer to the next, ten months in Vienna and then summer by the sea in Dalmatia, and soon it would be over for ever.

"Maybe none of this will be here next year," she said. "And it's never been as beautiful as it is now."

That was the end of the conversation. She waited till the next morning to make another call, to Philadelphia, where Lorena sounded anxious again. Another woman's voice answered the phone and Marija was about to hang up, then decided to ask for her daughter anyway, and for a long while only indistinct words were audible, as if the two of them were bickering, then a giggle that burst out and died, and finally Lorena's distant "Hello". She had not given much thought to Lorena's friends, but it struck her that whoever this person with her was, she must have just slept with her, her voice sounded so gentle and velvety and slow.

"Mum, do you know how late it is here?"

The time difference hadn't occurred to her, and she felt as though she had walked into her daughter's bedroom without knocking and been confronted with the certainty that everything she thought she knew about Lorena was wrong.

"I'm sorry, I'd forgotten where you are."

Hearing how melancholy she herself sounded, she paused.

"I'm in Croatia," she said, as if to prove that at least she knew where she was. "Maybe that's why I'm a bit confused at the moment."

The same question came again.

"Is everything alright?"

It didn't mean anything in particular, yet the following day she wondered how she could have said yes, it was, after she arrived back in Zagreb and saw how much the city had changed in the three weeks she had been away. At first she felt an involuntary resistance, thinking she must have wandered onto a film set by mistake, so exaggerated did the roadblocks, the sandbags, the taped windows seem to her, not to mention the patrols she encountered everywhere she went, the gun emplacements on the roofs, all the men in uniform. She did not react to the first air-raid warning, but then from the Kaptol district saw a bomber squadron making its approach, flying low as it swept over the buildings, and felt the ground shake under her feet as the noise reached her, passed over her and, seconds later, the aircraft shrank soundlessly in the distance, until they looked no bigger in the clear blue sky than a swarm of gnats. The subsequent silence was overwhelming, as though for a moment no-one and nothing dared make the smallest movement, in case there appeared out of that blue sky something more than a passing numbness that left the air throbbing for a while.

Marija spent her first two days back at the Palace Hotel, then found an apartment in the east of the city, a place where there was no trace of Zagreb's often invoked Austrian past and whole streets lined with dismal buildings had been erected in a hurry. The doctor who had lived in the apartment with his family until a few weeks before had moved to Belgrade, and she picked up the key from the neighbours and suddenly lived among the possessions of strangers. She looked around to discover anything unusual, but apart from an Orthodox crucifix on the T.V. and a collection of cheap erotic fiction, she found only an edition of the works of Tito in a glass-fronted bookcase, nothing more exciting than that, not even the family album in which a man smiled gently, his arm lightly around a woman whose expression was equally gentle, and a little girl with another smile that made her want to try it out for herself in the mirror. She ignored the "Chetniks" sprayed on the apartment door and again downstairs next to the front bell, until it was supplemented by a "Serbian whore" like a shriek that was doubtless meant for her, but a few days later all of it disappeared under a few hastily applied brushstrokes of blood-red paint. By then she had got to know the fellow who patrolled the street outside the estate every evening as its self-appointed warden, and to all appearances passed his test, which consisted of demanding that she cross herself so that he could see if she did it correctly or the wrong way around, like a barbarian.

Behind the block and a short distance up a hill was the hospital where the doctor had worked before he left in a hurry, and Marija did not need to turn on the T.V. or read the newspaper to know what was happening in the areas where there was fighting, because every day she could hear the cars bringing the wounded in from Slavonia and the Krajina through her closed windows. Some days they came without end, and as soon as it was silent for a few minutes on the usually empty access road the soft rumble of cars could be heard again in the distance, steadily amplifying and then ripping into the silence with an urgency that made her glance out of the window or run downstairs and watch where the cars came into view again as they turned into the last bend. For her this was a moment of grace, the passing from the bend till they disappeared under the trees, and she could hear her heart beating at the thought that not a hundred metres from where she stood a human being was arriving, a human being who would be unloaded, whoever he was and in whatever state between life and death, and someone else with him to look after him, at which she caught herself in mid-thought, that she must hurry there and lay a hand on the wounded man's forehead, telling him he mustn't be afraid, everything would be alright.

It wasn't clear to her why she felt so drawn to this idea, whether it was just the fear that gripped her, the indefinable unease whenever she thought about what was going on behind the hospital walls, and she only began to understand the feelings that had taken hold of her when, in the nearby Maksimir Park where she had started to spend half an hour or so before dusk, she met a soldier who was recovering after an operation and was due to go back to the front in a few days' time. She had been back in the city two weeks, but there was no question of returning to Vienna soon, despite the new semester about to start, she wanted to stay, she felt so sure that she was in the right place when, walking down from the pavilion, she bumped straight into him. Who spoke to whom she couldn't say, whether he spoke to her or she spoke to him, the one thing she remembered was that they had approached each other from a distance and then just stopped and looked at one another for so long that they both began apologising.

Somehow it was no surprise that his name was Angelo, and the many efforts she made to explain to herself what was happening over the next forty-eight hours, when they did not once leave the apartment, seemed like attempts to save herself from total oblivion, automatic, half-hearted bearings taken in the sudden expanse where she found herself cast up with him. When she told him he reminded her of her father, he laughed and she too was surprised, wondering what had made her say it, and buried her nose and face deep in the hollow of his throat and smelt him and had to restrain herself so that she didn't tell him the whole story at once, the scant memories she had of the man in uniform who used to throw her up in the air and catch her again safely in his arms. It didn't stop her exclaiming the next moment, "But you could be my son!" and then, showing him a picture of her daughter as if to assure him that she too had been young once, realising what a muddled state of mind she had worked herself into. She felt like putting her hand over her mouth and keeping it there, but then he kissed her, kissed her behind her ears, kissed the nape of her neck, kissed her breasts, covered her from head to toe with kisses, and she said no, said yes, said here, Angelo, here, and then he had already buried his head between her legs and he was kissing her as no-one had ever kissed her before.

It was day, it was night, it was day again, and though she knew it couldn't be, she thought she heard helicopters now instead of cars as she lay in the bedroom with her head on his chest, staring at the happy bride and bridegroom in front of the Jajce waterfalls. She slept, then, waking, felt his breathing while the space around her filled with the staccato of their rotors, as if someone had installed an enormous, noisily clattering ceiling fan in the room, and she curled herself up very small next to him. He gave no sign of being at all tired, but when he did once doze off she sat up in the morning light, pulled him to her lap and stroked his hair so that he woke with a start, telling her she didn't have to hold him as if she had just taken him down from the cross, he was still alive, then pulled her down and lay on top of her, burying her underneath him, his arms stretched out like the Redeemer's, her hands in his hands, to keep hold of her always and never let her go. Peering out from where she lay beneath him, she saw a patch of sky through the window and thought that the world could come to an end, shrink to a dot in that endless blue, and she would never know if she was afraid of it or wished it for herself. Pinned by his weight, she lay motionless until, disengaging one hand, she started to trace with her fingertips, over and over again, the newly healed wound in his shoulder, from which dozens of tiny splinters of shrapnel had been removed, leaving a sprinkling of discoloured bluish marks that spread in a gentle curve.

The incident that had wounded Angelo, in one of the combat zones in Slavonia, was so horrible that when he told her about it at first Marija couldn't believe it, and afterwards she couldn't get the image of the woman at the beginning of the story out of her head. The woman had been taken prisoner and had then been sent over from the enemy lines to the small position barely fifty metres away where Angelo and his troop were dug in, and that was the image Marija saw in her mind's eye later, of the lonely figure placing one foot in front of another on the flat land under the huge sky, moving heavily between the two lines like a pregnant woman. For she had a pack of explosives strapped to her stomach, with a cable running behind her, and Angelo didn't need to say any more, it was clear to Marija what that had meant for her, it made no difference whether she decided to stand still or keep walking.

"She had no choice."

The story was terrifyingly simple, and Angelo just nodded. He lay silently beside her, reached for her hand and pressed it. Then he let it go again and sat up.

"She was one of us."

He wiped his eyes with both hands.

"We waited until the last second, watched her coming closer and closer," he said. "In the end she was only a few steps away, and we heard her praying."

He looked at Marija with a tormented expression, and without thinking she tried to outdo him in the awfulness of what he was about to say.

"Then you shot her."

He said yes, then said no and shook his head.

"I don't know."

His voice was hoarse.

"We had been ordered to shoot and had taken cover," he went on, after sitting for a moment with his eyes closed, listening to the silence. "Then everything in front of us went up."

For a moment she thought he was going to cry, but he didn't, and she realised that she had wanted him to, so that she could comfort him, and then she cried herself and was surprised that he moved away from her and stood up and stayed standing naked beside the bed, waiting for her to stop. Although he said nothing, she apologised, and it was the only time she wondered what she was really doing here in a strange apartment with a strange man, almost a boy still, who was half her age and now looking at her as though he were thinking the same, wondering what had brought him here. She pulled the bedclothes up over her breasts to hide herself from his gaze, and then he lay down beside her again and asked her to hold him, and she clung tightly to him and held him and was held by him, until she slept again, and was woken once more by a constant droning that seemed to fill the room, though no helicopters were flying and it was nothing but the fancy of her imagination.

It was then that she beseeched him, implored him with all her might not to go back to the front, and was rebuffed for the first time.

"Don't throw your life away for these old men and their feuds," she said. "Whichever way you look at it, it's not your war."

At first he listened to her with an amused smile, but when she went on begging him, suggesting they run away together, he suddenly stopped finding her funny.

"What makes you so sure it's not my war?"

Now he was being serious, in a way that made her laugh aloud.

"It *isn't* your war," she said when she calmed down. "Please believe me, and don't go running into something you may never find your way out of again."

Then she said that he could go to America with her, and he became furious. He had told her that he dreamed of going there, and she was mocking him. As he lay beside her, she felt him hardening, but when she put her hand on his arm he pushed it away and it was over.

"If you can explain that to my friends I'll be very grateful," he said, "and just remember, the most important thing is, try not to get too over-excited and probably don't tell them that you could be my mother."

He raised himself abruptly and looked down at her.

"Or maybe they won't understand why I'm getting the hell out with you and leaving them to die alone."

She did not reply, and the next four days, which they spent mostly out of doors, not coming back to her apartment until late at night, seemed to her like a continuous state of emergency, a succession of smoke-filled bars that wouldn't end, in all of which he seemed to know someone, or soon did know someone, and was immediately plunged into argument. With no way of knowing in advance which way it would go, the same arguments could lead to sentimental embraces or to sudden differences of opinion, and once they had to make themselves scarce very suddenly to avoid physical violence. The talk was always about the same things, the situation in Slavonia, the Army's bombardment of the villages, the siege of Vukovar, and whether the men fighting at the front were right to feel the government had abandoned them, as was being said on all sides, and in the heat of the moment he frequently seemed to have forgotten her, but then he felt for her hand again or turned to her and kissed her in mid-exchange, and, thinking that everyone would be surprised, she learnt otherwise. They took it entirely for granted that she should be with them and drink with them, so she drank whatever was put in front of her and when, as it got later and later, she hung around his neck, her eyes closed and head swimming, at least her drunkenness came with an end to all understanding, and without having to say a word herself she sank into the muddle of voices, at her most exalted when she felt most lost, like a child meekly accepting everything that's happening as long as she is allowed to stay with the grown-ups.

Angelo bought her a red dress, and at his insistence she put it on in the shop, with nothing on underneath, and with bare shoulders stepped out into the late summer afternoon. In the street the heat hit her like a punch, and as she teetered beside him on extravagantly high heels, her swinging of her hips was not wholly successful, more like a staggering attempt to raise herself off the ground, without a sideways glance for the refugees by the roadside, hands outstretched, who stared after her like someone trying to show them that the bad times need not mean bad luck for everyone. Her state was one in which even she hardly recognised herself, and as she reflected a few days later on the figure she had cut that afternoon, an excited woman *entre deux âges* escorted by a young man brimming with health and strength yet still barely grown-up, who liked to place his hand possessively on her bottom as they walked along, the expression "soldier's sweetheart" popped into her head from her childhood in Vienna after the war, but when she afterwards asked Angelo to be a bit less obvious, he just laughed at her, refusing to listen when she said that that was what their Viennese female neighbours had called her mother, after they started to see an English officer's car standing outside their building.

She might have disregarded his nonchalance, but one afternoon it became impossible to ignore, as she sat with him at a café on Jelačić Square and recognised her husband among the passers-by outside. She pointed him out to Angelo, who hardly looked up. Hidden behind his sunglasses he carried on turning the pages of the newspaper while she stared, more astonished than shocked, and her husband seemed, at that precise moment, to be looking back at her.

"He's looking for me," she said with deliberate calm. "If he comes in here I'll have to think of something."

They had agreed that she would call him every day, but of course she hadn't, and this was the result. He had most likely seen the news, heard talk of a threat to Zagreb, and started worrying, yet she could not get it into her head that he was standing there, it was a weekday and he ought to be busy at the newspaper, or at home writing his column for posterity, or doing something else that wouldn't permit such excursions. He was no more than twenty metres away and seemed undecided, looking around him and then, jacket slung over his shoulder, making for a newspaper kiosk, where she saw him hunt around in his briefcase and pull something out of it that he showed to the woman while he talked to her. She nodded, and he busied himself for a few moments pinning a sheet of paper to the outer wall of the wooden kiosk, and although she was too far away to recognise the face, she sensed that the photo on the paper was of her and that it was a "Missing" notice.

"Should I go out and talk to him?"

She suddenly realised that she was whispering, and as she looked questioningly at Angelo she felt him grip her wrist, without seeming to have moved at all.

"That's exactly what you won't do." He too had lowered his voice. "You stay here like a good girl."

He finally looked out of the window, got her to show him again where her husband was, then took no notice of her while he stared at her husband for a long time. There was an amused expression around his mouth that unsettled her, and he looked aggressively casual as he examined the other man from head to foot. He had a matchstick in his mouth and was rolling and chewing it, and she was about to ask him to go easy on her husband when, thumb raised and forefinger pointing forward, he took aim at him.

"So that's Mr Journalist, eh," he said. "Looks as though he could write something pretty good if someone gave him a helping hand."

He mimed firing a shot, making a soundless "Bang!" with his lips, and his hand went up as if from its recoil.

"How about 'The Return of Fascism to Croatia' or some other crap? Sure to appeal to the pharmacists and the lady librarians."

His voice was full of scorn, and as he went on speaking it was obvious it was not the first time he had talked about the subject.

"It's the hot story, and your old man would be in good company with all the other pricks in the world who can't get enough of it, and actually he'd have a head start on most of them, having been here at least once before."

She hadn't told him very much about her husband but now regretted every word she had said. Hearing Angelo's mocking laughter left her unable to shake off the feeling that she had handed her husband over to him. It hurt her to see him so vulnerable, and she wanted to protect him.

"Can't you keep your unpleasant thoughts to yourself?"

She tried in vain to free herself from his grip.

"Let me talk to him and I'll come straight back," she said. "I won't leave you on your own, don't worry."

Her husband was now wrestling with a map, and as he tried to unfold it he kept looking around, expecting someone to come to his aid, and she saw that the expression on his face had something desperate about it. He kept mopping the sweat from his forehead, then finally brought out a handkerchief that he used to dab the back of his neck as damp patches began spreading under his armpits. She was afraid that any moment now he might knot the handkerchief at its corners and drape it over his head. But he took a few steps across the square, then came back again and stayed standing there, as if it had just occurred to him that this was the very centre of the city and she would have to come past it eventually, so it would be best for him to stay here at least for a while and not move from the spot.

He had put his right hand on his heart and was breathing through his open mouth, and because the gesture made her feel pain there too, she tried again.

"I'll tell him he should go home."

She might have been speaking to a brick wall, from the way Angelo continued to sit completely unmoved. He was still gripping her wrist, and almost unnoticeably he increased the pressure of his hand. As he did so, he glanced at her with an expression that did nothing to conceal his amusement at the situation.

"He'll do that sooner or later anyway," he said, his cynical tone unchanged. "In the end there'll be nothing else he can do."

Without warning he suddenly hauled her up from her chair. He had spat out his matchstick and was smiling invitingly at her. As he pointed behind her with his free hand, he pushed her in that direction with the other.

"Give the problem a little time, and it'll solve itself."

He steered her ahead of him, and when they were in the toilets she let it happen, let him pull her knickers down to her knees, and with one hand on her mouth press her back with all his weight against the cubicle door, which couldn't be locked, and when they came back into the bar her husband had gone.

"You see."

Her husband might have been a ghost, the way he said it. Angelo lit himself a cigarette, pressed a glass into her hand, and waited for her to drink it. Then he went on smoking, unruffled, sitting blowing smoke rings into the air and watching them rise, as she licked her lips and kept touching the corners of her mouth with her tongue, as if she couldn't believe that there was no blood there. She looked away from him and felt so naked that she kept tugging at her dress, pulling it down over her legs and up to cover her breasts, and hiding behind her hair, and she couldn't wait to get up and go.

Outside, she walked quickly to the nearest phone booth, and while Angelo, the butt of the cigarette he had been smoking still in the corner of his mouth, both hands dug deeply in his trouser pockets, walked up and down, watching her, she called the newspaper offices in Vienna and got the secretary to tell her the name and phone number of her husband's hotel in Zagreb. She hung up at once, dialled the number, and asked for him. It turned out that he had just come through the door, and the next moment she had him on the line.

"What are you doing here?"

She made an effort to keep calm.

"I saw you," she said, and between the individual words there seemed to be real empty spaces in her voice. "Are you spying on me?"

She heard him breathing heavily, as though he had been running. His hotel must be very close, perhaps even somewhere on the square, and at the idea she ducked and looked around, but there was nothing, just the usual passers-by, always the same people, it seemed to her, a half-dozen of them sent past again and again, supposed to simulate normal life, while everyone else had packed their bags and gone long ago. There was no sign of him, and it struck her that it would all turn out to be an illusion and that he was really sitting in Vienna on a perfectly ordinary afternoon, unable to work out why she was so agitated, and then he spoke her name and it sounded so strained that she instantly returned to reality.

"I've been trying to reach you for days."

His breathlessness had gone.

"Haven't you got a T.V.?"

He hesitated, perhaps wondering whether to show his relief or to heap reproaches on her, but in the end he just sounded glad to hear she was safe.

"You don't seem to understand what's going on here," he said, making an effort not to sound critical. "Are you living on the moon?"

She would have liked to say yes as she looked out and saw Angelo, not ten paces away, tapping his wrist with his forefinger to tell her to hurry up, and then she heard the uncertainty in her husband's voice. He hadn't spoken to her like that since the very beginning of their relationship, and she was moved by the raw undertone to his voice and thought, he has no idea what I've just been doing, although in the past he had been just as obsessed with getting into her knickers in the most impossible places, once even in the choir of a church, unfastening one hook after another and not so much proving his love for her in the process but breaking away from his petit bourgeois origins, as he would probably have said himself, escaping the beds where his parents and grandparents had been born, consummated their marriages, and died. It was heartbreaking to think how much time had passed since then, but in remembering it she had a feeling that she had to protect him now, as though he still had it all to come, and would either be initiated into the mysteries of life soon enough, or be spared them for ever.

"Go home," she said. "Go home."

He couldn't possibly hear how weightily her instruction rang in her own ears, a command that he must obey at all costs to ward off disaster.

"I need a few more days."

Before he could reply, she rang off, but kept the receiver to her ear as she turned towards Angelo, who had started kicking pebbles across the square. As soon as he looked back at her she nodded to him, and pretended she was still talking, moving her mouth, and then stood there with her eyes closed and wished she could sink to the floor and huddle there while the world went on turning without her, as she used to do when she was a child and hid in the cupboard under the stairs in their first apartment in Vienna, staying in the cramped cubbyhole until she heard her mother's steps above her, or her voice calling her. The effect now was the same, as if she had been holding her breath and could decide in the bat of an eyelid to stop breathing, or had stopped and was waiting to see what would happen, and Angelo no longer existed for her, and she surrendered to the feeling that time was standing still, or would move indecisively back and forth for a few moments, and only then make up its mind to go in one direction or the other.

That evening she asked Angelo to hit her. As soon as they were back in the apartment he had literally torn her clothes off her body, but he suddenly paused when she made the request, surprised herself, wondering what had come over her. At first that was his only reaction, and then, when she repeated it, he turned his head to her and looked at her, and she gradually realised that it was not sadness in his eyes but horror. Slowly he moved away from her, sat down and, with his arms propped on his knees and head in his hands, could not be induced to lie down again, and shook off her hand when she started to stroke his back and his wounded shoulder.

"I'm not doing that for you," he said at last, controlling himself with an effort. "What do you think I am?"

She didn't know what to say to him, and in her helplessness murmured alternately "Angelo" and "Love", but this made him genuinely angry.

"Where did you get the idea from? Some women's magazine?"

He was silent for a moment, and then spoke in a made-up voice, as though he had to extol himself as the very latest thing, the *ne plus ultra* in the market of sexual relations, the dream or nightmare of all girls of good family and not yet fallen angels with a migraine and too much time on their hands.

"Try it out one day, with a real savage."

His laughter switched to derision.

"If your husband can't do it for you, go to a combat zone," he shouted. "With a bit of luck you'll have no trouble finding the brute you've always wanted there."

Then he told her to bend down, and she did, although she was suddenly afraid of him, right by the bed, as he wanted, her legs spread wide, her upper body stretched out, her hands above her head. She asked him not to hurt her, but felt as if she had been impaled, split in two, every thrust going straight up past her coccyx, through her spine and into her brain as he pushed into her. She didn't hear what he was saying, didn't want to hear what he called her, a cascade of abuse that poured from him as if he didn't trust the strength of his body alone and needed to dominate her even more completely. It had nothing to do with either the woman she had been before, or the woman she would be afterwards, and while it went on she clung to the idea of being exactly the lifeless doll he had made of her, making an effort not to utter a sound, as if she wasn't there at all, and instead biting her forearm, so hard that the blue marks left by her teeth still showed days later, and closing her eyes.

When it was over she didn't move, but listened as he left the bedroom, went into the living room, and did something at the bar. She heard him fill a glass, come back, and sink into the armchair behind her with a groan. It didn't trouble her that he could stare at her, and when he immediately stood up again, picked up the quilt that had fallen to the floor and threw it casually over her, she understood the gesture without turning to him. For she knew that he would have covered up a sweating horse ridden half to death and worth no more effort with the same contempt.

"I won't hit you," he said, stretching the words out as if unsure of the right tone for them. "I won't hit you."

He bent over her and sought her eyes.

"You'll have to ask your husband for that."

It had been quiet all this time, and only now did she notice that she couldn't hear the drone of apparently approaching helicopters that she had got used to over the past few days. Not the slightest sound came in from outside, only a car now and then, steps outside the open window, nothing more. Once there was a far-off howl of an ambulance siren, then it ebbed away almost as soon as it began, leaving behind the vagueness of silence, and much later, after she must have dropped off to sleep and then woken to find herself alone in the apartment and finally stood up, gone to the window and looked out, the sky had long been dark.

"They won't be flying today," she said to herself, and by "they" she meant angels. "It must be quiet at the front."

This was not something she could have told her girlfriends

about, nor probably how, a few days later and in spite of everything, she was in the square outside the railway station just before midday, waiting to say goodbye to Angelo because he had to go back to the front. Small groups had gathered around two clapped-out Austrian post buses, with their engines running, and the first men, mainly in uniform but some in civilian clothes, were already beginning to climb on board when she saw him. He was getting out of a taxi that had been standing there for some time, and perhaps he had been watching her, perhaps even hoped that she would leave soon, but when he came up to her it wasn't like that at all, it was instead like their first meeting in the park as she walked quickly towards him and stopped in front of him without saying anything. Then she put her arms around him, and as astonished as she was at herself later, in retrospect, it felt the most natural thing in the world to do amidst all the embraces, tears and promises around her. She liked the feel of his stubble against her cheek, and smelt the warmth coming from him, his cigarette smoke and lack of sleep, a slightly sour smell she hadn't noticed on him before, and thought she also smelt something quite new in the canvas of his jacket, the dust and dryness of a past time, and didn't know whether she was actually remembering the morning of more than forty-five years ago when she had seen her father for the last time, or whether she was just imagining something about her father's kisses and the sun and the sea back then, and did not really have any memory of them at all.

"You could be my son."

There it was again, the same phrase, the same confusion as in the first hours with him, but this time she did not ask him to stay. Before she could stop to think what she was doing, she had made the sign of the cross on his forehead with the thumb of her right hand. He pushed her away and looked around to see if anyone had been watching them, and only then did she grasp the misunderstanding and wished she could undo the gesture as she saw the fear in his eyes, saw that it had been not so much a sign to preserve him from danger as a mark visible from a long way off and a target for any sniper.

"I don't know what I can wish you," she said. "If I try to picture where you have to go, nothing seems enough."

The first bus was already pulling away while the second hooted impatiently, showing that it wanted to get going, and then, as she stood, weak at the knees on the pavement, moved away before her eyes before the door had fully closed behind him. It was already hot, and those who had been left behind stood in the sun for a moment before some of them broke away and ran after the buses, women and children and, if she was not mistaken, three pregnant women among them, and her first impulse was to run with them, but she stayed where she was and raised a hand to wave, and although she knew no-one could see her, she remained like that, her eyes raised up to the sky, a cloudless blue dissolving again and again into new layers.

FIVE

AFTER HIS FIRST VISIT DON FILIP REAPPEARED EVERY FEW DAYS, but each time Ludwig drove him back into the city he kept a low profile, saying very little, and if he did talk he kept to safe subjects, relying on the series of anecdotes that linked him to the old man, in the telling of which he was as predictable as if there really had been only a sea voyage, three weeks and a few thousand kilometres, between their last weeks together in Europe and their new life in the southern hemisphere. If he was playing a part, that of the friendly, slightly absent-minded and rather superficial man of the cloth who liked to indulge in harmless reminiscence, Ludwig could hardly detect it, though it made him all the more sensitive to the fact that at the end of each drive Don Filip sat waiting in the back of the car until Ludwig opened the door for him, making it clear that he had not forgotten their first journey.

At home, Ludwig could be sure that Claudia was only waiting for Don Filip and the old man to be settled in the living room together, and then a nod was enough and he followed her down to the cellar. He had never before known a woman cheat on her husband with as much enthusiasm as Claudia, nor one so unfailing in her invention, as if there were as many ways of being unfaithful as the contortions of the human anatomy would allow, in addition to which she made – wanted to make – so much noise about it that Ludwig found himself watching the door the whole time and hoping that as little of it seeped out as the sound of shots from the room next door. If he put his hand over her mouth she bit him, breathing through his fingers, and so hard that the pain made him take it away again, letting her scream rip, a long drawn-out howl that sounded to him as though she meant it to pierce her husband to the marrow.

"Tell me something nice," she always asked afterwards, her voice coming from far away, as if nothing could reach her anyway. "Tell me lies."

The more over-excited she was, the more Ludwig thought about Nina, who had stifled the faintest moan, Nina for whom it had been a matter of honour not to let anything show, not a sound, just her trembling that became more intense, the look in her eyes and the way she counted out the seconds between her half-closed lips when he wanted to know how much longer before she came, and remembering her he found Claudia's noisy outbursts embarrassing. He was careful not to offend her, but whenever he promised her he loved her or uttered some similar phrase to keep her happy, he always had in his mind something that Nina used to say, that she didn't want him telling her any fairy tales, and he longed for her clarity.

They were weeks that Ludwig lived in an unbroken frenzy, weeks when the old man could summon him to the shooting range and he would come straight from sex with Claudia, weak at the knees and his head spinning from her, to another crazy contest with the two old men, in which it was all but impossible to beat Don Filip. He was the one they had to thank for the idea of shooting at candles instead of targets, and the expression on his face as a trembling thread of smoke rose to the ceiling from the place where a flame had just been burning was nothing short of bliss. He refused the pistols the old man offered him, producing his own weapon from under his soutane and applying himself to the task with a single-mindedness that impressed Ludwig and provoked new bursts of enthusiasm from the old man each time.

Ludwig was just glad not to be caught *in flagrante*, glad to manage to act as if his mind were fully on the competition in hand, as Claudia grabbed her clothes and scurried out of the next room and upstairs to greet them all half an hour later like the perfect housewife, her cheeks perhaps a little flushed, with lipstick newly applied and perfect hair that swung wide every time she turned her head. On these occasions Ludwig scrupulously avoided her gaze, concentrating fully on the two old men, but the more aware he became of Don Filip's purpose in soliciting donations, the longer the list of what was intended to be purchased with them grew, the more unreal it seemed simultaneously to recall how Claudia's body had just been stuck fast to his. It was a crazy sort of reversal effect, making the two old men and their intended enterprise seem like a couple of children playing in a sandpit and producing an outrageous sensation of superiority, at least as long as Claudia's smell remained on him, which finally tipped over into comic opera the day a marine officer turned up, a man with supposedly excellent connections in the government who had come to help them get their aid parcels moving, but who turned out to be, above all, a pomaded and polished dandy from the top of his head to the soles of his boots, who bowed deeply to the lady of the house, kissed her hand, and seemed to belong to real life far less than even Don Filip and her husband.

The old man described him as a hero of the Malvinas War, but Ludwig couldn't imagine that he had ever been anything other than an orderly-room stud, with his close-fitting uniform stretched over his pot belly. He had a girl's narrow hips, knock-knees exaggerated by his boots, an impenetrable leathery face with deeply sunken little slits of eyes, and kept looking around as if he were being followed. As nervous as he was, Ludwig would have guessed him to be in the cavalry rather than the marines, keeping a parade-ground mount that was good for nothing else and perhaps a whip for his mistress.

Conversation with the officer also took place behind closed doors, and after he had gone the old man and Don Filip made fun of him, confirming Ludwig's impression of all three of them. They described him as old-school, out of the same mould as those colonels and generals in various branches of the Army who until a few years before had vied for power, showing up outside the presidential offices at Casa Rosada with their toy tanks every few weeks and, without a shot being fired, overthrowing the government, deposing the president and placing him under house arrest on full salary. Ludwig had heard the old man's opinion of the junta more than once, that compared to all the other alternatives, especially the "gentlemen *guerrilleros*" as they called themselves, it had been a stroke of luck for the country, and he could tell that, however much he made fun of him, the old man liked the figure the dandified officer presented, as if you only needed perfect manners, the possession of perhaps two pairs of white gloves for every eventuality, and sufficient French to know how to invite a lady to dance, to render all further questions superfluous.

It seemed appropriate that he now began to come out with his own bizarre ideas more and more often, like a barrage laid down to cover the busy intrigues on which he and Don Filip were bent, and the whole faintly ridiculous spectacle of belligerence touched another low point when one weekend two men came to the house, whose showy appearance visibly identified them as villains and who were apparently to form the nucleus of a future rapid-reaction force. They had the fighting-dog look of bodybuilders of long standing who had become pot-bellied and slow, and they came with the appropriate references. One boasted of having taken part in half a dozen Antarctic expeditions while the other claimed, without irony, to be a former member of the paramilitary death squads maintained by the state in the '70s, and as proof showed the three "A"s sewn into the lining of his jacket, standing for "Alianza Anticomunista Argentina" and certifying that he was licensed to kill. The pair smirked at the old man's salute when he greeted them, and stood with folded arms, scratching their biceps, left and right, and listening to what he had to say in silence. They summoned a weary smile for the Second World War map of the "Independent State of Croatia" that he spread out in front of them, showing the country extending over all of Bosnia and as far as Belgrade, and the same smile at the sight of the shooting range, and when Ludwig was introduced to them as the instructor with whom they would practise combat operations on the banks of the Plata, they were already bored with the whole thing. They drew a month's pay in advance that evening, casually stuck the pistols that were their basic equipment into their belts, and when they failed to turn up next morning to get better acquainted and with the vague idea of reconnoitring the terrain, there was little doubt that they wouldn't be back.

In spite of these farcical plans, which inevitably ended in setbacks, when the old man was alone with Ludwig he was much the same, at most a little more sentimental, the way he had been before Don Filip had become a regular visitor. Their expeditions into the city together were not so frequent, but when they went the trips lasted longer, the old man happy to take any detour, to show Ludwig a view over the harbour from somewhere up in Barrio Norte, or a bar in La Boca or Barracas where he once used to drink, or in the evening direct him along the banks of the river to the city airport, where they would sit in the car as only lovers usually sat, or sometimes families with children at weekends if they had no money for the zoo or anything else, watching the planes coming in to land over the coffee-coloured water. The only thing Ludwig dreaded was when the old man harped on about his status as an outsider, its symbol being the Hotel de Inmigrantes where he had spent his first days in the city and to which he sometimes requested Ludwig to drive him when they were in Retiro, an extended barracks-like building on the Dársena Norte that was now a museum but in the past had been the reception hostel for new arrivals in the country, that additionally stood in a street called Avenida Antártida Argentina, so that every immigrant who harboured any illusions was clearly apprised of the reality that he had come to the ends of the earth, and not heat but cold would reign in his private hell. At home too the old man now often asked Ludwig to keep him company, and although he did not talk much he was friendlier than before, like an old dog who had been kicked about and left home recently, not half a century ago, and so did everything he could to keep alive the pain of his loss that was all he had in life, bringing out again the pictures of the village where he had grown up, a shabby-looking collection of houses on a bleak, stony hillside, and his parents' house a little over to one side with a view of the sea.

On the days when Don Filip stayed away, the old man even spent some time with the little girls. One day Ludwig drove all three of them to the run-down area around the bus station, close to the Yacht Club, which was usually out of bounds for them, and watched the girls standing on the edge of the harbour basin and looking up at their father, as if waiting for instructions, although none came. The old man led them back through the poor area at the foot of the cliff – when the wind blew from the river, the howling of the dogs here could be heard at night, even in the house on the heights – and as they were going along the dusty street that would turn to mud in the rain, with dogs barking at them from all sides, and certainly under observation from inside the dark hovels, he reached for the pistol he was carrying under his jacket. It was an unobtrusive gesture, which Ludwig saw reflected, even long afterwards, in everything their father did with the two little girls, and although he often seemed to be just making up for earlier neglect when he pushed them on the swing in the garden, sat them on his shoulders, or carried them through the house like two sacks of flour until he had to sit down exhausted, at these moments he also called them by their names and joined in their laughter. It was natural for him to test their Croatian, and natural for him to show affection when they replied correctly, and whenever there was a word they didn't know Ludwig had to come into the breach and be shown them as an example, and the old man would tell them, jokingly, what an impertinence it was, how disgraceful for two girls from Dalmatia, as he called them, although they had never been out of Argentina, for two daughters of the Adriatic not to know the Croatian words for moonbeam, honey, light, when even a former policeman from Austria knew those terms.

It was on such a day that the old man asked Ludwig to take a photograph of them all, he himself immediately uncomfortable with his own wish, brusquely requesting Claudia and the little girls to take up a position in the garden, where he joined them. Then he called the dogs, and when they too had lain down in front of the group, panting, their muzzles raised in the air, their ears pricked, the picture couldn't be taken quickly enough. They stood together, the old man in a suit, the two little girls in the innocent dresses they always wore, even Claudia in something old-fashioned for the occasion, and to anyone who saw the picture and did not know better it might have looked as though it were taken more than a human lifespan ago, so that they might all be dead, and just before Ludwig pressed the shutter he saw that not one of their faces bore even the ghost of a smile.

This sort of unreality now seemed to have been part of his life for a long time. He no longer thought it exceptional, it felt normal to drive the increasingly reserved Don Filip back to the city at night or to chauffeur the old man around after sleeping with his wife, with his employer resorting to sententious maxims to avoid saying what really moved him as night fell and the lights came on in the streets. On one occasion he said abruptly that what he had not done in his life, what he had missed out on, had failed to do, was as important to him as everything else, because his longing for it was much greater than a genuine memory could ever be, but even before Ludwig could work out what he meant he saw his despondent look and knew it was nonsense. Afterwards he always thought of that moment of non-disclosure, when he drove to the San Isidro house in the evening and saw the light in the windows and had to fight off the feeling that he was coming home, or when he went for a walk along the banks of the river and the high-rise blocks in the city centre seemed to tremble on the water in the distance, and he wished that his own state of suspension in which he found himself, his muted, almost drugged state of feeling, his painless existence without memory of Nina or of his daughter in Graz or anyone else from his former life, would never end.

There was no shortage of warnings that he was simply pretending to himself, but he was unprepared for the encounter with the old man that wrenched him out of his reverie, down in the shooting range one morning. He had spent a sleepless night, and been firing a few rounds to calm his nerves, alone in the room for the first time – in the flickering neon light it radiated the chill of a refrigerator – when the old man came in and asked if there was something wrong with his nerves, firing a gun at this hour like a madman. Without answering, he let the old man take the pistol from him, unclip the magazine, and empty it round by round, as inoffensive-looking as he could be in his dark blue pyjamas with the two white stripes on the sleeves and the slippers that he wore.

"You're surely not going to profane the Lord's Day?" he said, and there was a dangerous quiver in his voice. "Had it escaped your notice that it's Sunday today?"

He waited, looking around the room in apparent embarrassment, although there was nothing to be seen here that he didn't know inside out, then out it came, each word like a blow.

"You're sleeping with my wife."

This was after a week when Ludwig had been into the city with Claudia almost every day, having a couple of drinks at the Plaza, the Alvear Palace or the Café de la Paix, and then letting her take the wheel and, squeezing his hand firmly between her legs, drive for fun up and down the wide Avenida 9 de Julio and, tyres squealing, a couple of times around the obelisk in the middle as if it were a golden calf, before they finally took a room in Recoleta, in one of the hotels in the Calle de Azcuénaga where they were rented by the hour, with a view of the afternoon light on the gravestones in the nearby cemetery. He remembered the expression of the porter-receptionist, to whom he would have liked to apologise for their comings and goings, doubly melancholy behind his dark glasses and the toughened glass of his lodge, and did not dare glance at the old man. For at the same time he was thinking of the way Claudia's pupils rolled up so that only the whites of her eyes showed, whenever her breathing quickened and rasped, as though she were going to die lying there under him, her hands gripping his back and letting rip like a police siren in the streets of San

Francisco, as she laughingly said herself, her face empty and angular with desolation.

The experience had been so weird that Ludwig smiled as he thought of it, and didn't know what he should find more absurd, that sense of humour or the situation he now found himself in.

"I'm not sure I understand you," he said at last, stumbling over his words. "Is this meant to be some kind of joke?"

It was all he could say in his own defence, and the old man left him in uncertainty for some time. He seemed detached, just looking at Ludwig and appearing to enjoy his confusion. Then he held the unloaded pistol to Ludwig's temple and pulled the trigger twice, accompanying each click with a dry "Bang!"

"You're lucky you're not the first," he said as he looked away again. "Or you'd be a dead man by now."

It was a few moments before Ludwig realised that this was just a macabre attempt to frighten him. Hearing the old man's laughter, as if from a distance, and feeling a hand on his shoulder, he badly wanted to walk away without a word and sit with a cigarette on the toilet, such was his urge to empty his bowels. He knew that there were no rounds left in the magazine but the threat remained, and he made a strenuous effort to control the shaking that spread out from his heart through his whole body and the next moment collapsed again to a burning point somewhere deep inside him.

"You shouldn't play with that," he said, unable to make his words sound as relaxed as he intended. "You know it brings bad luck."

All his helplessness, all his feeling of being at the old man's mercy, was in the remark, and his longing for a world in which you could make things unhappen over and over again.

"I don't imagine you'd like to be in my place, with me having a laugh at your expense."

Real cramps were running through him, and he could not calm

down, despite the old man apologising and, when that didn't help, addressing him in a tone of exasperation.

"Don't get so excited about it," he said, throwing up both hands and lowering his head in excuse. "You're still alive."

He pushed the pistol into his own mouth and looked at Ludwig for a long time before, closing his eyes, he pulled the trigger with a theatrical gesture.

"Well, are we quits now?"

The story he told then had nothing to do with the incident, but he imbued it with as much meaning as if it were supposed to be some sort of commentary. Pointing to the picture of the condor on the wall, he said that there were stories of members of the species who, when they felt the approach of death, soared as high as possible in the sky and then dived down to smash themselves to pieces on the bare rocks. Despite its irrelevance, there was something unpleasantly symbolic about the idea, and while Ludwig gazed again with mixed fascination and disgust at the bird's blood-red head, looking as if it had been skinned and then replaced on the white ruff at its neck, its head turned away to one side in flight, he could not rid himself of the impression that the old man was talking about himself.

In contrast he had felt, whenever he looked at the photograph, that condors were creatures who would still be hovering high in the air, their cold eyes sweeping empty expanses before and after all time, when nothing else was moving on earth, angels and creatures of hell in one. He tried to explain this to the old man.

"They remind me more that eternal life and death are the same thing," he said. "As far as I know, the Indians saw them as messengers of the gods."

The old man looked at him askance, as if he had lost his mind, and Ludwig switched tack in an effort to strike a lighter note.

"Have you seen any in real life?"

The old man nodded.

"There was no avoiding them whenever I went up into the mountains," he said. "Just don't ask me if I went looking for them, or if I'd rather not have seen them, given the choice."

Although this seemed to be the end of the incident, Ludwig was sure that it was on his account when, a few days later, he came on the old man and Claudia quarrelling. They were glaring silently at each other when he came into the living room, and he realised at once what he had walked into. Claudia had been drinking and looked unnaturally vivacious, and the old man seemed to be seeking an answer to something she had just said, and relieved that he could turn to Ludwig.

Addressing him by his police rank of major, which he had never done before, he adopted a formal and old-fashioned manner, as if that alone proved him to be a man of honour.

"Forgive me if I send you away, but we have a few matters to settle," he said. "Would you be so kind as to stretch your legs for a while until we call you?"

With that he stood up and led Ludwig to the door into the garden. He was hardly outside when Claudia started to howl. He had caught her eye in passing, and suddenly all the old defiance in her expression had gone, without even a plea to him not to leave her alone, only a submission he had never known in her before, and it shocked him because he had never before felt such a need to embrace her, yet he had merely bowed his head and walked away at the first sound she uttered. The dogs trotted behind him, and stopped when he stopped, apparently untroubled by the sobbing that came again and again, while he walked the whole length of the garden wall but could not find anywhere, even in the remotest corner, where the sound didn't reach him. At one corner there was a place where you could see a triangular sliver of the river's mouth, and he looked intently into the distance until the last of the whimpering had died away and been replaced by the sound of music coming from the house, which made him shiver because it reminded him of what it had meant in the time of the generals, a gramophone turned up to ear-splitting volume in a police station, or a car parked outside it with the engine in neutral at maximum revs.

Perhaps half an hour had gone by, and around him the afternoon had come to a stop, when the old man came across the garden and stood next to him.

"Don't worry too much."

He put a hand on Ludwig's shoulder.

"Maybe you'd like a few days off," he said, "if all this is getting a bit too much for you. You could take a boat trip upriver."

He tried to justify himself.

"As you know, my wife has problems."

He tried a joke about her psychiatrist in Palermo who wasn't just supposed to be drying her out but straightening her out to boot, as he put it, while all the time he was just making her crazier than ever, but Ludwig couldn't listen to him any more.

"It's your business," he said, trying in vain to speak firmly, hearing his voice breaking. "You'll have to deal with it on your own."

He carried on staring out over the water, until he became aware that the old man was holding something in his hand. It was three hundred-dollar bills, uncreased and fresh from the bank, and he held them out as he might just have held out a piece of sausage to the dogs, and when Ludwig did not reach for them he simply put them down on the balustrade, where the first breath of wind would blow them away. Then he walked back again, but not without turning when he was halfway to the house to see if Ludwig had moved, and shaking his head before going on his way, calling once each to Capitán and Teniente, though the two animals were following him anyway.

This was another occasion when Ludwig might have backed out of the whole business, but when he finally went back into the house and found Claudia wandering around with a bruise under her left eye and holding a bottle of wine from which she drank from time to time, while the old man sat in an armchair and watched her, he dismissed the possibility from his mind. Keeping his eye on the dogs, who lay sleepily on the floor and raised their heads apathetically when he came in, he walked past them without a word and withdrew to the cellar room. He felt glad that the two little girls were out with their nanny and had not witnessed any of the scene, and over the next few days he ensured that, as far as possible, things carried on that way. Claudia did not want to talk to him, just looking at him half-pityingly, half-contemptuously when he spoke to her and dabbing at the swelling on her face that slowly turned every colour of the rainbow beneath a thick layer of make-up, while the old man left him to his own devices with a condescension that was intended to show Ludwig how sure of himself he was, and also perhaps connected with a disappointment that Ludwig hadn't put up more opposition. Husband and wife both kept their distance, sometimes treating him as though he didn't exist at all, but instead of using it as an opportunity to withdraw he kept himself at a sort of heightened readiness, enquiring several times a day whether he was needed for anything, and making himself visible, providing a presence as he self-mockingly put it, acting the part of the man who was ever-available and, more and more, ready for anything.

He couldn't explain his reaction, and probably there was nothing to explain. Sometimes spending hours in the company of the two little girls, he only knew that he was waiting, and with each day that passed he felt a piece of his former life break off, as if another had lived it, a police officer with an apartment in Hütteldorf who just happened to share the same age and name as him, had the same child by the same wife, and the same memories of a lover who had bled to death as he watched. For the first time since he left Vienna he had not forgotten his dreams when he woke up, though he had no idea what to do with them, with the fact that now, night after night, he was taking Nina's service pistol away from her again before he hugged her, and at the same time bringing his daughter back to Graz after an afternoon in the Prater with two pistols that fired blanks, an enormous cartridge belt, and strict instructions not to address him as Ludwig anymore, as her mother wanted, but to call him Daddy. Then, on top of this, Don Filip sat down with him one evening and asked if he would like to make confession, and the question seemed so absurd to him (and not just on account of the priest's excessively implausible character) that he was profoundly relieved when at last the old man asked him to go down to the shooting range with him again and shortly afterwards Claudia too, as if it were pre-arranged, stopped sulking and came back to his bed.

So life was almost back to the way it had been before, and the only marked difference was her insistence on choosing the El Tropezón as the place to sleep with him again for the first time, as if the occasion required special staging, at an old-fashioned hotel in Tigre with a view of the river that enjoyed a certain notoriety among lovers with a taste for the macabre, because in the 1930s a writer had poisoned himself there.

His name was Leopoldo Lugones, and on the way there she told Ludwig that he had been the father of the police chief of the same name, a man who had the dubious reputation of finding inspiration in the techniques of butchers whenever he wanted to make people talk.

"Not that his father was any shrinking violet either."

There was a certain smug superiority in the way she talked about him and consciously dramatised his last moments.

"Apparently the poor man did away with himself because he was getting nowhere with his biography of General Roca," she said, repressing a theatrical sniff. "Isn't it sad that he couldn't think up a better reason?"

Very little interested Ludwig less at that moment than speculating about a writer's suicide, but he kept the tedious conversation going.

"Who was General Roca?"

This earned him a speech about Roca's legendary campaign to eradicate the Indians, ended by Claudia with some fanciful remarks about the Argentine soul, which he only half understood and only half wanted to.

"Every schoolchild knows General Roca," she said. "He thought up the basis of the ideas that convinced a lot of people here that they have no connection with the rest of the continent, because in reality they are blond and blue-eyed and belong to Europe."

Fortuitously the room itself was available, and before Claudia undressed she insisted, waving away his reluctance, on reading aloud the suicide note that was hung there. It was wild stuff, and at first Ludwig couldn't work out how to take her idiosyncratic passion for death, then he decided just to keep quiet and let it wash over him. After she finished reading, she announced pompously that you could tell a real man from his willingness to die for a cause, and he was relieved as she dropped her fervent tone and added laughingly that it didn't have to be a book.

"I'd like to know what your cause would be."

She lay stretched out on the bed, damp with sweat in the afternoon heat, looking at him with an expression that momentarily made him want to exist as no more than her image of him. Feeling her way, like a blind person, but without taking her eyes off him, she had had her hands on his face all this time, and only now did she remove them, and laid her head on his chest, where he felt her warm breath.

"You could claim that I'm your cause," she said. "Of course I wouldn't believe a word of it, but at least you'd be having a shot at the romantic touch, for a change."

This was a bit too gushing for Ludwig's taste, though notable for the fact that the same week he had had a conversation with the old man that had taken a similar turn, except that he had wanted to know something rather different from him.

"You've proved you can kill someone for the sake of a woman," he said, as though going back to the question of his most important qualification. "But would you do it for me?"

They had been down in the shooting range, firing at the cardboard figures supplied by Don Filip via his Army connections, lifesize dummies with targets over their hearts, and the old man had been demanding that Ludwig give them names before he took aim. He himself had had no difficulty christening them, and gave Ludwig a long list of candidates, among whom there always featured a former partisan general or a minister of the People's Republic of Yugoslavia whom he hadn't managed to dispatch himself yet, until Ludwig too knew the names of all these prominent figures by heart, consoling himself with the afterthought that many of these World War Two heroes and postwar fighters were already dead anyway.

So he didn't answer, hoping the old man did not mean it seriously, for the obsessiveness with which he was applying himself to the shooting range these days was making him anxious. Observing his shooting, he saw that the usual alternation between tension and relaxation, the old rhythm of his target practice, was gone, replaced by a cold precision, an unconditionality and determination, from which all playful elements had vanished. But after a few more shots it reached the point where after each shot he shrugged off his ear protectors, waited for Ludwig to follow suit, and repeated the question.

"Would you?"

It wasn't the first time Ludwig had encountered such fury. In the police there was always the odd officer with a restless trigger finger, who might suddenly snap, and he knew not to intervene under any circumstances, it was too dangerous, you simply waited, as you would with a sleepwalker, for the person in its grip to wake up. So he said neither yes or no as he observed the old man's perform-ance with increasing dismay.

In the end the old man turned to him, pressed his loaded pistol into his hand, guided his finger decisively to the trigger, and targeted the barrel to point at his own heart.

"Or maybe that would be easier for you," he said, breathing heavily in his agitation. "Wouldn't you at least like to try it?"

It ended in a bottle of slivovitz that they drank together to fallen comrades, but perhaps the old man's excessiveness was precisely the reason why two days later Ludwig did not hesitate to prove his loyalty to him in a slightly less dramatic way. He had been told to be ready that evening, and when the old man appeared he had driven him to one of the most disreputable parts of the city, right behind the Constitución railway station, where they parked the car on the potholed pavement and, in the dark, observed the noctur-nal bustle that was playing out around the pitches of a few ten-peso tarts, as the old man scornfully called them. Yet despite his contempt he had clearly picked one of them up the day before, after his lady friend in the Calle Maipú had stood him up, though as Ludwig instinctively unholstered his pistol and laid it on his lap, ready to shoot, the old man, fiddling with his cuffs and squinting up and down the street, was unforthcoming about why he wanted another word with her.

"You'll see everything soon enough," he said. "You'd better be ready for a surprise."

Ludwig had to be satisfied with that, and about an hour later he knew what to do when a blonde appeared in the lights of the service station across the street and the old man nudged him. He jumped out of the car, following the old man and staying close, and barred the girl's way, hands on hips and elbows so far out that his jacket parted and she saw the butt of his pistol that he had tucked into his waistband as he got out. The old man himself drew her attention to it by glancing repeatedly to assure himself that Ludwig was still with him.

"What a beautiful evening for two turtledoves like us to take a walk," he said. "Shall we look for somewhere quieter, where we shan't be disturbed?"

Acquiescing at once, she let him guide her towards a dark side-street, panic in her eyes. She turned into it, stalking ahead of him, a ghost in her boots, her fishnet stockings and a miniskirt that only just covered her bottom. She seemed to duck at each step, pulling the long, bright red feather boa that she had had around her neck behind her like a dead animal that she was trying to drag away from him to safety. The clicking of her heels on the asphalt continued for a few steps, an unreal echo, until the old man forced her into the entrance of a building where there was hardly any light. After that all was still, and she stood in the doorway with her arms hanging, giving way at the knees now and then as he talked to her.

It was no more than a whisper, and Ludwig, who was standing a few steps behind him, could hardly hear what he was saying, but it didn't escape his notice that she flinched before carrying out each instruction. She pulled the wig off her head and dropped it heedlessly on the ground beside her, and all the remaining light was concentrated on the shaved skull that became visible, as if it were shining from inside. Before he realised what was going on, she had also unbuttoned her short jacket and exposed her breasts, and then pulled up her skirt, insofar as that was possible, and pushed her knickers down to her knees, holding her breath.

The old man was speaking louder now, gesticulating with both hands and pointing again and again to the place between her legs.

"What is that?"

He was now so close to her that Ludwig had no illusions about what was going to happen, and when a light suddenly came on in the building opposite and its beam fell on her, he saw her bloody face.

"By all the saints in heaven," she said, "I beg you," as though determined to keep the dramatic manners of a diva even in this situation, and now there was no doubt about it, it was a man's voice. "If you have a heart in your body, have pity on me."

He hadn't seen the blow struck, but blood was flowing freely from her nose, and the old man stood in front of her, dabbing the jacket of his suit with his handkerchief. He took a couple of steps back, like a connoisseur intending to appreciate a work of art from the right distance, and when it went dark again at the same moment, Ludwig heard her slide down the door to the ground. She crouched there, cowering, and he stayed where he was as the old man bent over her and tried to pull away the hands she was holding over her penis to protect it.

"Look at this filthy creature," he said, gesturing with both hands again. "Did you ever see such filth?"

This time Ludwig took the three banknotes, again as smooth as if they had been ironed, that the old man pressed into his hand. It was evidently his way of seeking, or expressing, fraternity after an outburst, and afterwards Ludwig was relieved that for a long time on the drive home he said not a word and that, even so, theirs wasn't the conspiratorial silence he had experienced when one of his police colleagues had done something they shouldn't, that over-inflated sense of belonging, of being welded together by a secret. The old man sat beside him, rubbing his hands with satisfaction until Ludwig looked at him, when he started fiddling with his cuffs again then took a comb from his trouser pocket and ran it over his hair, before finally allowing himself to make a statement.

"You just cannot show any weakness at all in these situations," he said. "Once you do, you're lost."

The following day Don Filip paid his last visit before setting out for Uruguay and Chile on another fundraising expedition, from which he did not expect to be back for a few weeks, and on a sudden impulse Ludwig handed him the money the old man had given him the day before.

"Light a candle for me."

The response was all of a piece, the blessing that Don Filip casually traced in the air and the comment that accompanied it as he stood there, legs apart and smiling.

"That ought to be enough for a flame-thrower," he said, and if he was acting the part of the hooligan the next minute he reverted to his mild, kindly veneer. "May the enemies of freedom roast in hellfire."

He insisted on going down to the shooting range one last time before he left, and heard the confessions of everyone in the house, although Ludwig refused to take part, despite the old man's urging. Instead he watched as first the two little girls and then Claudia and her husband went into the living room, one by one, emerging a few minutes later with their eyes downcast and withdrawing to sit quietly in a chosen corner. Somehow the old man turned the atmosphere into one of himself going off to battle next morning, and after Don Filip had left he summoned Ludwig and asked him not to be so godless and at least say an Our Father with him. When he added that it was an order, it wasn't clear whether he meant it as a joke or not, but if Ludwig had imagined that now his employer was no longer under Don Filip's direct influence, he might be more relaxed, he was mistaken. The exact opposite happened, and with the old man's conversational partner gone he needed someone to talk to, so that from then on, not a day passed when he didn't confide the latest news from Yugoslavia to Ludwig and press him for his view of the situation there. By now it was intensifying, with the Army intervening in the fighting at Plitvice and the deaths that had resulted, and Ludwig felt it was his duty to try to restrain the old man one lunchtime when, far more triumphant than concerned, he described images showing blood in the snow, and the two little girls pushed their plates away and wouldn't eat any more.

His drums of war, however, had little to do with the reality of late summer in Argentina, and they remained a muted, unreal background noise to the still warm and mild March evenings, when you could sit out of doors and watch the stars appear after dusk, following them in their course, as Ludwig frequently did, feeling he would be perfectly at home anywhere beneath them. Claudia now came to him in his room in the cellar night after night, and when they had sex there was something desperate about the way she clung to him, apparently determined to leave scratch marks all over his back and renew them every few days, as if she too had to have something visible and equally bloodstained to set against the old man's version of events. At these moments everything the old man said abruptly retreated into the furthest distance, and Ludwig let himself be lulled into a false sense of security that, far away as it was and so unreal, none of it was anything to do with him, but was happening on a dark barbaric continent named Europe that he had left behind him, possibly for ever.

SIX

IN EARLY APRIL THE OLD MAN FLEW TO CHICAGO FOR A WEEK, then on to Toronto for a reunion with friends he hadn't seen since the war, while Ludwig drove Claudia and the little girls to Villa Gesell, where they had first met three and a half months before. They were blessed days, with the last swimming in an ice-cold ocean and the first autumn storms that made the great barn of a hotel where they stayed creak and groan like a slave-ship in a heavy swell, so that Ludwig had the impression it might break free from its moorings, windows banging, at any time and float off into the open sea. When the weather died down, the beach was left behind under a boundless sky that looked as Ludwig had never seen it before, the most delicate pale blue, shot with streaks of white, which exerted such a powerful pull that the surly earth seemed to have lost its gravity overnight and you were left with the choice of either believing in God or buying watercolours and paintbrushes and making an idiot of yourself in front of an improvised easel.

On such a day Ludwig stepped out onto the balcony early in the morning and on the beach directly in front of him, rippled with fresh rivulets and streams, saw the nanny with the two little girls, playing barefoot hopscotch from patch to patch of sand in black shorts and sleeveless vests, the kind of kit he had once worn himself for school P.E. lessons. As if they had been waiting for him, they looked up at that moment. He waved back, but despite the wind having dropped he couldn't hear their calls. Apart from them there was no-one else down by the water, and as they gradually moved away he took fright, thinking for no clear reason that there would be nothing he could do if harm came to them now. There was something heartbreakingly brave about their almost unrecognisable little figures, and as he watched them go and felt himself no longer at their side, he knew he had started to say goodbye. He kept them in view for as long as he could, and when he finally turned round and went back into his room he couldn't shake off the memory of how his own daughter, when she was three months old and on her first trip to the seaside, had sucked his forearm so hard in the roaring surf that she had left a visible imprint of her mouth for ever on his skin.

This mood stayed with him for the rest of the vacation, and it was all the harder for him when the old man met them on their return, full of plans. After his trip to Chicago and Toronto he gave the impression that people really were converging on Zagreb from all over the world, as Don Filip had said they would, old comrades in arms who just like him hadn't seen their homeland for forty-five years and were determined to be there now that the struggle, unfinished all those years ago, was being resumed. At least, that was what he said, not seeming to shrink from the implication of his words, and in fact looking like a man just back and newly inspired from a training course, to judge by the way his words carried him away. Now he too shook his fist like Don Filip in full flow, cursing the Byzantine barbarians on the far bank of the Drina, and at such moments they all knew it was better not to provoke him but to avoid him or wait in silence until he had calmed down of his own accord or disappeared to the shooting range to work off his feelings there. He spread such general restlessness through the house that Ludwig yearned to be back next to the Atlantic, yearned for the haziness of those days by the sea and the blurry, vague watercolour-like feelings they had invoked instead of the decisiveness that was now required from him all over again.

They had been back in San Isidro for a few days when the old man announced that he was taking them all with him on an excursion to the opposite bank of the Plata, to Real de San Carlos on the Uruguayan shore, where at the turn of the century a businessman from Dalmatia had built a colossal amusement park whose ruins had become a destination for sightseers from Buenos Aires. It was a sense of past and future greatness in which he himself didn't fully believe, but he was nevertheless full of anticipation when they went by taxi the few kilometres upriver from the ferry landing and then, dressed in their Sunday best like a family of pioneers or settlers, arrived at the abandoned fairy-tale landscape where visitors had amused themselves in their thousands a lifetime ago, and which was now a patch of no man's land on the edge of the world, with the darkness of a continent beyond it. Its hub was a gigantic bullring that was reminiscent of a Roman amphitheatre, its walls crumbling and separated by a palm grove from a barricaded building that had once been a hotel and casino, and they walked back and forth between the two for a long time, thinking that somewhere they would find a perfect vantage point from which they could properly view the whole complex. It was midday, and although an untidy cluster of container-shaped houses could be seen half-hidden in the bushes and at times they could hear children's voices, dogs barking, and the crowing of a nearby cockerel, they met nobody. The only living creature seemed to be an anaemic-looking horse, tethered to a post and standing motionless in a small field, but, like everything else, it could have been no more than a hallucination as they passed by.

While they were strolling down the avenue that led to the river

Ludwig dropped a little way behind the others, and as he did so he realised that he was seeing them for the first time as a family. (The nanny was absent, occupied with a visit from her cousin from Rosario.) Yet watching them he found he could not imagine a place where they all belonged together, and when he saw the old man grasp the two little girls' hands as he walked between them, all he felt was a fear that they would break away from him and run to Claudia. Physical contact seemed not to reduce the distance between the three of them at all, and it disturbed him that they could walk hand in hand and simultaneously seem to be completely separate as they stood at the waterside and looked out at the remains of the pier that had once extended the avenue, a double line of wooden posts often no more than knee-high but sometimes taller and still even linked together in some places, a line that you could imagine geometrically continuing on from its end as far as the Argentinian shore.

The old man couldn't have chosen a less appropriate place to deliver a sentimental speech, but Ludwig realised that that had been his reason for bringing them here from the beginning, as the old man, probably not quite believing his own words, kept coming back to the same point over and over again.

"One of us created all this."

He had not let go of the two little girls, and glanced at one of them and then the other, as his evident need to make a speech weighed him down and he groped for the right words.

"But I'm afraid it was all over and done with a long time ago, and probably nothing like it will ever come again," he said. "So you should see what's left of his creation."

He crouched down to tell them about his countryman, born in Dubrovnik, who had worked to realise his dream on this part of the coast. He had deserted from an Austrian warship, so the story went, and come to Argentina where he had made a fortune as a shipowner, and the old man was full of admiration for him. Staring out at the river as though he could see a steamer strung with a tiara of coloured lights there, its presence announced by the music from its band drifting across the water, he said that in those early days boats had plied between the two riverbanks several times a day, and called the Dalmatian businessman a great visionary and praised the century to the skies for those days' youth and innocence, declaring that there had been no more such men since then.

It must have sounded absurd to the little girls, and he seemed to have forgotten who he was talking to as he started to lecture them about how a legal ban on bullfighting had been the beginning of the end after fewer than a dozen bullfights in the ring, and tearfully hugged the two of them close.

"It's always the same, whenever one of us starts something," he said. "Before long, envy and resentment bring him down."

The little girls did not react, just exchanged glances, wondering what he was talking about, while he, looking around and seeing what had become of the place, suddenly became aware of the futility of his remarks. He let the girls go and looked up and down the narrow sandy beach on both sides of the pier, a hand raised to shield his eyes from the sun as the girls moved away from him. They walked to the muddy water's edge and began dropping stones into it while he stood watching them, not moving, until Claudia went up to him and put her arm round his shoulders.

"They're very young," she said. "Give them time."

He made a dismissive gesture with his hand.

"They're old enough."

The two girls were throwing sand at each other, and he turned his gaze away from them and looked at Claudia for the first time, as though they were her children alone and not his too.

"I don't ask much from them," he said, and in reality had already given them up. "So long as they don't forget where they come from, I'm happy."

With these words he looked around again, up the avenue with the bullring at the end, then out over the water and the half-ruined, half-rotting pier with its wooden pilings nailed in place. If it hadn't been for the waves lapping against the shore it would have been completely still, the stillness deepened by the far-off barking of a dog and the rapid, glass-clear chiming of a bell from somewhere in the bush, and against the boundless sky he looked like a biblical figure undergoing a trial sent by God that threatened to crush him. The way he stood there, he might suddenly have sunk to his knees, a conqueror returning to the scene of his heroic deeds only to discover that in his absence everything had slipped from his grasp and he would have to begin again from the beginning, but no longer had the strength for it.

They were on the homeward ferry when he sat down with the two little girls again. He asked them about what he had told them that day, but either they really didn't know because they had already forgotten or just hadn't been listening, or they were feeling defiant, looking at him with their big, doll-like eyes. Then he asked them which were the biggest cities in Slavonia, Dalmatia and Istria, and when he got no answer to that either he told them to count up to a hundred, in Croatian of course, so that by the time they got home that evening he was so cross with them that he smashed their piggy banks with a hammer and said that if they didn't understand what it was all about, they should at least give their few pesos for the cause, like everyone else.

But even this seemed almost a game, in comparison with the terrible news he had gleaned from his newspapers, the accounts of refugees from the Krajina and Slavonia who had retreated to the shelter of the cities or to the hotels that stood empty by the Adriatic. Events reached a flashpoint at the beginning of May when a squad of policemen was lured into an ambush at Borovo Selo and, according to some estimates, twelve men lost their lives (other sources put the casualties even higher). By now it was not just the facts that upset him about such stories but their specific background, and he spent days trying to find out more details, apparently phoning around the world, and in the end had the full story, which he had feared as much as he longed for it, an account of the men wounded in a shoot-out then laid side by side for trucks to run over them, mutilated corpses, pictures the T.V. stations had not dared to show, and rumours that the bodies, packed in boxes, had been sent to the Defence Ministry at Zagreb. In many towns there were demonstrations against the Army, and although up till then he had sometimes said that despite appearances it might still all blow over, now he was sure it was too late for that, and that war had begun.

By this time he had started talking about it outside the house, and it did not bother him that the elderly gentlemen who sought shelter from the daylight in his favourite café in the Calle Lavalle retreated from him at the bar or eyed him suspiciously, afraid that his eccentricity might turn to dangerous craziness at any moment, with him producing a gun from nowhere and opening fire at random. Every day the waiters asked him if he had heard any more news, and as they wiped tables around him, whether bored or genuinely curious, they all seemed only to be waiting for a sign from him to put on their jackets, step outside, and with the dignity of undertakers head any funeral procession he might care to assemble. He answered them as studiously as he ignored the amused smiles that lingered at the corners of their mouths, looking past them at one of the café's many mirrors or at the four wall clocks, sponsored by a coffee company, that showed the time in Buenos Aires, New York, London and Moscow, until at last, at the other regulars' urging, a fifth dummy clock, with a cardboard dial and two cardboard hands pointing ominously to five past twelve, was added to show the time in Zagreb. After that he reverted for a while to the mute, darkly brooding stranger he had been until not long before, when no-one had known anything about him except that he always drank a double espresso and asked for a little dish of olives with it, which he usually left untouched.

Weeks passed, weeks full of lamentation when the news increasingly appeared to vindicate his story and his café audience at last offered him their ear, and Ludwig began to think that he would finally adapt to playing the exiled outcast, suffering comfortably from his lost origins, the man who talked about nothing but going back soon but in reality had no plans to do anything about it. The first cold days of June arrived, and the old man still made no move, and because Ludwig himself felt more and more restless, it was he who urged him on now, who reminded him about his daughter whose birthday was in a few weeks' time, who kept bending his ear about summer at home, but got only vague answers from the old man, muttering that they could be off at any time. When the time to do something finally arrived, he both appeared to have purposely chosen the least favourable moment and took Ludwig by surprise with his urgency.

It seemed that way partly because less than a week earlier he had sent Ludwig, with Claudia and the two children, to Bariloche for the start of the winter season, and suddenly there was no more talk about the place's dubious virtues, it was all wild enthusiasm and cheerfulness, the fresh air would do the girls such good, so that his phone call, when it came, reached Ludwig as if from another world.

It was late afternoon, he was tired after skiing, looking out at the lake beyond his window and the mountains just recognisable on the far side through the sleet that had begun to fall, when the phone rang and the old man came on the line. His voice sounded very close as he asked Ludwig if everything was alright, and then, as soon as he had finished a few temporising remarks evidently intended to allay Ludwig's suspicions, he broke the news.

"Get back to Buenos Aires as quickly as you can," he said in a tone of great decisiveness. "You're flying to Zagreb with me the day after tomorrow."

Ludwig had so swiftly got used to the holiday atmosphere at Bariloche without the old man's constant whims to contend with, that the prospect did not gladden his heart. He would have liked to go on spending time out in the snow, enjoying the all-over thorough weariness that came from physical exercise out of doors and that he thought he had forgotten, although it had been the best feeling of his childhood, the happiness of coming home after spending hours and hours out in the cold. He thought of the trip he and Claudia and the little girls had taken up to the pistes of the Cerro Catedral that morning, when they had made him stop halfway, at a grotto in the middle of nowhere, and he was about to tell the old man about it, but bit his tongue and instead offered the first excuse that came to mind.

"I don't know what your wife will think if I just disappear and leave her alone with the children."

Claudia had climbed the steps up to the statue of the Virgin in the grotto, and he had to smile as he remembered how she had struck a pose there, an apparition herself in her white all-in-one snowsuit against the background of black rock, and he felt an urge to defend this absurd image, to which the girls had reacted in unison with a yelled *"puta madre, puta madre"*, with all his might.

"I'm back in the city next weekend anyway," he said, already guessing he would get nowhere. "Can't it wait till then?"

He could positively hear the disapproval in the silence, but refused to leave anything untried.

"How am I going to get there in such a short time anyway?"

The old man let him speak, and at first refused to respond. He said only that their flights were booked, and Ludwig pictured him sitting in his study, looking out at the garden and trying hard to suppress his displeasure as he presented him with a fait accompli. Then he cut the discussion short, giving Ludwig no more chance to object and sounding so sure of himself that Ludwig realised he probably hadn't chosen the timing of his phone call at random but had arranged it carefully so that his wife and children would be away from the house when he left, two weeks' holiday up in the Andes so that they wouldn't be in San Isidro, trying to stop him going.

"The best thing would be for you to get straight in the car and drive through the night," he said, and it was more than a suggestion. "Otherwise you could end up very pushed for time."

He began to talk long-windedly around the arrangements, and when he finally interrupted himself Ludwig understood that he was not playing a game.

"There's another thing."

Whether he intended to or not, he sounded solemn.

"You can consider yourself a soldier from now on."

In the old man's world this was clearly as good as formally swearing someone in, and afterwards he paused so that there was no sound on the line but a long crackling, like a lit fuse inexorably eating its way through empty space. Suddenly the distance between them seemed tangible, the hundreds and hundreds of kilometres back to the Atlantic coast. Then the old man's voice came again, as though he were in the next room.

"By the way, you can forget my suspicions about my wife."

Something in his voice made Ludwig wary.

"If you're sleeping with her, that's your problem," he said. "But you should know when it's time to say goodbye, and not take me for a fool."

He hung up, and three hours later Ludwig was on the road, still annoyed at the old man's way of dealing with him. He had been rash enough to tell Claudia about the conversation, and she had asked him whether he didn't feel he was being treated like a child and then called him a loser when he didn't answer her immediately, threatening to scream if he so much as tried to touch her, and now he drove through the thickening sleet and remembered how she had suddenly changed and clung to him, finally lying on his chest, sad and dazed by the violence of her own protestations that he couldn't let her husband push him around like that. The memory of this scene set Ludwig against the old man more than everything his employer had said to him, and by the time dawn was breaking after an endless night he had made up his mind that this time he really would end his service with him at the earliest opportunity and, thus reconciled to himself, stared ahead into the weary light in which the flat land extended for hours and hours without the slightest contour, as far as the horizon.

When he arrived at San Isidro in the evening, however, he did nothing of the sort when the old man asked if he had scared him yet again, and made no further reference to their conversation. The old man had collected all of Ludwig's things from the apartment in town and told him to pack at once. Then he made him sit in an armchair, cut his hair with electric clippers in his own razor-cut style, handed him a black suit that he had bought him, and didn't let him out of his sight, not just dressing him himself but helping him tie the necktie that of course went with it. In memory of his very first years in the country he had reserved a table at a small restaurant at La Boca, by the waterfront in the Vuelta de Rocha with a view of the old transporter bridge, and as they sat with the stink of the Riachuelo river in their nostrils despite the closed windows and the cold, he told Ludwig that the parliament in Zagreb now intended to declare independence within days.

He looked at him expectantly and seemed disappointed when he failed to share his enthusiasm.

"Don't you understand what that means?"

Ludwig was afraid he was about to go into his performance of centuries of oppression all over again, with full accounts of every martyr who had spilled his blood for the country since the Middle Ages, but fortunately he restrained himself.

"It wipes out the last forty-five years at a stroke," he said. "It will be as though they had never been."

The old man himself noticed how false this sounded and looked at his hands, embarrassed, as though he were ashamed that hope had run away with him.

"Of course, you can't give someone a new life."

Ludwig watched his eyes stray restlessly around the room, and though he had resolved not to let himself be taken in by the old man's sentimentalities anymore, he fell back into the trap.

"Is that what you'd like to do?"

Instead of an answer he received yet another roll-call of all the old man's compatriots, scattered across the continents of the world, which always culminated in the same question: "Do you know how many of them there are?"

The old man had recounted the saga over and over again, but now really seemed to want to restore to each of them individually their lost honour, never mind the different reasons for it.

"As many of them as are still living there," he said. "Which makes the idea that's now going around, of chartering ships to bring them back in the largest possible numbers, sound pretty adventurous."

Only then did he admit his fear that in the end the Yugoslav Army would come out of its barracks with tanks to prevent the country from breaking up, yet despite the depressing prospect he painted, it wasn't that that kept Ludwig awake that night when they finally returned to San Isidro. More from a kind of indecision than because he wanted to, he had suggested a last session in the shooting range, and when the old man said no he found himself alone in his room again, where the few remaining hours still gave him too much time to think, so that eventually he had to stop himself knocking on the old man's door at the crack of dawn. He had been able to repress his panic as long as he was not alone, but now he wondered how he was going to account to himself for the recent months, because if he carried out his idea of simply striking them out of his life then he was in a quandary, having to start all over again where he had left off and go right back to the Westbahnhof at Vienna, wishing that the bullet had struck him and not Nina.

In the morning the old man was attentive in a way that suggested he guessed how Ludwig had been agonising. In the taxi on the way to the airport he glanced at him every few minutes before turning and looking at length out of the window, where a layer of mist clung to the ground, and seemed absorbed in his own thoughts until he turned back to Ludwig again and tried to meet his eye.

They had left the city behind them when he finally broke his silence, and out in the open country the few houses and shacks that were visible stood in the rug of mist as if under water, rickety single-storey buildings whose gables still protruded.

"If I didn't know how unlikely it was, I'd bet on it snowing today," he said. "I can smell it in the air."

He was all emotion once more, or more truly it was his way of hiding it, but he didn't quite succeed as he continued in a quiet voice: "Winters in the south are terrible."

Ahead of them the landscape lay colourless, shades of grey in the lingering morning gloom of a day that refused to dawn properly, and later, imperceptibly, would pass into an equally indistinct evening, and he immediately fell silent again. It was so cold he had kept his overcoat on, and it made him seem faintly impatient, although he was visibly enjoying the drive. When a squall of raindrops gusted occasionally against the car, showering the windows, he was unmoved, seeming to have expected it and finding the unfriendly weather entirely appropriate to the circumstances of his departure.

When they arrived at the airport he rushed to Don Filip, waiting in the departures hall after interrupting his fundraising tour to wish them safe passage, and what a reunion it was after so many weeks, the old man hugging the priest with eyes closed, as the only way he could guard against the strength of his own emotions. He would not let go of him for a very long time, and kept pulling him back to hug him again each time he tried to free himself. Don Filip waited until his friend had subsided before he went into action himself, putting on a great show and fuss to bless them both that culminated in a piece of near-black magic at the check-in desk when he produced a screw-topped silver container and sprinkled them with holy water.

He then handed the old man two black folders.

"This is all I could find."

They were held together, bursting at the edges, with thick red rubber bands like the seals on preserving jars. Papers spilled out, newspaper cuttings and handwritten pages that looked as if they had been stuffed into the folders in haste. On the covers were the words in Gothic script "Bleiburg I" and "Bleiburg II", making a sharp contrast with the contents by the terrific care that had been taken with the calligraphy, as if the titles had been composed for all eternity in a gleaming permanent blue-black ink that stood out in relief, the upstrokes razor-sharp, the downstrokes broad as the blunt back of a knife.

The old man clutched them to him with both hands.

"Should be enough for a modest bang, anyhow!"

He laughed the way you might expect cartoon characters to laugh, if you could hear them, and fitted with the stylised picture he seemed to have of certain gentlemen's reactions when he opened the folders' covers and the contents blew up in their faces.

"It won't do them any good not listening anymore."

With each thing he said he seemed to want to outdo himself. When he at last remembered where he was, he kissed Don Filip again left and right on the cheek, his eyes popping a little and breathing through his mouth, which gave him an inane expression. Then he calmed down and stood in the middle of the waiting passengers, suddenly almost inconspicuous, a face lost in the crowd and as dangerous as anyone else.

"In my book we're good to go," he kept saying, like an invocation, causing people to turn and look at him. "I'm all set."

Although Ludwig was mortified to witness this outburst of emotion, when his turn came he didn't protest, allowing Don Filip to embrace him without a word. In retrospect he considered himself lucky, because as he hugged Don Filip the priest discovered the pistol he had unthinkingly brought with him, took it and hid it under his soutane. It was swiftly done, and Ludwig only found out when he was through security and had lost sight of Don Filip that in the pistol's place in his inside jacket pocket was a small wooden crucifix, a roughly carved object with the dates 1945 and

1991 burned into it and the words "I am with you", which Ludwig involuntarily repeated out loud.

The sense of oppression that he felt didn't leave him until they took off, and as the plane banked sharply to the left and climbed over the city and the river it didn't escape his notice that the old man too was looking back at the expanse of the pampas like a tract of scorched earth that he was leaving behind him. Ludwig had never seen such rapture, mingled with something that struck him as a glinting beneath the surface, he had never seen anyone so beside themselves and at the same time deep in themselves, except perhaps a woman who thought she was unobserved at the climax of her lovemaking, and the more reflective he himself became in the following hours, the more he noticed the old man seeming to revel in this euphoria that kept rekindling itself again and again. He spoke to Ludwig almost exclusively in Croatian, not bothering to ask whether he understood the half of it, ordered one gin and tonic after another, and flirted continually with the stewardesses, who put up with it as though he were in a state of grace and could do no wrong. Then he would take Ludwig's arm again, and when Ludwig turned to him he saw that he had closed his eyes or was looking out of the window as if it were his first time in a plane, though in reality it was to hide his face and avoid bringing on himself the stigma of a lunatic about to say outrageous things he would regret later.

Darkness was falling as they flew out over the ocean, and Ludwig was glad to see the old man eventually fall asleep as the plane droned on through the night and stay sleeping as the first lights of the European mainland showed. The black folders had been on his lap throughout the flight, and despite Ludwig's efforts to relieve him of them he had continued to clutch them, as he had clutched his rug, which he pulled back up to his chin each time it slipped until he finally laid his head on Ludwig's shoulder, breathing like a child, and Ludwig dared not move. Sitting quietly beside him for what seemed like hours, he gave himself up to contemplating how one of the shortest days of the year could turn into one of the longest as you crossed the equator, but this made him dizzy and as it gradually grew light and he stared outside he could have sworn, against all the evidence, that what he saw either wasn't blue or wasn't the sky, it was so unlike the soft transparency of the sky above the pampas, where there was nothing to catch or hold the eye.

He no longer had any doubt about what he must do, and as they were changing planes at Frankfurt he said, this time without hesitation, "I'm not going to Zagreb with you."

The old man looked at him uncomprehendingly, and he stammered, "You'll have to go on alone."

He had expected him to protest, to try to make him change his mind, but the old man just nodded, and in the terminal building's artificial light he looked grey and genuinely old for the first time.

"I thought you might say that," he said, although he couldn't conceal his surprise, and looked around searchingly, as if for help. "I'll be alright."

His eyes were full of scorn and his face showed what he thought of Ludwig's announcement, but Ludwig also saw his satisfaction, the self-pity of all who feel themselves betrayed and the warm glow of having had his darkest convictions confirmed. He watched him turn and walk away, and wavered between relief that this was probably the end of the story and the sudden thought that he might be the closest person to him in the world. He was no good at partings, even if he usually wanted them sooner rather than later, and wanted to run after the old man down the long corridor, but waited instead and counted to a hundred with his eyes closed, knowing that the old man would have disappeared into the airport crowd by the time he opened them again.

Yet it was not just his manner of departure that made Ludwig susceptible again to his former employer's overtures at the end of the summer, which he spent in Vienna after a fashion, it was also the feeling that he owed the old man something. In the meantime he had tried his hand at various less than laudable occupations, from bouncer in a nightclub to chauffeur and chaperon for the ladies of an escort service, and had already lost hope of shaking off the role of the policeman involved in the fatal shooting at the Westbahnhof, which made him ideal for such employment and at the same time marked him for ever, when the old man called. He blurted out what he wanted, and Ludwig didn't take long to think it over when he asked him to join him again, in fact he was glad to have the chance because now his daughter knew the story too and on his last visit to Graz had asked him whether it was true that he had killed a man in Vienna, and had recoiled from him in horror when he tried to stroke her hair and reassure her.

His memories of Nina were slightly different. He avoided places where they had spent time together after he walked in the Prater one day and almost burst into tears in the middle of the Hauptallee, yet he also found that he could suddenly feel her walking beside him anywhere in the city. She and he had been the same height, and he had always loved being eye to eye with her, the crazy delight at the way their sight line tipped out of the horizontal, the up-and-down of each step which had felt like a running leap to him, but now when he awoke from his daydream he was pulled up short before slinking on his way. He had a girl in the Siebensterngasse whom he saw from time to time, a masseuse with half a dozen diplomas on the wall and wonderful hands, and who, although neither he nor she really wanted it, became his girlfriend in the end, but one day as he talked to her about Nina she cut him short and he found himself back out in the street, on the grounds that she had enough work to do bringing him back to life every time he turned up at her place like a dead man, and she wasn't having that as well.

The old man assured him it was nothing major he wanted him to undertake, just to keep someone under surveillance. He seemed not to doubt that Ludwig would accept and referred to the job casually, as though it were much more important that the two of them saw each other again after all this time. Then he teased Ludwig for having left him in the lurch so suddenly, and Ludwig thought that either he really bore him no grudge about it or he hid it very well.

"If you wriggled out of it because you were afraid, I can re-assure you," he said. "The war's not coming to Zagreb, and if it does you can go straight home."

Ludwig didn't know where the old man had found his telephone number, but he didn't mind. He offered to start the next day, and the old man laughed. Then he said that Vienna didn't seem to be exactly an earthly paradise for him if he was in such a hurry to leave, and Ludwig agreed, and just as the old man was about to hang up he asked who his target was.

The old man hesitated.

"Do you have to know?"

He cleared his throat, and his voice sounded irresolute.

"My daughter."

SEVEN

BEFORE SHE MET ANGELO MARIJA HAD, JUST ONCE, GONE AS FAR as the hospital buildings on her evening walk, and after he left she remembered the piece of paper she had picked up in the entrance hall of the main building and carried around with her ever since. It was an advertisement, neatly handwritten, by a doctor offering his psychiatric services gratis (he underlined the word) to those fighting at the front, and also looking for a receptionist and assistant willing to work gratis (again underlined), and she went to see him that afternoon. The address that was given was not far from the former Victims of Fascism Square, now Great Croatians Square, on Bauerova Street, and the gentleman who opened the door to her after she climbed the broad staircase to the third floor must have retired from his practice some years ago, a small man with still thick white hair and a moustache, wearing a neatly knotted tie under his faded smock of surgical green. He took her on as soon as he heard that she was from Vienna because he had studied there for a few years before the Second World War, and for the next few days she arrived punctually at eleven at his rambling, book-crammed apartment. Two of its rooms were for consulting, one of which contained a couch, and for the next five hours she sat there with him, though she soon knew as well as he did that no-one would arrive except for his friends, a journalist no longer in regular work, but who apparently had articles published now and then, and an emeritus professor of Slavonic Studies, the only company he had left, whom he used to take into a separate waiting room where at around three in the afternoon he would entertain them with coffee and cakes, followed later by white wine and a sweetish liqueur. He complained to her only once that, at his age, there was nothing he could do, or he would have been the first to volunteer, and she decided that if it helped him to offer his hypothetical services she understood exactly how it was, and so would knock from time to time at the door of the room where he sat playing cards with his friends and ask him to come, "If you don't mind, Doctor . . .", and he would put down his hand of cards, excuse himself and go out to smoke a cigarette with her in the hallway or just wait in silence until exactly thirty minutes were up and he could rejoin the others as if he had just finished with a patient.

That she herself might end up being the one to turn to him was the last thing she expected. She hadn't intended to, but one day, after the other two failed to turn up, she started to talk about herself in such a vague and ambiguous way that it seemed it was her only reason for coming to him. To begin with, he interrupted her from time to time, then he just listened, sitting opposite her at his desk, and she saw the nature of his interest change, as what had begun as a private conversation gradually turned into a professional appointment, with him scribbling a note on a sheet of paper with one of the neatly sharpened pencils lined up in front of him and then, as she fell silent, apologising before finally, almost as if going on the offensive, asking her the decisive question.

"What about the soldier?"

It was impossible for her to really say anything about Angelo, and she regretted having mentioned him at all, for the more she had tried to force herself not to think about him the less she had succeeded, and she knew that the first wrong word would bring it all pouring out, which she absolutely did not want. The phone number he had given her didn't answer, and as soon as she realised that she couldn't reach him she felt wretched – she had never asked his surname, nor did she know where he was from or which unit he belonged to – and now she reproached herself bitterly for just letting him go, as she followed the news from Slavonia with ever-increasing anxiety, unable to look at the T.V. pictures of the destruction there and then looking all the same, as if he were sure to appear among the ruins at any moment.

"What do you mean, what about him?"

At the end of a long working life the doctor knew very well that he couldn't insist, but he couldn't conceal his curiosity to hear something new, something different from the usual dances men and women led each other, in all their complications, of which there were perhaps no more than half a dozen variants and he was familiar with them all, however outlandish, however apocryphal.

"I noticed how you talked about him."

He had a concerned expression, and she looked at him in surprise, immediately on her guard against professional sympathy.

"I didn't say anything."

He agreed with her.

"But you couldn't have been more eloquent," he added. "I feel that I know your whole story."

This struck her as so brazen that she laughed.

"My whole story?"

She shook off the hand that he placed on her arm, and didn't know whether to be touched or repelled by the sadness that he radiated at that moment.

"Aren't you confusing something?"

She found the pompous warmth of his comprehension dis-agreeable, and when he finally added that it was always like that and she didn't need to feel ashamed about being taken in by an illusion, she let him know what she thought.

"Maybe it's really your story, and you've got some sort of transference going on," she said. "I hope you're at least aware of the possibility."

They both lapsed back into the silence in which they spent most of their time together and which she was already used to, it being her second week, the week the article was published about his practice, the one the journalist had said he was writing when she first met him (though he hadn't been taken particularly seriously in the bantering atmosphere of the three men's conversation), a panegyric to his friend's unselfish and patriotic work in this time of crisis, which he showed to her with visible pride. The snapshot he had taken of her and the doctor standing at the waiting-room door bore the caption "The doctor and his assistant from Vienna", and as she skimmed the couple of columns of well-turned phrases next to it he pointed to the picture as if she might otherwise miss it, a photo on the blurry side of sharp that annoyed her chiefly because without advance warning she would hardly have recognised herself in the woman who stared at the camera with a slightly crazed and hopelessly yearning expression. To top it all, the article gave her full name, which she had told him with some reluctance, and without knowing why she had used her maiden name and not the surname she had had for nearly twenty-five years, and this made her feel more defenceless, as though it were about another person, another life, with another past and future, whose naming in the newspaper was probably the trigger for everything that followed.

For two weeks later the first advertisement appeared, "Marija [. . .], your father is looking for you," and if she thought fleetingly that Angelo was behind it, making fun of her because she had kept on and on at him about her family history, she knew immediately that it couldn't have been him, for one thing he didn't have the money. The address for reply was the Hotel Esplanade, but she didn't answer, though she did go to the hotel that evening and stayed at the bar for a short time, barely even looking around to see if there was a man of the right age there, then leaving her drink half-finished and hurrying home as though she didn't want to be dragged into a story that was not her own. The person who placed the advertisement must have meant someone else of the same name, she reasoned, trying to reassure herself, after all, it wasn't such an uncommon name, even though she knew this to be a weak explanation that only meant the second and then the third advertisement hit her harder. By then at least it was clear she couldn't pretend to herself any longer, and that it was up to her and nobody else to discover what all this was about if she wanted to preserve her soul's peace.

The simplest thing would have been to reply immediately, but before she could persuade herself to do so, the journalist, whom she had told what had happened along with the professor and the doctor, brought her a double-page spread containing an interview that had appeared a couple of weeks earlier, and from that moment on there was no doubt.

"It's an interview with the man who placed those ads," the journalist said, his eyes hidden behind the rims of his glasses as he looked at her. "Seems an interesting fellow."

The first thing to catch her attention was the two photographs that accompanied the interview, in one of which she would have recognised her father even if she had been half-blind, because it had been with her through her entire childhood and youth in Vienna, on the chest of drawers in the bedroom she had shared with her mother and later in a place of honour under the crucifix, as long as they had one, in their various apartments, and finally framed and hung on the wall where their few visitors were bound to see it. It showed him as a young man, in 1942 or '43 as the caption said, standing on the left of the picture, knees bent, in paratrooper's overalls, one hand on his trouser seam, and in the other a fully open parachute that had just touched down and filled the rest of the picture. All the light seemed to be trapped in its nearly transparent hemisphere with its undulating hem and visible median seams, and she immediately remembered how, as a child saying her evening prayers, she had sat on the edge of her bed with her hands together and imagined that it was the sun, that her father could make it rise and set with a tug on the lines and that he watched over her sleep as the lord of light and darkness.

The journalist was waiting for her to say something, but the picture's impact was so strong that she closed her eyes and wished fervently that it could carry her away.

"Give it to me," she snapped at him, sounding more petulant than she wanted to. "Or do I have to beg you for it?"

She knew he had seen the picture's effect on her and hoped that he would now go away, but he stayed standing close to her, a chubby man with a shaven head and impassive eyes who was the one of the trio who sometimes looked at her as though he thought he stood a chance with her. He had never complimented or teased her or said anything saucy or insinuating, but even though she hardly felt his hand's pressure as he touched her forearm she was careful not to give way and lean on him for support as she could have done. Her distrust was not just because his look followed her whenever she fetched the doctor from the waiting room, there was his physiognomy too, the germ of hope in his face despite his age, which distinguished him from the other two, who both had something sexless about them and would hardly have addressed her with slight suggestiveness as "child", the way he did now.

"Do you feel unwell?"

He tried to persuade her to sit down, and when he saw how pale she had become he wanted to get her a glass of water, but she had stepped away and eluded his grasp and was already at the door.

"Don't worry," she said. "It's nothing."

Then she was outside the room, speaking to herself.

"It's only my father."

The doctor's apartment was large, and her heels clacked on its parquet floor as she hurried through its rooms, trying to find somewhere she wouldn't be disturbed, until she finally came back to the consulting room and sat on the couch, her last possibility of escape exhausted, and waited quietly to meet her fate. There had been an air-raid warning earlier that morning, but neither she nor the three old men had reacted to it, and in the silence now the sound of traffic drifted up from the street and the sultry morning, announcing another hot day, treacherous and unbearable in its everyday idleness, and she wondered whether she should simply throw the newspaper pages away and pretend she had never seen them. She tried to calm herself, but she hardly knew where or how to start reflecting on what had happened without the pain of it overwhelming her, until she became unable to defend herself at all and started hearing her mother's voice, which had become softer and softer with the passage of time but had never stopped assuring her that her father might yet be alive, seducing her with more and more stories, all of them over and done with long ago and she herself hardly believing them anyway, though for her mother's sake she had carried on pretending to be waiting for his return, despite the fact that the war had literally swallowed him up and they had never heard another word from him. The notion that he might come swaying down from the sky beneath his parachute one fine day, knock on their door and walk in, had dominated her childhood, and she sensed that the weeks, months and ultimately years of her fears were all buried in that picture and she must never let them take her captive again.

But it was the second photograph in the newspaper that told the complete story, or as much as she needed to know, and again a glance had sufficed, so that she tried to blot it out as she unfolded the two pages again, but the fact that the man in the picture, undoubtedly her father, was standing next to a much younger woman kept drawing her back and, hard as she tried to resist the impulse, she found herself looking from one to the other and back again, the ageless man in sunglasses and a white, starched shirt, his sleeves rolled up, with what to all appearances was a bottle blonde in a pale blue summer dress, a few pounds overweight in the right places, and with more than enough gold around her neck and on all her fingers, and only after she had studied them both did she dare to lower her gaze to the two little girls squeezed in front of them, twins, indistinguishable from each other, with dreamy eyes and black, shoulder-length plaits. They must be five or six, the age she had been when she lost sight of her father, but although she instantly remembered being introduced to visitors on many occasions dressed in just the same way, it wasn't the little white dresses the girls wore or their white patent pumps, their white hair-slides or the crosses they wore around their necks, that her eyes lingered on. It was the unquestioning confidence in their eyes by which she most clearly recognised herself and which simultaneously hurt her the most, their certainty that he was standing behind them, they had no need to turn around, they took it for granted that he was there.

The realisation hit her with a delay, and she stared at the two children, refusing to let herself fully take it in. It might have been because the narrow strip of water in the photograph's background was the Río de la Plata, as the caption said, and that she could not bring near and far together in her mind so quickly, but eventually she could no longer refuse the idea that these little girls were her sisters, her little sisters at the other end of the world. The names played their part, Carmen María and Evita María, and no sooner had she absorbed them than she could not get her mother's words out of her head, that whenever she had asked why she was called Marija and not something else, her mother had always countered with the same answer: you're called after the Virgin, Marija, you're called after the Virgin.

The interview was headlined "Return from Argentina", and underneath it the standfirst "Croatian anti-Communist returns home after forty-five years in exile", and though she could hardly concentrate as she read it, one of the first things she registered was the true dates of her father's biography. If the article was factually correct, he hadn't been killed in the last days of the war or soon afterwards in Slovenia or Carinthia, as she had believed, but had fled from the advancing partisans first to Austria, from there to Rome, and finally overseas. The article carried a third illustration showing the back of a postcard sent from Italy, dated 10 March 1948 and addressed to his hand at the Basilica, Buenos Aires, but she could not make out either the significance the banal text was intended to have, giving expression to hopes of his safe arrival in the New World and good wishes for a new life, or the two blurred and barely legible signatures, one of which was allegedly that of Monsignore Giovanni Montini, later Pope Paul VI.

However, that was not what puzzled her, not what set her racking her brains, any more than the details of his life did. These were the usual kind of thing, there had been dozens of such stories about people who had returned to Zagreb in the last few months, and at first sight his seemed fundamentally the same to her, one of the muddled heroic legends of men who had waited for decades in some corner of the world and decided that their hour had come, and so were now hurriedly glossing over the dark matter in their biographies or so broadly reinterpreting it as to suggest that there was nothing to be glossed over, and if they were not exactly turning up in the city as brilliant victors, it was as the stubborn old warriors that they still were, whether history had vindicated them or not. Against this background his story seemed interchangeable, his job in the Buenos Aires slaughterhouses, the transport company that must have made him his fortune, even his time as a security consultant, apparently, it all added up to no more than his present desire to do his bit for his country in the war, to make a patriotic gesture that in no way distinguished him from the rest of his kind, and to which his private life was nothing more than a picturesque adjunct, his first wife in Argentina, who had died or from whom he was divorced, the happiness he had found in later years with a former model, as she was described, and their two children. It was standardised, intended to prove that he was a family man, nothing else, and therefore and not least well qualified for responsibility, even of the highest kind.

A notable feature of the interview was the way in which he shrugged off questions about the period before his flight, and Marija found herself reading his answers as though he meant them for her personally.

"Do we have to discuss that?"

The interviewer put no pressure on him, backing off the moment he showed the slightest reluctance, in fact to all appearances more than happy to steer his subject to safe ground whenever he himself ventured a step in the wrong direction. To hear the old fighter say that he had served in a paratroop unit during the war and been active in resistance against the partisans at the end of it seemed to make the interviewer uncomfortable in any case, and was clearly more than he had intended to get from him, so instead of pursuing the story he returned to more innocuous subjects.

"You come from Dalmatia," he said. "Is it true you want to buy back your family home on the coast from the present owners?"

Her father's "Yes!" came with an exclamation mark, but Marija thought she could hear him pause before answering the next question.

"You also had a wife and child back then?"

Three dots followed on the page.

"What happened to them?"

For her this was the moment of truth, and although his words were there on the page in black and white, she tried to think what else he could have said instead, because anything would have been better, any uncertainty, than his supposed assurance.

"They were killed."

Scarcely had she reached the words than she repeated them in a whisper, and the interviewer only seemed to reinforce her incredulity as he repeated them in turn.

"They were killed?"

She couldn't get it out of her head that her father had still had the chance to say no, to explain that he had been having a joke at their expense. As long as he was saying that he had sent them to Vienna six months before the war ended, meaning to follow on later, as long as she had not read on, everything would have been alright, she could have turned back the clock and lost herself in her dreams in which, as a child, she had asked perfect strangers when her father would finally be coming home, he must be coming home for her birthday, he must be coming for Christmas and for Easter, he would come if she ate up her supper and went to sleep, would come if she was good, if she went to church at the crack of dawn on Sunday after Sunday and prayed for him. For a moment she wished to herself that he could really have believed they were no longer alive, and that was why he had never shown his face, but as soon as she started thinking about it she knew it was almost impossible, given the assurances repeated again and again about where they were to meet him, the times and places set in stone during the war for ever afterwards, if not here then there, if not this day then that day, possibilities upon possibilities of outwitting reality, all the way to her mother's annual appointment to meet him in front of St Stephen's Cathedral, where until the very last years before she died she had always gone, promptly, at eleven o'clock on their wedding anniversary, to wait, if all else failed, as they had agreed, until the stroke of twelve on that day, though in reality she used to carry on waiting for him all afternoon.

There was nothing about any of that in the interview, however, and it made Marija shiver to think of the fate he had intended for them when she read that she and her mother had fallen into the hands of the partisans, though he fortunately only let himself hint at what that had meant and did not spell it out in graphic detail.

"My daughter was just five years old at the time," the interview said, and even in written form she could picture the sentimentality that had clearly gripped him. "No-one is going to tell me that she was guilty and deserved to die."

This threw her completely, and she didn't know whether she might not have preferred him to be dead after all, as she had always thought he was. At least then she wouldn't have had to come to terms with these fabrications, she told herself, as she listened to the sounds from the rest of the apartment, the footsteps approaching along the corridor, going away and coming back again. For the first time since arriving in Zagreb she felt she would have been better off in Vienna, where she wouldn't have had to deal with this, and as she was considering what she should do, whether to dash into the street and walk around for as long as it took her to start thinking clearly again, or to stay sitting where she was and watch it turn into a nightmare from which she only had to wake up, there was a knock at the door. The three old men all stood there, waiting for her to invite them in, and when she didn't react they shuffled in anyway, the doctor, holding a liqueur bottle, a step ahead of the other two, who made no sound and looked as though they would have very much preferred to be invisible.

"Can we do anything for you?"

The way they looked at her made her think of Angelo. She didn't know why, it must have had something to do with the forlornly resigned conviction that they radiated, a sort of presumed certainty that it must be their fault if they couldn't help her, and she suddenly wished that he were there and would take her in his arms. Studiously not looking any of them in the eye, she folded the sheet of newspaper till it was small enough to hide in her fist and pictured leaving them, and their helpless attentiveness, behind and speeding out of the city, heading east on the motorway towards Slavonia until she reached the first roadblock, asking for Angelo, calling and calling his name and refusing to stop, as the ultimate proof that everything was futile.

"I need air."

The doctor had been trying to press a glass into her hand, but she was already at the door by the time she got the words out, and she looked around, touched to see how tender he looked standing between the other two.

"Have a drink for me, gentlemen," she said, without sarcasm. "I'm afraid that's all you can do for me."

Her voice shrank to a whisper.

"If I'm not mistaken, there's something to celebrate."

Outside it was still the same day, still the same coming and going of people, the same anxious anticipation of the next air-raid warning, which she was coming to accept as if it were nothing out of the ordinary and part of everyday life, and she waited for a moment at the building's entrance and wondered where she should go. To go back to her apartment was out of the question, everything in it was so bound up with Angelo and the sudden intuition that it had all started with him, with his turning up and the way he reminded her of her father, as if she had brought everything else about by that one meeting. The Hotel Esplanade was about a quarter of an hour's walk, and on the way she started to work out what to say, but passing the station she went in and looked up the departure times of the trains to Vienna, before crossing Tomislav Square and Strossmayer Square and making a beeline for the Palace Hotel, where she took another room, indifferent to the way the desk clerk regarded her, officious as it was, and even relishing his unconcealed disdain, as though he were in no doubt that she was either on the game or he would have to cut her down, blue and swollen, from the ceiling later, a woman without luggage who at the beginning of the century would probably have been courteously or even discourteously shown the door, but these days could afford to snub the clerk by saying in answer to his question that she planned an indefinite stay.

It wasn't far to the lift, but she knew that she had to avoid conversation if she didn't want to run the risk of losing her grip. It was the middle of the day, but half the hotel staff seemed to have assembled at reception, four people, two men and two women, both smoking in a bored way, and in front of them a waitress and a chambermaid who seemed to have been especially summoned to welcome her, plus the porter who hurried on ahead of her, acting with a greater sense of his own importance the less he was needed. These people were staff, employees whom she was paying for their services, but she felt she had to be careful not to hug one of them as other people might hug a horse or a tree, so close was she to crumbling at any word spoken to her, like the clients of her girl-friend who worked in a luxury boutique and had told her how sometimes on Mondays she could spot them from a distance, the desperately sad wives who were allowed to come and choose something new for themselves because their husband had spent the weekend with his lover and who then, as they tried things on, trembling like babies, shuddered at the slightest chance touch as though being touched was something that had only ever happened to them in another life and their skin had retained no memory of it.

Not until she was in her room, as she stood by the window looking out over the rooftops and caught herself thinking that this would be the moment when planes would materialise in the afternoon sky (which made her feel neither fear nor hope but only indifference), did she fully realise the state of panic she had worked herself into. As if the facts weren't enough, she felt she was waiting for something else to catch up with her at any moment, something that had been sown in the past, something that would be more serious than mere knowledge, and it wasn't any help to lie on her bed as she then did, playing dead, one wrong thought would be enough to set off a process that would relentlessly expunge her life, dissolving the complex assembly of connections that held its tissue together so that not a single thread would be left, only a heap of tangled fluff. For a long time it didn't even occur to her that she was still clutching the newspaper in her fist, and when she then unfolded it and looked once more at the photograph of her father with his wife and their two children, it seemed to her that that was literally the one tangible thing she had in her hands, if she was going to insist on there being a connection where there was none, their little white dresses in her sweat-damp, printer's ink-blackened fingers.

It was more of a reflex than a conscious decision to call her husband, but she had hardly dialled the number when he was picking up the phone, and of course not only wanted to know the whole story but confidently chipped in with instant advice.

"Don't make the mistake of getting in touch with him."

She might have agreed with him, but could not help bridling at his self-assurance.

"He's my father."

This elicited a scornful snort.

"Your father?"

He seemed to have decided to treat the whole story as ridiculous, from the way he asked her please not to be childish, and mockingly wanted to know if she really needed this kind of thing at her age, before he suddenly turned perfectly serious.

"Someone like that just can't be your father," he said. "Why would you still want to have anything to do with him after all these years?"

It would not have surprised her to hear him bang on again about her father the way he had at the beginning of their relationship, before she reined in his mythomania, telling him that he could call her Partisan Girl as much as he liked if that was what he really wanted, but that she had to disappoint him about her father, who was no Communist. She recalled his reaction when she had told him, the incredulity with which he had questioned her, what side had her father been on in the war, the right side or the wrong side?, his annoyance at her vague answers, and the way he had tried to construct his own picture out of the few fragments that were all she could supply, and now she feared she was about to hear another outburst. He said nothing more, and she could not even hear his breathing, but it was the same old trepidation she felt, the same feeling of being trapped and confined that she had had in the months when he had taken her father to task again and again, and with him of course herself as well, and she realised that not for anything in the world would she listen to his lectures again, and told him so.

"That's not what you used to say."

And in her mind's eye she suddenly had the image of the long afternoons spent sitting in the bath together that autumn, when she had received her schooling in revolutionary theory. He had always worn his peaked cap with the red star and sometimes even had a cigar in his hand, the very picture of a smooth-talking chief ideologist, and she had been young, naïve, eager to drink in even the most boring procedural nonsense, easy prey for any kind of indoctrination, just so long as a moment came when he stopped talking, leaned towards her and whispered in her ear that he loved her. She would have put up with everything else just to have that, and when she thought back to that time now, however great her aversion she couldn't help feeling a wave of yearning.

"Perhaps you really don't remember, but for a long time my father was your explanation for all my failings and weaknesses," she said. "More than once when you wanted to have the last word, you called me flesh of his flesh."

She didn't want to remind him of the fights they had had over some detail, or of his evasiveness when he had felt driven into a corner or his unvarying verdict whenever he had wanted to hit her where it hurt most, that with a background like hers she was bound to be unreliable, but before she had properly reflected the words had slipped out. He had had other maxims to hand too, but she bit them back and only told him that he had been unable to think up anything better than going on at her in that vein until she felt her background made her guilty of everything. Then she fell silent, and in the silence she heard his lips opening and closing, and the nervous clearing of his throat before he tried to calm her down.

"Forget those old stories."

But he no longer had the same assurance.

"Surely what matters is that he never existed for you," he said. "So why would you put yourself in the power of a phantom now?"

It would have been easy for her to retort that it was more a question of finally freeing herself from her father, and her past, by facing him after all these years and asking him, begging him to explain why he had left her alone as a child and why he had now betrayed her again by claiming that she was dead. Precisely because nothing he could say would ever be enough, she wanted to hear it from his lips, imagining that she would then find release because, whatever he did say to her, she would only laugh. From her point of view, his one and only course of action was to say nothing, but then she would absolutely make him say something, and as soon as he opened his mouth he would be finished in her eyes.

She was, in short, wholly uninterested in where her husband's logic might lead, which she also told him before she said goodbye.

"Maybe he wouldn't have been in my head so much if he had been around the whole time, but the way things are, he has existed for me much more by not being there, as I imagine you can understand," she said, and couldn't keep a dismissive note out of her voice. "Put it this way, every day that I was with you, I was thinking about him."

Then, because she hung up before he could answer, she was filled with groundless euphoria, and when a while later she called Lorena in the same exuberant mood, she initially composed herself to ask her daughter in a very easygoing sort of way whether she had any desire to get to know her grandfather. But as soon as she heard the first ringing tone, which seemed to come not just from another place but from another time, she felt she was pushing her luck, and then it wasn't her daughter who came on the line but another woman again, though whether it was the same one as when she had last tried to call she couldn't say, but if it was, she made it even harder this time for Marija to get through to Lorena.

The phrase the woman repeated, several times, stuck in her memory for days afterwards, it sounded so categorical.

"She can't come to the phone right now."

Between these words she heard the woman repeat, in whispered asides, "It's your mother, sweetie, it's your mother," and then Lorena eventually came on the line, sounding tired and distracted and as though, despite the woman having told her, she didn't know who she was talking to. Her first words were addressed to the other woman, after which she said yes and waited, suggesting that there must be a special reason for Marija to disturb her at this moment. Once again she sounded like someone who had just got out of bed or been out late the night before, and her unwillingness was audible in her silence.

"Do you know how late it is?"

Marija tried to forestall her by asking the same question she expected from her, but she didn't succeed in sounding as relaxed as she would have liked, and the answer came so promptly and was spoken so cuttingly that tears sprang to her eyes.

"Five to midnight, Mother."

She looked at her watch and worked out the time difference, yes, it must be exactly five to midnight in Philadelphia, and just as she told herself to stay calm and not read anything into it, Lorena's next words took the wind out of her sails.

"It's always five to midnight when you call," she heard her daughter say, and quickly covered the mouthpiece with her hand, feeling she could not trust her reactions. "What's the matter with you?"

That was the end of all her father- and grandfather-related bliss, she ended the conversation as quickly as she could and without apologising or letting her daughter know that she was crying, rushed out of her room, along the corridor, down the stairs, through the now empty lobby and outside, and not ten minutes later was at the Hotel Esplanade, asking for him. The desk clerk leafed through his bookings at length, looked at her and went away to telephone where she couldn't hear what he said, and finally came back to tell her he had gone out, and when she asked when he would be back, just shrugged his shoulders and added that she would be better off not waiting for him. Something about the way he kept glancing at her gave her the feeling that someone else had been expected, and sure enough, at that moment, a woman hurried in to whom he spoke in a whisper, a girl really, blonde and in a flimsy dress, with long, slender limbs, who carried her trainers slung over her shoulder with their laces tied together and walked with excessively long strides in her high heels.

There was nothing very peculiar about it, not the place or the time, as she told herself, yet a glimpse that she caught of the young woman as she was on her way out would not go away. She had turned around once to look back, and couldn't decide whether the young woman was staring at her by accident or whether she had been watching her the whole time. Whatever the truth, she felt she was being looked at, but could see no sign of it in the woman's gaze, not the smile she often elicited from other girls of that age, nor the slightest sign of sympathy or even a hint of conspiracy. There was interestedness without interest, a demonstrative detachedness that missed nothing, and it reminded her of the black-uniformed, heavily armed men who had been guarding a building on the far side of the street as she arrived and with an identical watchful lethargy keeping the hotel entrance under surveillance at the same time.

Perhaps it was because of the young woman, and a vague curiosity that she had aroused in her, that wholly contrary to her original intention of just letting some time pass, she returned to the hotel lobby as dusk was falling and asked for her father again. This time she was served by a different reception clerk, who apparently did not need to spend very long consulting records but informed her in a provocatively clipped tone that there was no-one of that name staying at the hotel, although she could leave a message for him if she liked. He then repeated this, word for word, adding was there anything he should pass on to the person?, and when she wanted to know how, in view of what he had said, he could do any such thing, he busied himself behind his counter and refused to look up as long as she remained in front of him, undecided whether to stay or leave.

This time, as she stood there it was a man who caught her eye. He was sitting in one of the armchairs, his hair cut so short that his scalp shimmered, and slightly greying, watching her over the top of his newspaper without trying to conceal the fact, and it was not so much that he was reading an Austrian newspaper that attracted her attention, and linked his presence with her own, as the directness of his gaze, which had something shameless about it. His face reminded her of the faces of the men in mail-order catalogues with their well-groomed looks, who smelled of aftershave even on the odourless pages, and if she might have found it hard to place him in peacetime, now, with a war going on, he could have been absolutely anything or nothing. He seemed ill at ease in his dark suit, as if it weren't the kind of thing he usually wore, and she caught herself trying to visualise how he would look if he stood up, how he would move, how he would stand, bending slightly at the hips, how he would shift his weight from one leg to the other foot, his arms folded high across his chest. All the time she was speaking to the desk clerk she had been unable to rid herself of the impression that he was listening to her intently, and the clerk himself had enunciated so clearly that not a word could have escaped him, yet she rejected the idea that he might be a detective, possibly sent by her husband, if only because it was all too obvious and he would never have passed as a detective, even in a film.

As she walked past on her way to the door, he said good evening to her, and there was more than familiarity to his tone (which she found completely unjustified), there was the outrageous insinuation of a certain kind of man who gave others the impression, merely by the way he smiled even at a woman he didn't know, that he had slept with her, or could, any time he wanted to. She had no intention at all of returning his greeting, and wouldn't even have glanced at him in passing, but just as she walked past she thought she heard her name spoken, and hesitated. She walked on, and even before she felt his presence behind her she knew that he would come after her and that he didn't mind her knowing, judging by the way he coughed and made no attempt to walk quietly. She didn't go via the station this time but up Gajeva Street, taking care not to hurry, all the time wondering what she could do, until on the corner of Trenkova Street she finally waited and let him catch up, despite there being no-one else on the street and knowing that passing motorists had learnt long ago to close their eyes at the important moment, or at least not to look or, if they did look, to prefer not to see anything or say later that they had seen nothing.

It might have been half a minute that she stood there, her head down, staring at the ground as though she could make him vanish into it, and then she still didn't turn to face him.

"Why are you following me?"

He didn't answer, and it reassured her to hear him fumbling, apparently looking for cigarettes and matches in his trouser pockets, because the next thing she heard was the scrape of a match on the side of a box, the faint hiss of the flame, how he inhaled and then blew out the smoke almost soundlessly. The smell reached her at the same moment, and she sensed how closely he was standing behind her, observing herself as she registered the most unimportant details around her, a chance pattern on the pavement, a handkerchief lying there, as though she needed to collect them for a witness statement later. She knew that she had time, that nothing would happen till he had finished his cigarette, but then she would have to decide one way or the other, to run away or to face him and take him on, if no alternative presented itself.

"I don't know what you want from me," she said and still did not dare raise her head, even to catch a glimpse of the scrap of night sky at the end of the street. "If I have offended you in some way, I'm sorry."

At first his only answer was to laugh, but then came his murmur. "Look at me."

He placed a hand on her shoulder, and she turned so slowly that in the end he took hold of her upper arms and helped her to turn.

"Please don't be afraid of me," he said, raising both hands in the air to cancel his grip on her or at least eliminate any threat from himself. "I'm the last person who wants to harm you."

He let one hand sink down to her arm again.

"I have a message from your father."

He looked at her the way he might have looked at a child, and started speaking with a great effort at clarity, which seemed exaggerated to her only because he was standing less than a metre away.

"It's his wish that you stop trying to see him," he said, after a deliberate pause for effect. "Better to wait till he gets in touch with you."

He turned away, and she watched him walk back down the street at his slow pace, dragging his feet a little, hunching his shoulders, like a man leaning into the warm evening air as though it offered some resistance. She waited till he had disappeared, then set off to walk the short distance back to her own hotel. She was afraid that he might reappear and kept turning around to see, but just as though a curfew had been enforced there was again no-one to be seen on the deserted street and she was entirely alone.

In her hotel room she went straight to the table to write a letter to her father, the way she had always written to him on his birthday when she was a child after the war until her mother had stopped her, telling her that she was old enough now to give up believing he would ever write back and that all these years it had been she herself who had replied to her in his name. As easy as it had been for her to write to him then, telling him about the little things that interested her, now it was equally difficult for her to say what really mattered. In the past, whenever she couldn't think of anything else to say, she had always done him a drawing in coloured crayons, a child holding a man's hand, a picture full of meaning but lightly done, the sun or a bunch of flowers, and she would have preferred to take refuge in some such thing now, in a picture that left everything open and lacked the clarity of words. Because however she started, it sounded wrong, different from even the clumsiest sentences that her girlish imagination had once devised, like her wish, which she had never spoken out loud, to marry him when she grew up, and at length she felt she could just as easily write "Dear Papa, I'm glad you are alive" as "Dear Sir, how I wish you were dead", for both sounded equally inappropriate, on the airmail-thin hotel notepaper with the golden crest held by two rampant lions with lolling tongues, and the date 1907, which alone made her dizzy with longing.

EIGHT

FROM THE MOMENT LUDWIG ARRIVED IN ZAGREB HE HAD GOOD reason to think that there was something wrong with the old man, and not just because for a long time he failed to mention his daughter at all, about whom he had spoken with such urgency on the phone. Outwardly he had not changed, he was still the imposing figure for his years that Ludwig remembered, but there was something painstakingly fussy about his behaviour that diminished him. He met Ludwig at the railway station, and as he began immediately reeling off everything he had been busy with in the last few weeks, as though he needed to answer to Ludwig, of all people, it sounded less like boasting and more like someone establishing a series of alibis, and as he informed Ludwig that he had now built up a picture of the situation in the combat zones and was in contact with the people who mattered there, and similar bits of nonsense, Ludwig wondered what exactly he was trying to prove. The brisk manner in which he said it Ludwig remembered very well from Buenos Aires, but now it was without any naturalness or irony, and the old man might have been the most peaceable of people, acting out a perverse whim to see what it felt like to talk in an emphatically belligerent way.

The impression that he was watching a strange theatrical performance was intensified by the old man not taking him straight to the hotel but first giving him a guided tour of the traces of his past, as he pompously put it. All of Ludwig's objections were in vain, and, hungry and tired from the journey, he found himself sitting next to the old man and watching him fall more and more mute from one landmark to the next as he directed the taxi through the city centre and out to Maksimir, where his unit of paratroopers had been billeted in the war, and from there led Ludwig on foot to the neighbouring district of Borongai. Here the old man wanted to show him the airfield over which he and his comrades had put on more than one display jump, a place that might have been prepared specifically for the purposes of his tour, because when they finally reached a barracks gate a soldier on guard indicated that they should not loiter but clear the area as quickly as possible. From over the walls they could hear constant engine noise, the persistent grumble of several vehicles, and shouted orders, although outside, apart from themselves, there wasn't another person in sight. Suddenly a truck approached at speed, and the recruits sitting side by side on the flatbed behind the cab, their rifles upright between their legs, shouted something to them that Ludwig didn't understand, but the old man acknowledged it with a wave.

"They're doing well," he said when they were out of sight and the road lay peaceful once more in the last of the sunlight. "I've been able to convince myself of that with my own eyes."

As he proudly told the story of how, some weeks before, he had had the chance to spend the night with a group of fighters barely old enough to enlist, at a position near the Serbian border, it was noticeable how much it mattered to him to establish immediately a link across the decades with his own former unit. As he described it, the night had been a baptism of fire for most of them but they had all stood their ground and had probably cut a fine figure under his wing too, if only such expressions and the intention behind them weren't suspect these days. What he meant was that they deserved the highest praise, and he wanted to offer them his respect, or whatever word it was he used, at the same time counting himself as part of their combat unit, as though fifty years later the battles of that era were still being fought.

The effect on Ludwig was of the same flipping backwards and forwards in time that he had experienced before. It reminded him of the cross with burnt-on dates that Don Filip had slipped into his pocket before their flight took off from Buenos Aires, to the point where he felt as uncomfortable as when he had first touched that object. Having been too superstitious simply to throw it in a rubbish bin, he had left it on the baggage conveyor when they arrived at Frankfurt instead, hoping that someone would take it for themselves, but as he listened to the old man it occurred to him that his action might have been futile and he was still under the cross's curse.

With each word the old man was now contradicting the twaddle that had passed his lips not half an hour before, the harmless stories of the war with which he had adorned his guided tour, and in the end Ludwig felt he had to point this out.

"I thought you didn't fight at all back then."

He was trying to provoke him, and though the old man seemed well aware of this, he smiled in a way that was intended to show Ludwig he knew what he was up to, then looked around to make sure no-one was listening, and indeed the buildings did seem to be abandoned, their shutters still closed in the afternoon, their flowers withered in the flowerbeds, their flags hanging limply from their flagpoles like the sad relics of a failed revolution.

"Ah, so you've the urge to investigate me yet again," he said. "When you're done with your fifteen minutes of moralising, do let me know."

He turned his head away, looking amused.

"How do you come to that conclusion?"

Ludwig couldn't be bothered to remind the old man of the anecdotes he had shared with him from that part of his life, his flimsy stories of never-ending youth, of preparations for an emergency that wouldn't come and similar inventions. He hadn't believed for a moment in the artificial tranquillity of his barracks idyll, when mishaps during training jumps had supposedly provided the only excitement, he had viewed his stories of weekends spent with a convent schoolgirl while his wife and child waited for him in Dalmatia as exactly the diversionary tactic that they probably were, and he could only marvel at the old man now behaving as though he knew nothing about any of it, looking Ludwig straight in the eye with an expression that could not have been more blank and laughing in a way that finally Ludwig allowed to get to him.

"To hear you, anyone would think you never had anything to do but form the guard of honour at funerals and parades," he said. "Didn't you say you were still sure in the last year of the war that you could survive anything in your smart blue dress uniform, and that right to the end you wouldn't have to get your hands dirty, even with the world going to hell around you?"

The tales of the impressive tasks entrusted to the old man and his comrades had created an image in his mind of them as a music-hall company from the First World War, all bright buttons and colourfully plumed helmets, rather than a paratroop unit from twenty-five years later, and now he mocked him.

"You must have looked like a real pantomime."

They were still walking, and the old man paused in mid-stride when Ludwig said this. He turned to him and stared with a look intended to convey that he considered him beneath consideration, then raised his head and looked beyond him with narrowed eyes into the distance, as though he had every reason to suppose that somewhere beyond the horizon was an authority who could assess the injustice being done to him.

"A pantomime?"

His voice expressed scornful disbelief.

"You shouldn't make the mistake of underestimating us just because we learnt how to salute and march in step."

He glanced at him again.

"What do you know about the last year of the war?"

He was standing in front of an abandoned car, stripped down to its bare panels, tyres missing, bonnet open, and he stood as though a camera were pointed at him and he wanted to do nothing less than issue a communiqué to posterity.

"In the last year of the war the whole country was contaminated by partisans," he said, putting his emphasis on the word "contaminated". "If you can't imagine what that means, then you'd better inform yourself before you start opening your mouth."

His vanity had got the better of him, and for a moment Ludwig thought he was about to say more, for in the past he had often managed to make people talk by doubting their competence, but the old man was too clever for that, he was not one of those petty criminals who were vulnerable to taunts and that notorious sense of inferiority that made them liable to confess to crimes that existed in no statute book. He said simply that Ludwig's private lesson was over and they had both better let the past be the past, though he then immediately returned to the subject of the recruits, explaining that all they really lacked today was the right kind of basic training, including drill, and that because they were often sent to the front without it they didn't know the most elementary things, sometimes not even how to ensure the best way of staying alive.

He was getting as excited as if he were about to lead a unit into combat himself, yet the truly fraudulent aspect of his behaviour didn't strike Ludwig until that evening, when he invited him to his suite and he happened to eavesdrop on a conversation with Don Filip. He had just entered the room as the phone rang, and while the call went on he stared around it in irritation, not wanting to hear the old man compromising himself in front of him. Something defensive had come into his voice from the start, something that didn't suit him or his physical presence, and his tone remained so soft that he had to repeat almost everything he said, and whenever he raised his voice a little he seemed afraid that he might not sound co-operative enough and lowered it again immediately.

"Believing in the Lord and praying are all very well," he said, after listening for a while and saying nothing, just nodding and shaking his head, "but I'm ruined. If something doesn't happen soon I might as well kill myself."

The source of his complaint was that he had been waiting in vain for the money collected by Don Filip on his begging trips to arrive, and the weeks of discussion between them on the subject, arguing it this way and that, seemed to have worn him down. He had arrived in the city with great plans, and so long as it was believed that he had funds available to get something started, people had courted him, he had eaten with senior officers, had contacts, all the way up to the anteroom of the president's office as he emphasised, had been assured that he would receive every kind of support for his plan to rent an office in the city centre and start recruiting volunteers for the fighting by paying them a cash bonus, as he had tried to do, albeit half-heartedly, in Buenos Aires, and now here he stood with nothing to show for all his talk. The result was not just that he was no longer welcome anywhere and feared being a laughing-stock in the cafés if someone recognised him from his picture in the newspapers, he was also getting phone calls telling him that it was time he coughed up some money at long last, after proclaiming for weeks that he was going to do great things for his homeland, or at least explained how he justified staying at the most expensive hotel in Zagreb and talking big but doing nothing while day after day people were being butchered in Slavonia and the Krajina.

Ludwig guessed straight away that this was not the first time he had had such a conversation with Don Filip, and also knew this would not be the last time he heard the old man's words as he hung up.

"There are some problems, but the money will be here next week."

But he was unable to explain why it was taking so long, and spoke without conviction about difficulties with the bank, which didn't want to action a transfer of such magnitude to a country currently in a state of war, and when he said that it sometimes seemed to him that Don Filip had had a vision and that must be at the root of the trouble, though it was no more than a despairing joke it might have been the literal truth.

"You saw for yourself how crazy he is about his pistol, but right now he's behaving so piously I could believe him capable of any mischief," he said. "Let's say that I wouldn't be surprised if he's taken a unilateral decision to divert those donations and get some new cathedral built in honour of the Virgin Mary somewhere in Patagonia."

He was making an effort to keep up a convivial atmosphere, little as he believed in any of it. His hand still on the receiver, as though thinking about whether to call back and talk to Don Filip more sternly, he sat for a moment, seeming to need to calm himself, and looking suddenly exposed in the room, which was at odds with the usual standards of a luxury hotel by looking as bleak as an interrogation cell, having probably been furnished like that at the old man's instructions for the duration of his stay. Two folding chairs and a table were its only furniture (which made the bedroom next door and its huge bed and lavish flounces look baroque by comparison) and under the deliberately bare tungsten bulb above his head he looked like a man who had survived a powerful explosion and without his sense of hearing, balance or direction, and vaguely aware that he himself has caused it, had to find a new bearing in a life that was not his own and had nothing to do with him.

An enormous map of the surroundings of Bleiburg hung on the wall behind his back, dotted with red, blue and green map pins, and every time Ludwig glanced at it the old man fidgeted with the two black folders that he had brought from Argentina and were lying on the table in front of him, pushing them to its lip and then pulling them back immediately, knocking their edges firmly together with the flat of his hand. Directly in front of him he also had the photograph of his daughters that had stood on the mantelpiece at San Isidro, but he did not seem to see it when he looked at it. Instead his expression acquired an absence, a sort of emptiness, and his gaze roved restlessly around the room, only focusing again as it stopped at the framed picture by the door, a print of a turn-of-the-century poster advertising the Österreichischer Lloyd steamship company and its postal service between Trieste and Dalmatia. Its view of Dubrovnik seemed to calm him greatly, and indeed the first thing he had said to Ludwig when they came into the room was that the picture had been taken from a hill to the south at exactly the angle from which guns were now being fired every day across the rooftops of the old town at the harbour, at which he could not hide a certain satisfaction.

It had almost sounded as if he were pleased about the bombardment, and Ludwig thought that only now did he understand what made him feel that way. It was not just out of a hope that the world would stop closing its eyes to such excesses as it had when the towns of Slavonia were under fire, to say nothing of the wretched villages of the karst country, not just that the world would no longer be able to look away, now that the "pearl of the Adriatic" and its great history were involved, it was also from a macabre sense of assurance that now at least something was happening. In short, his burning desire for action was like that of the proverbial fireman who willingly sets his own house on fire in order to have his conflagration at last, whose flames he might choose to quench or just to watch with the happy eyes of a child, and so to Ludwig he embodied the very picture of a desperate man for whom any act was justified that freed him from the inactivity to which he had been condemned.

He could not shake off a feeling that that was also why he was looking for his daughter, that he would never have begun looking for her otherwise. Only now did he raise the subject again, and it did not seem to weigh on his mind much, judging by the way he opened the table drawer, put a newspaper cutting in front of Ludwig and looked at him as though he wanted to palm something off on him. He pointed casually at the grainy photo, giving him time to study its subject, a woman of unclear age who stood next to an elderly gentleman, looking undecided as to whether she should move closer to him or further away for the photo to be taken.

"That's her."

She had been caught at an unfortunate moment, wearing the forced smile of a snapshot that in her case had something pinched about it and seemed simultaneously to welcome any and every catastrophe, a look that, from the way the old man bent over it as if to confirm something, probably matched his own mood.

"It's not very recognisable, but you'll manage," he said. "The less you know, the better."

He wrote down the address where she worked and said that would probably be the best place to pick up her trail, but Ludwig interrupted him.

"Perhaps I should at least know how she comes to be alive, when you've always claimed that she was dead," he said. "You knew it wasn't true all along, and the story you told me about the partisans is a fairy tale."

At first the old man was unperturbed.

"Does it change anything for you?"

He would clearly have preferred not to talk about it, and when he did, it was the unwilling and reticent confession of a man who had used the war as an opportunity to leave his wife and child. The explanation that he offered was more of a pretext for not having to confront any of his actions, as he assured Ludwig that he had only understood his own intentions when what was done was done and at first he just hadn't sent them word for two years while he was on the run, so that he never gave away where he was staying. But he seemed not to believe this himself and kept waving his hand dismissively, as though shooing his genuine memories away, as he related that the idea of burning all his bridges and starting again had occurred to him only when he arrived in Argentina, and then it hadn't needed much of a decision to let his wife and daughter go on thinking that he was no longer alive, because in all probability they had got used to the idea by then, and for him to declare them officially dead in turn.

"Of course, I could have arranged for them to follow me," he said. "But I was always putting it off, and then the moment passed and it would have done them more harm than good."

It was not Ludwig's place to judge him, and although he couldn't explain the old man's thinking to himself, he at least understood why he was now expending such effort to find his daughter, why he had put two advertisements in the paper for her and arranged for a third when he knew where she worked and could easily go there, and it also explained why he had employed him, Ludwig, to do the job. The father had had no intention of getting in contact with his daughter when he first planned his return, it was only after seeing her photograph in the paper that the idea had come into his head, and since he knew that he couldn't assume she would welcome him with open arms after all these years if he turned up at the drop of a hat to tell his side of the story, he wanted to find out how things stood before he made a move. That was all the secret there was about his method, odd as it might seem, and Ludwig felt glad that it was neither a cynical game he was involving her in, nor a querulous old man's way of passing the time when he was at a loose end and, from sheer boredom, decided to start moving the people around him back and forth like chess pieces.

Although Ludwig had reservations about having let himself in for the job at all, he waited for her outside the address he had been given the following morning in a mood of excited anticipation. His mission could hardly have been vaguer, to find out everything he could about her, and for that reason alone, out of sheer bloody-mindedness, even before he caught sight of her for the first time he felt a great sympathy for her. He had not slept much the night before, unable to ignore the noises from the old man's bedroom, adjacent to his, the popping of gunfire that could as easily have been from a Western or a thriller as from T.V. news from the combat zones, and as he lay awake he had spent a long time reflecting whether it might not be best to tell her the whole story and then disappear, never to be seen again, but now here he was and no longer thinking any such thing. He watched people as they ascended and descended the building's broad stairs and instantly his hunting instinct awakened, he felt under his arm for the pistol that the old man had pressed into his hand as he left the hotel, and when he saw her face he knew that he would stay. He had left the photograph back at the hotel, its quality so poor it would hardly have helped him, and instead was relying on his skill to identify her, but he had not the least doubt that it was her, if only because of the way she kept turning round, as though she knew she was being watched.

From the moment she came into his field of vision until she disappeared into the building's entrance was only a few seconds, but in the afternoon he again saw her exactly where he had lost sight of her that morning, having left his observation post only once in the hours between to go and get a coffee, although he knew her working hours and that the risk of missing her if he hadn't stayed was small. When she reappeared it was already past four-thirty, and there was the same restlessness about her, a harassed glance to the left and right as she paused at the top of the stairs and then she looked straight in his direction before she walked down. At pavement level she stopped, supporting herself against the wall of the building for a while, one knee bent, as though she was doing it just for him, and he had time to observe her calmly as she first threw back her head and scanned the sky for a long time, then lit a cigarette and stood motionless in the sun, her eyes closed, and from second to second the tension seemed to drain away from her and only from the forced calm with which she smoked could he guess that something was upsetting her.

Although he subsequently followed her home, his later observations felt contrived in comparison to the clarity of those first few moments. He knew it was absurd of him to note, about the way she walked, that it was as though she were expecting to experience a different force of gravity, or to see in the way she crossed a road a paradoxical mixture of indecision and haste, not to mention his earth-shaking confirmation that she could stop in front of a shop window and not seem to know what had first attracted her attention. In the tram he noted the profound concentration with which she crossed her legs and immersed herself in a book, and afterwards was unable to read any of what he had written down without shaking his head at himself, whether it was the erect posture of her back as she got in and out of the tram, the pronounced bobbing of her shoulder-length hair, the salaciousness with which she renewed her lipstick or the huskiness of her voice as she asked the person next to her the time. All these things might be true, but they were all false too, they might, even allowing for his self-conscious efforts to evoke something particular and striking, be correct, but still added nothing to what he felt he had seen when she had stood leaning against the wall as if just for him. For there had been something disturbingly youthful about her which he had not expected, an unfinished look, as if not every part of her had yet found its place, and it had been reinforced by the dress she wore, black with yellow spots and close-fitting, and the flip-flops on her feet, whose slap-slapping as she got up and he walked behind her reminded him of his adolescent summers by the swimming pool, long afternoons that never ended and girls much younger than her, softly lit and lethargic as reptiles as they basked in the sun.

At first the old man stared at him, dumbfounded, as he tried to explain what had fascinated him so much about her. He had gone straight back to the hotel to make his report, and the moment he sat down he heard himself talking about how a touch of weariness had given her something pure, some inner composure that had raised her up from the rest of the world, and immediately felt uncomfortable as he sat on his folding chair because he could picture how it must sound to the old man. He clearly hadn't left the hotel all day, because he was still wearing the blue velour kimono and yellow crocodile slippers turned up at the toes that he had had on in the morning, but just as Ludwig felt he couldn't listen to his own nebulous remarks any longer and fell silent, the old man indicated with a barely perceptible gesture that he should go on, raising the forefinger and middle finger of his right hand, which lay on the table, as if to beckon Ludwig closer because he couldn't hear what he was saying, then letting his hand fall again.

"They lost a poet when they made you."

He leaned back and folded his arms, apparently to give Ludwig an opportunity to justify himself, but the next moment leaned forward again and gripped the table's nearest edge with both hands, ready to get to his feet.

"What you say about her is a bit vague, to say the least," he said, and if he was at all agitated he succeeded in concealing it well behind an aggressive show of boredom. "Can't you try to pull your-self together and just say straight out how she seems to you?"

It was still light outside, but the old man had drawn the curtains and switched on the light as though in preparation for an interro-gation, and Ludwig could have sworn that the light bulb had been changed, its light much dimmer than the day before, and for the first time the air in the room struck him as stale and musty, like somewhere where the window hadn't been opened for weeks. He hadn't thought about what to say, let alone shown the old man the self-conscious notes he had made, and he realised that whatever he said he stood no chance of satisfying his employer. The thought also occurred to him that his daughter wasn't in the least like him, and it wouldn't have surprised him if she weren't his daughter at all, but he felt he needn't be the first to say it, if it had to be men-tioned at all. It didn't escape his notice that the old man had let his arms fall limp at his sides, dangling as though they didn't belong to his body, and when his hands twitched a little, Ludwig remembered how he was always petting the two dogs at the San Isidro house and shivered, but at the same time felt secure.

"I don't know," he said. "What do you want me to say?"

He looked at the map behind the old man's back, as if he could obtain some kind of answer from its pattern of red, blue and green map pins, in places so close together that their heads touched.

"She looks lonely to me."

He had meant to avoid saying anything definite, but he had said it, and the moment he said it he wished he could take it back.

"Do you know what I mean?"

The old man peered at him over the rim of an invisible pair of glasses, refraining from any sarcastic response, although he could hardly control the sudden twitching at the corners of his mouth.

"She looks lonely to you?"

He spoke it like a foreign word, and there was something about him that suggested a man forgotten by God and everyone else, banished to a post in the depths of the provinces, who has just been informed that the transfer he has been longing for for so long has been postponed and he will have to sit tight for a few months longer. In an effort to preserve his composure, he straightened his spine and sat well forward from the back of the chair, and briefly maintained that position before rising with a sudden movement. He reached for the phone, ordered coffee and went into the next room, coming back with a cigar that he lit distractedly after biting the end off and spitting it into the waste-paper basket. Then he sat down again, picked up the photograph of his daughters from the table and looked at it, shaking his head as he puffed blue, earthy smoke into the air.

"If that's intended to be an allusion to the poor fatherless child, you can forget it," he said, talking with the cigar in the corner of his mouth. "You have a daughter yourself, so you must know how robust is the will to live."

Ludwig hadn't meant to say anything of the kind, but before he could explain the old man turned away and said he would like to be left alone, and each time Ludwig came to him over the next few days he had the impression that the old man no longer took his reports very seriously. He received him in the same informal clothing, sat and listened to what he had to tell him, but rapidly made his lack of interest clear, and in truth there wasn't a great deal to say anyway, as the appearances of the old man's daughter were more or less interchangeable from one day to the next. She arrived just before eleven, disappeared into the building, and when she came out again after four o'clock went straight home by tram, giving him the same impression of restlessness as on the very first occasion, and anything else Ludwig might have added to this account would only have roused the old man's displeasure again. The additions would have included that the word "fragile" occurred to him whenever he saw her and that at the same time he felt he perceived a defiance in her, and although he waited near her apartment building in case she came out again later, or perhaps appeared at the window, and never experienced another situation like the one there had been the first time he saw her, he considered carefully when the old man asked him whether she had looked lonely to him again or not, as in the end he inevitably did. By now, however, the old man no longer wanted to know whether Ludwig had spoken to her, and it was clear that after his first disappointment he had given up expecting anything much from this sort of observation and in reality was only waiting for the weekend to come, when the third advertisement was to appear.

Until then he continued to devote himself to his other businesses, as he still called them to keep up appearances, and in the process Ludwig began to understand the kind of isolation he had manoeuvred himself into during the three and a half months since his arrival in Zagreb. He no longer left the hotel and, if asked, the question of what it had felt like to set foot on his native soil again after so long elicited only a grim look. He stayed in his suite with the curtains drawn until nearly midday, then came downstairs for lunch with not a hair out of place (as though the strictest dress code applied in wartime) or had Ludwig fetch him something when he returned from his first watch, and sat on the bed to eat it in his dressing gown or pyjama trousers and a jogging top bearing the words "Boca Juniors", yet despite the clothes he still looked like someone from the beginning of the century and could, in fact, have been one of the passengers on the Orient Express for whom the hotel had been built, a gentleman from Paris or London who did not belong here and would reboard the train the next day and disappear into the blue distance in the saloon car, safe behind its panoramic windows. When he told Ludwig he ought to take it easy, it was said ironically, though he then acted as if he meant it seriously, in keeping with his own strategy that the worse the news was, the more comfortable he made himself, having apparently grasped once and for all that the best protection against bombs and shells was not steel walls, however thick, but the amenities of this grand hotel that stood like a fortress in the middle of the city, along with his own suite's makeover to look like an interrogation cell as the last shred of a façade intended to make him look soldierly. It seemed to offer him the greatest comfort to know that he was staying where Gestapo headquarters had been in the Second World War, and when he boasted to Ludwig that the concierge could get him a flak jacket as easily as a tailcoat, an anti-tank rocket as easily as a diamond-studded evening gown, and that a Kalashnikov ordered from reception cost less than a woman for the night, or then again it might be the other way round, it filled him with absurd pride.

The truth was that he had bid this war farewell long before, once he had realised that he could not take part in it himself, and increasingly he sought his salvation in the past. He felt he had been cheated in some undefined way, and whereas from a distance the smallest piece of news had once had meaning for him, now he had the T.V. set on from early morning until it closed down after the late-night news with the words "Goodnight, defenders of Croatia, wherever you are", which he stood up to hear, but was often not watching at all when pictures came in from the combat zones with always the same shots, the menacing views of maize fields with little white clouds exploding over them, the soldiers ducking low as they ran, or the already hackneyed panning shot to the empty, black-gaping windows of a building, its walls densely pitted with bullet-holes. He had grasped that tanks were advancing in the east, that many towns and villages on the Drava and Danube had been under fire for weeks and Vukovar would soon be encircled, but it seemed to move him as little as if it were in another country. He talked about the war like a disappointed lover, and the most emotion he showed was when he raised his voice as he talked about the bombs that had fallen in the Zagreb suburbs and said, as if moved by his own words, that once immediately after an air raid he had not only visited a fortune teller but lit a candle in the cathedral and then gone on a pilgrimage to Marija Bistrica, a few kilometres up Mount Medvenica, the local mountain, to kneel at the feet of the Black Madonna.

All that remained was his regular phone conversations with Don Filip, which reminded him why he was here in the first place and which, Ludwig guessed, also supplied him with a pretext for retreat, proving to himself every few days that he was doing all he could and then leaving him free to immerse himself again in the two black folders he had brought with him from Argentina. That had become his main occupation when he stayed in his suite, his new obsession with reconstructing from the newspaper cuttings and personal accounts he had before him, down to the smallest detail, what had happened at Bleiburg on 15 May 1945, and to Ludwig it made him look like a grown-up playing with toy soldiers as he stood in front of his map, explaining the positions of the British and the partisans, and pointing repeatedly at the area outside the city gates where the flight from Yugoslavia had ended for tens of thousands of refugees. That was the day when their fate was to be decided, and he spoke of it with the same bitterness Ludwig had detected in Buenos Aires when they went together to the cattle market and the old man had told him the story for the first time, except that now it was even clearer that he refused to see everything that had preceded it, and would have preferred to rewrite the whole story.

It was clear too that he needed no other conflict now, and he sprang to life when he reconstructed the scene for Ludwig's benefit, beginning with the constant comings and goings on the road to the city that day from early in the morning, to the Yugoslavian reconnaissance planes flying over the Karawanken mountains and the loudspeaker vans that appeared at regular intervals, instructing the refugees to lay down their arms. On the map he showed Ludwig the castle where the British commander was quartered and where negotiators from the Croatian Army had made a last-ditch attempt to avert catastrophe, and pointed out roughly where the British tanks that had come up were positioned, their guns trained on the crowd to prevent it from breaking out, looking at him pointedly because all commentary was superfluous. He said that before the unconditional surrender, at some time between four and four-thirty that afternoon, he had already known how it would finish when at midday he heard church bells ringing in the distance and the ensuing silence was broken by the drone of Spitfires flying in a show of strength overhead, turning and looping and coming back again, their wings quivering.

Ludwig had heard more than enough of this, and was relieved when he could get away from the old man's lectures by glancing at his watch and reminding him that it was nearly four, time for him to get back to his observation post, or when something else happened to interrupt these hapless sessions. He insisted on continuing with his job even when the old man said it wasn't important anymore, and in his relief at having got away again almost ran after his daughter, leaving him alone to go about his gloomy business in his interrogation cell, where the heat seemed to become denser and denser, as though tiny droplets in the air made breathing difficult. Yet they were half-hearted efforts to escape his employer, and as soon as he was back he sat down dutifully on his folding chair again, listening for footsteps out in the corridor that never halted at the door with a knock to rescue him from the worst of these obsessive ramblings, and each time the disappointment made him close his eyes for a few seconds and with small, hardly perceptible mouthings gasp for breath.

He felt the same sense of all-round unreality whenever Claudia phoned and the old man passed him the receiver, saying she wanted to speak to him, and then she was on the line asking whether he was letting her husband twist him round his little finger again, while the two little girls could be heard laughing in the background. Ludwig didn't answer, just stood with the receiver in his hand and felt a crazy nostalgia for his months in Argentina, when it had so often all seemed to him like a game, even wishing himself back at the shooting range in the cellar where there might have been something demonic about the old man under the neon lighting, but not the resignation he was showing now that made him truly dangerous. He watched him across the table as he asked how the girls were, and when Claudia wondered aloud whether she should say something to make him blush, he just laughed and waited till he was in his own room later before imagining how he would sleep with her under the open window and afterwards lie beneath the cool sheets with his hand on her stomach, and he felt the contingency of his existence more strongly than ever.

He had only been in Zagreb a week but he had lost all sense of time, and when the day of the third advertisement finally arrived he was glad to be roused from his increasing lethargy and, having been woken by the old man at the crack of dawn, was in position outside his daughter's apartment building at six-thirty. The plan was that he should not let her out of his sight that morning and should make sure she saw the newspaper, if necessary act like a hawker, hand her a free copy and tell her she ought to try it at least once. He did not have long to wait, and this time when she came out he didn't bother to stay out of sight or disappear into the doorway of a building when she turned round, but walked along the pavement for a while beside her, as if they were together, then sat down directly facing her in the café, with only a small marble-topped table between them, so that when he placed the newspaper in front of her, as if by chance, it was logical that she should ask if she could have a look at it.

He had often been the bearer of bad news, but had never seen someone react the way she did on seeing her father's advertisement. Whenever he and a police colleague had rung a doorbell, merely asking whether they could come in had usually been enough to spread consternation and terror, but if he had thought that the old man's daughter would clap a hand over her mouth, scream or burst into tears, reactions he had encountered many times in the past, he was wrong. She stared at him instead with an oddly distracted expression, then looked around the café for a long moment as though misfortune might not reach her, just so long as no-one noticed anything, so he immediately knew she had seen at least one of the other two advertisements. He asked if he could help her but she shook her head, and although she went on staring at him, her eyes now full of tears, he felt sure that within seconds she would have forgotten his question and that she would not recognise him in any future encounter. She hunted in her handbag for a handkerchief, unfolded it and left it on the table, stayed sitting with her legs at an angle under her pencil skirt, and put out her hand to fend him off, even though he hadn't moved. Finally she dropped her hand, stood up, and walked with stiff steps to the ladies' where she remained for so long that he was about to go and look for her, and when she did come back he almost failed to recognise her. She had tied her hair back and painted her lips with a loud red lipstick, was wearing sunglasses, and looked around as though she felt that everyone in the café was following her but then gave him, of all of them, a nod as she left, seemingly inviting him to come with her.

The old man was calm when Ludwig recounted his meeting. He put the paper away after examining the advertisement again and asked him if he wasn't over-dramatising the whole thing a bit, but Ludwig stuck to his version. It had happened exactly as he told it, he said, and when the old man objected that it didn't sound as though his daughter had been exactly pleased, he was so irritated that he couldn't work out whether the old man was being serious or not.

"What did you expect?"

The old man didn't answer, and his self-satisfaction as he sat facing him, hands linked behind his neck, enraged Ludwig. He had too clear a picture in his memory of the old man's daughter leaving the café, groping her way around the tables like a blind person, to retaliate with his usual sarcasm. He had stood to open the door for her, and now he was glad that he had sat down again and couldn't tell the old man anything of what had happened next, even if he had wanted to, and however much he might be waiting for more.

"It wouldn't have been right for me to take advantage of the state she was in," he said, unhappy that it sounded so slight a reason. "I let her go."

He had acted without thinking, but the memory of her trembling lips made him feel a need to explain why.

"I'm sure you'd have felt sorry for her too."

He said it so quietly that it came out almost inaudibly, and he was waiting for the old man's laughter when he was astonished to hear him agree instead and praise his sensitive handling of the situation.

"Relax, it was the right decision. Believe it or not, your hesitating makes me a lot happier than if you'd tried to be forceful."

He was hardly recognisable in this state of unaccustomed understanding, and if it was intended to be ironic he gave Ludwig no sign of it. The only way Ludwig knew that there was also a lot about the result that hadn't pleased him was when he then rose to his feet and thanked him distantly and formally for his work, which was not his style. He came towards Ludwig, hand outstretched, as if this were goodbye and they were unlikely to see each other again.

"With a bit of luck from here on everything will sort itself out, all we have to do is keep calm and wait."

With this he steered Ludwig towards the exit.

"What's the betting she'll come running through the door any minute now?"

That had been on the Saturday, and after Ludwig had sat out

Sunday in front of her apartment building without result, things did indeed happen fast on the Monday. In the morning he watched her go into the building where she worked as though nothing had changed, but that afternoon, as he was about to leave the hotel to resume his position, he suddenly saw her standing in the lobby. He couldn't hear what she was saying, but he saw her negotiating with the desk clerk, who was under strict instructions, and as she turned to leave empty-handed she brushed past him but didn't see him. She only had eyes for a girl who had just come in and almost run him down, a tall, lanky creature, blonde with a vengeance and gawky movements and absolutely no breasts, who intercepted her look and glared back like an adversary, watching until the door had closed behind her.

He wanted to follow her, but considered for a moment and called up to the suite, and the old man instructed him to stay where he was, he might need him at any moment.

"If she turns up here again, send her away."

His voice was loud and croaky, like a sound coming over a pair of scratchy loudspeakers with a tiny delay between them, yet though this was clearly an extraordinary situation Ludwig was unable to account for his sudden agitation. He watched the girl, who had been wordlessly waved ahead by the desk clerk and was now waiting at the lift, looking across at him as though she understood every word, while the old man talked on and on and he barely managed to toss a "yes" or "very good" into the harangue. The old man continued to repeat himself in an endless loop, saying the same thing over and over, and for the first time in a long time again addressed him as Major.

"Be very kind and make sure she doesn't come up here, whatever happens," he said. "You'll think of some way to get rid of her."

NINE

LUDWIG COULD PERHAPS HAVE BEEN BETTER PREPARED FOR THE absurd scene that awaited him when the old man had him paged nearly an hour later. After all, his employer's sentimental side was nothing new, and from the very first day Ludwig had been back with him again, whenever he felt like breathing some life into the stalemate of his Zagreb existence he talked about Buenos Aires in the same homesick way he had talked about Croatia back in Argentina, fantasising about how it would be spring there any day now and he really fancied seeing the trees in blossom on the Plaza San Martín at least once more in his life, or going to a race day at San Isidro or the Palermo hippodrome, or driving out to Quilmes just to stroll up and down the promenade. In Argentina he had never shown the faintest interest in any of these things, they were activities that in the full possession of his powers he would have dismissed as an utter waste of time, for weaklings. The nostalgia had reached a climax when one morning Ludwig went into his suite and he was still in bed, and he told him to open all the curtains and windows, sank back into his pillows with eyes closed and said that he wouldn't be surprised if the last few weeks, when there had been intermittent air-raid warnings every day, turned out to be one long hallucination and instead of the threatened city of Zagreb out there, it was the snow-covered Andes that rose into view, or the sea, white and empty as a millpond, the way he had once seen it back in the '50s near Bahía Blanca. He then asked Ludwig, in all seriousness, whether he could envisage going back to Argentina with him, but when Ludwig didn't answer he abruptly cut short his rhapsodies about what they might all do there together, looked at him from under flickering eyelids, and sent him away without a word.

These were signs of progressive decline, and if Ludwig had sometimes doubted the old man's sanity in the past he was, now, forced to admit that he had underestimated his craziness in every respect. For when his employer opened the door to him he was met by the wail of a tango, and even before he saw the contents of the two black folders spread across the floor, the newspaper cuttings and other papers, many obviously torn, lying around in deliberate chaos, his gaze fell on the gramophone that sat on the folding table next to an empty champagne bottle and two glasses, probably just another item that was child's play for the hotel management to supply, although more or less the last thing he would have expected. Gesturing to him to come in, the old man was sweating and dabbing his forehead with a handkerchief, his collar too tight, the necktie he wore with his suit knotted so firmly that it was cutting off his air supply, his face flushed with red spots. He was breathing heavily, whether from excitement or because he had been exerting himself was hard to say, and he seemed unable to make up his mind, first getting between Ludwig and the bedroom doorway, then with his free hand pointing to it and to the girl standing there, her gaze fixed on the floor and apparently frozen in mid-movement.

"The lady would like to go home," he said, and although his voice was flat and purged of highs and lows, it sounded like an order. "Be very kind and show her out."

It looked very much as though she had just been dancing with him, and the idea made Ludwig shudder. He saw that her hair, which she had worn loose when she marched into the lobby, was now in two braids, and he knew that the old man must have asked her to plait it like that and in all likelihood, overcome by nostalgia, he had told her about his little daughters too, saying it would remind him of them. She no longer wore her miniskirt either, but a black dress with a slit up the side that in her frozen position, bobbing awkwardly as though to make herself shorter, bared her thigh almost to the hip, and Ludwig imagined her movements, first drawn-out then harsh, as he had sometimes watched other women performing them in Buenos Aires when he had stumbled on couples dancing a tango for tourists, in all its paradoxical mix of unapproachability and longing for intimacy, in the middle of the day somewhere in the pedestrian zone of the Calle Florida or on Sundays near the Plaza Dorrego, as though they had got their midnights and middays confused.

The girl might not have moved for only a couple of seconds, but he experienced the time as particularly drawn-out, like the scene of a crime at which she was keeping still until he had secured the evidence. The old man meanwhile had sat down on one of the folding chairs and was nodding to him impatiently, so Ludwig knew what was expected of him and moved closer towards the girl, but he hadn't even put out a hand when she snapped at him, her eyes flashing like those of an actress who intended her glance to scorch the audience all the way to the back row, "Don't you dare touch me."

The old man laughed as Ludwig flinched. He rubbed his hands, the way he did in Buenos Aires when they came up from the shooting range and Claudia nagged him please to go and get clean before he even thought of sitting down at the table or coming near her or one of his daughters. From the way he looked at Ludwig he might have been remembering the same situation and how furious it always made him, and possibly for that reason he now spoke decisively.

"Just don't let her intimidate you."

He had tipped his uncomfortable chair backwards and half lay on it as if it were an armchair, looking ready to enjoy a spectacle that was no longer of any concern to him.

"Don't handle her with kid gloves either," he said, and for a few moments listened to the silence that followed a high-pitched click and the music cutting out. "She'd only misunderstand."

He laughed again, but before Ludwig could think how to get out of the situation the girl had set herself in motion, and he watched her as she swept up the shoes standing on the floor in front of her and walked past him on stockinged feet. She didn't look at him and nor did she seem to see the old man when, after he told her sarcastically to give her mother his best wishes, she stopped in front of him and spat, very matter-of-factly, almost like a form of greeting with which he must be very familiar. Turning away, she then dragged her feet deliberately and with a lengthy rustling noise across the mess of scattered papers, not picking them up until she was out in the corridor with Ludwig behind her.

Here she went to the other extreme and began to walk almost as if she were on a catwalk, putting one foot forward over the instep of the other, and turning around every few steps to glance at Ludwig. Whenever he seemed not to leave sufficient distance between them, she stopped dead and held up her hand defensively, with the same flashing of her eyes that amused rather than scared him. Although they were on the fourth floor she took the stairs, still holding her shoes and going down them as if on high heels, still taking care the whole time that he didn't come too close, and only in the lobby did she wave him towards her.

"You've done your job now," she said, as if it were up to her to dismiss him. "You'd better stay here."

There was little reason for Ludwig to give it any more thought, but when he got back to the old man's suite his curiosity got the better of him and he asked who she was, having thought it odd for there to be a car waiting for her at the hotel entrance, an aggressive-looking black limousine with heavy bodywork and narrow tinted side windows.

"You got yourself a proper scrubber there," he said, with ironic approval. "Careful she doesn't take you for a ride."

He still saw the limousine's rear passenger door opening, apparently automatically, for her, and her climbing in without another glance at him and being driven away, defiant astonishment and horror mingling on her face as though she had just discovered that the world was flat after all, and she might spin off it at any time, and that everything intelligent people had ever tried to tell her to the contrary was nonsense.

"Is she a tart?"

The old man waved him down.

"What do you mean?"

He was kneeling on the floor, having started to clear up the mess, and did not wish to be interrupted in his retrieval of one document after another, glancing at each sheet briefly then either putting it on the desk or crumpling and tossing it into the waste-paper basket.

"She's anything but," he said, and there was something reluctantly paternal in his voice. "She's the learned lady's daughter."

This was his disparaging term for the historian from the university whom he had asked to come once a week to help him get his papers in order and organise them, as he put it, on a scholarly basis. Ludwig found it hard to relate the girl to this woman in any degree, having seen her once in the interrogation cell as she was just taking off a huge sleeveless overall of plastified fabric that she wore for her job, to show that she was not only engaged on dirty work but also wouldn't be surprised if she were actually asked to handle the dead themselves whose names she was listing for the old man, and seeing her standing there with her legs solidly apart and hips thrust forward he would have taken her for a man, had she not been wearing a dark brown jacket and skirt under her idiosyncratic work clothes. Nor had she looked to him like the studies supervisor that she was, but more like an ex-athlete with her muscular arms and legs, short severe hairstyle, and chronically melancholy, clown-like face that didn't match the rest at all. It had immediately been clear to him what she must think of the two black folders, so little did she try to keep her disgust secret, but then he was amazed to hear the old man say that she was a hundred per cent Communist, and had only taken on this work because she had lost her job, and she couldn't wait to get out in the street and get her loathing out of her system at the first opportunity.

"In this learned lady you have a wonderful opportunity to study what political convictions are worth," he had said, while she was in the room. "Yesterday in every respect she was toeing the party line, today she will rewrite history for you any way you want it."

As if this weren't enough of a taunt, he had demanded her agreement and not stopped pressing her when she didn't answer.

"Am I right, Doctor? Yes or no?"

The dalliance with her daughter that had gone so spectacularly wrong that afternoon was part of the same miserable game-playing. For it had not been the girl's first visit either, and at the same time as he was buying the learned lady's academic authority while hardly believing in it in the slightest, it was the girl's friendliness he really cared about, the way she called him *señor* and he could call her his *chica* or *niña* in return, and perhaps it was her innocence too, at least in his dreams, an innocence by which he was so taken that he felt he had to prove his own virtuousness back to her, so that the furthest he had ever gone when his feelings overcame him was to stroke a strand of hair back from her forehead. She smiled radiantly at him whenever he waxed lyrical about the great wide world of Argentina, as though it didn't mean the boundless melancholy of the pampas, like the biggest chump he had champagne served to impress her, and everything had gone fairly well until he had the idea of the tango and made the mistake of telling her more about her mother than she wanted to hear.

In any case that was how he portrayed the situation when Ludwig asked him what had happened, while he continued to crawl across the floor picking up the scattered papers.

"I told her the sort of work her mother is doing for me," he said. "It made her fly into a rage."

As if he wanted, quite seriously, to express his admiration for her temper, he clicked his tongue and flicked his fingers up and down, making a little fluttering sound.

"You should have seen her going for me, fists first, then grabbing both folders and tossing them across the room."

He stood slowly back up, supporting himself on the table with one hand while he rubbed the other across his eyes in a tired gesture, then massaged the root of his nose with his thumb and forefinger.

"I understand nothing about the ideals of today's youth, but I find their single-mindedness very touching," he said patronisingly. "On the other hand I was already starting to think she was a bit crazy."

That was the end of the conversation, because he suddenly felt dizzy and when he said that he was going to lie down on his bed for a while Ludwig saw that he was swaying. He went over to support him, and only as he was about to draw the curtains did it strike him that they had been open all the time, and so the idea that the old man could have been dancing with the girl seemed to him all the more absurd, recalling again the couples he had seen in the glaring sunlight of Buenos Aires and his *idée fixe* about the angular syncopation of their steps, that that was how the dead would move if they rose again. He was about to say something to the old man, but, as if reading his thoughts, his employer pointed to the gramophone, asked him to take it back down to reception, and indicated the broken record that lay next to it on the table, its sleeve crumpled so that only part of the title stood out, "*Mi vida . . .*"

"I've no use for it," he said, as though he hadn't sent for either item himself. "Why would I want to listen to that stuff?"

Ludwig saw his opportunity to slip away, and as he was sitting reading the newspaper in the lobby a while later and the old man's daughter suddenly came back through the door, he was still thinking about the girl. It was impossible that the old man had arranged for the pair of them to appear hard on each other's heels like that, so it had to be one of those dramatic coincidences that are only believable in reality, but now he couldn't discard the thought that she had come too late, that the meeting with her father had already taken place, with an understudy playing her part, after a fashion. He watched the desk clerk turn her away again, nodded involuntarily to her as she left empty-handed, then followed her, making sure that she was aware he was with her. It was already getting dark, and she seemed unable to decide whether to hurry and shake him off if she could, or to pretend to be perfectly relaxed, taking a few hasty steps and then reverting to a slow stroll again, and with her anxious air as she pressed close to the walls of the buildings she could have been indistinguishable from the young woman who had earlier made such a spectacle of her exit from the hotel.

It was an impossible situation, and Ludwig probably would not have spoken to her at all if she had not suddenly stopped and asked him, staring fixedly at the ground, why he was following her, his own intention, if he had one, having been just to follow her to her destination then go back to the old man and give him one of his vague reports. As it was, she took him by surprise, and when she finally turned round and her eyes reminded him of a cornered animal, he had to stop himself from hugging her to him and holding her close. He wanted to warn her against the old man as she stood before him, to tell her he was crazy and that she should take herself away somewhere she would be safe from him, but once more he remained loyal to his employer's interests, keeping her at arm's length, saying only what was most essential.

"Take care of yourself," he did finally say, but by then he had already turned away from her and she didn't hear him. "You only have one life."

The old man made no reference to her or the girl when Ludwig returned to him, but he was suddenly filled with a desire for action, as if the brooding passivity that had taken hold of him in the last few weeks had just as suddenly left him. It was time to go to Dalmatia, he announced, to finally see about his parents' house, and although he had mentioned it endlessly it struck Ludwig that he had chosen it as his way of escape, since it had to be done quickly. Yet each day before they left felt like a warm-up for what was to come, because all kinds of things suddenly occurred to the old man that he still had to deal with, although to Ludwig they simply proved that in reality they had no reason to be in the city and that it remained a questionable honour for him to stay by the old man's side.

So he went with him to inspect the soldiers arriving and leaving from the railway station, to check the anti-tank defences on the bridges over the Sava and, after ending up at the Mirogoj cemetery, to watch a guard of honour there. Afterwards the old man went in search of the graves of two friends, and asked Ludwig to wait for him at the entrance. As he returned and they left the cemetery together, he had something light and almost ethereal in his step, despite his bulky physique, and moved as if in a world of his own, resembling momentarily those night owls who still wandered the city centre's squares in the early morning before it was fully light, like a ghostly company of the resurrected or the living dead.

In the night there were shots close to the hotel, and at breakfast the old man was in a better temper than he had been for a long time, demanding to know how Ludwig had slept, and to his complaints about the noise said at once that he shouldn't let little things like that bother him, with an assumed cold-bloodedness that he maintained throughout their subsequent drive. He insisted on taking the wheel himself, and when, his arm casually dangling out of the window after negotiating his own conditions at the first roadblock, he raced towards the next checkpoints every few kilometres without slowing down, it seemed suicidal but he carried it off. The men in uniform, the approaching car in their gunsights, were impressed by his lunatic willingness to risk life and limb, lowered their weapons and waved him through, seeming to recognise something of themselves in him as they bent casually to inspect his papers, then radioed ahead to forewarn their colleagues at the next checkpoint. It probably helped that he was kitted out like them, that he had the same haircut and wore the same sunglasses and the same fingerless gloves, and Ludwig had the impression that he only had to offer the youngest of them a cigarette or show them a photograph of himself as a paratrooper, which he did more than once, proudly mentioning his unit, and they were overawed by him, staring at the bulge under his leather jacket as though they had forgotten their own equipment and were still children, just dreaming all this.

They had to travel via Pag island, because the direct land route had been impassable for weeks, and on the short ferry crossing the old man asked a woman to take a photograph of the two of them. He spoke to her from behind, making her jump with fright, and she looked visibly uneasy among the almost exclusively male passengers, but then agreed, and Ludwig tried hard to keep a straight face as the old man put an arm around his shoulders, also trying not to let it show that he was thinking that this would be the picture he would be presented with, when the time came for him to answer for everything. The way the woman evaded his glances was enough to give him an idea of that, and he could have done without the quips of the old man too, enjoying intimidating the woman with his rowdiness and fussing, laughing loudly as he directed her to the right position, saying that it was only for police purposes and didn't have to satisfy any artistic standards, so she should make it quick and painless.

Merely having a physical objective seemed to restore all the old man's energy, which made Ludwig fear, as they approached the village, that he might look for a confrontation. He had asked him why he was so sure he would get the house back, and his only reaction had been a slight smile, but he had looked at Ludwig in such a way that Ludwig immediately understood what he meant and felt profoundly uneasy at the weight of his pistol where he had casually put it that morning in his inside jacket pocket, over his heart.

"Don't ask me to be part of your dirty work again," he said. "You can't count on me this time."

The old man had hardly glanced at the landscape, but had

become less and less communicative as its bare barrenness became increasingly familiar, had hardly glanced at the sea either, calm and flat in front of them, the late afternoon sun already close to the horizon, and even when they reached the two-storey stone building with the green door and window frames it evoked no sign of recognition. They had left the car in the village and climbed up the steep gravel path to the house, followed by a dog that slunk along some way behind them, head bent and tail lowered, and to all appearances this was less of a return than a land-grab for the old man, who might have been striding over enemy territory, taking possession of it merely by contact with his feet. He was in such a hurry that he could hardly keep his breathing steady, and for a while he had to stop and stand with his hand on his hip, his back straight, staring at the sky as if completely disoriented.

The sun had just disappeared behind a cloud as they reached the house, and though it had been warm all day Ludwig thought he felt a breath of cold air. He looked up the wind-blasted hill, then down over the slope's expanse to the sea, and was seized by panic at the thought of having to live here day in, day out, with nothing but a stony wilderness behind the house and maybe a couple of dozen sheep. It frightened him to think of having only the changing seasons to look forward to, summer's oppressive stagnation without a breath of wind, the sudden violent weather in winter when the bora funnelled down from the mountains and the water far below turned to a black abyss with a surreal sprinkling of white before smoothing out again overnight and dissolving into its usual endless, indifferent blue, and he felt like leaving the place again as quickly as possible.

No-one in the house had stirred, but he was sure they were being watched because there was food on a table next to the door, as though the people who lived there had jumped up at their approach, leaving everything where it was to take refuge. The property was a humble one, hardly worth the waist-high wall that enclosed it, comprising a few square metres of parched pasture, a couple of wooden sheds next to the stone building, a well and a garden fenced with chicken wire where a few withered sunflowers had been left behind. Ludwig had a feeling that he was looking at a miniature world that could be obliterated with a single hasty kick. Washing was hung on a line slung between the house and an olive tree, and the children's toys scattered everywhere made him think of his daughter with a pang, remembering visiting her at Graz again for the first time after he came back from Argentina, when he had watched her from the garden gate for a long time as she played in her sandpit, undecided whether he should go in or just walk away again.

The old man was calling out, and almost at the same moment the door opened and a man appeared in the doorway, looking as though, despite his weedy figure, he intended to fill it, his legs apart, his hands above his head as if hooked on the wooden lintel. He could have been forty, gaunt, with thin hair and a harassed look in his eyes, and he made no response to the old man's greeting, not even with a nod, only giving both men a dismissive and hostile look intended to check them, as if they were dogs who might attack at any time. He was wearing a white undershirt and a faded blue apron around his waist, and twitched almost imperceptibly as the old man approached.

"Nice view you've got here."

On the way up he had not once turned to look at the sea, and nor did he now, staring instead at the toes of his shoes as he kicked at the sand.

"I'm interested in the house," he said, and although he raised his head he still did not look at the man. "How much do you want for it?"

This came out so unexpectedly that the man just opened and shut his mouth without a sound, and as he continued to hesitate he was pushed aside by a woman who must have been standing behind him in the house's dark interior and now came out. She placed herself in front of him, arms folded, and despite the flowered dress and gumboots she wore she was a strange sight, with her sharply chiselled features and hair pinned on top of her head that left her neck exposed as she turned to the man once more. She seemed to want to shield and control him, and from the way he accepted it, it was clear which of them had the final say.

"What do you want?"

She had a dark, almost masculine voice, dry and rough, and when the old man repeated his question she laughed disbelievingly.

"We've got no plans to sell."

She acted as if his brusqueness amused her, but she was wary. Wiping her hands on her dress, still watching him, she slowly seemed to grasp how serious he was. She laughed again when he suggested that she shouldn't make it a matter of pride, but it was a helpless laugh, the kind of laugh he'd been waiting for.

"You know yourself what this dump is worth, and if they set fire to the roof over your head you'll have nothing left at all," he said, as if he were being kind enough to give her one last chance. "How long do you think the fighting back there is going to last before the first men turn up who won't be as thoughtful as me?"

In his outstretched hand he proffered a bundle of notes he had fished out of his jacket pocket. They had a rubber band around them, and when she didn't put out her hand to take them he snapped it off, fanned out the notes, then placed them on the chopping block in front of the house and weighted them with a stone, not letting the woman out of his sight.

"My offer's good until the weekend."

Ludwig knew that her resistance had been broken when she looked at her husband and he avoided her eyes. She hesitated, but it was more to save face than anything else. It gave her a look of surprise, and as she glanced at Ludwig he turned away, but for a moment it had looked as though this business were just between him and her.

"Go," she said. "Go."

Her voice now lacked any force.

"We'll be out here at the weekend if you want us, but now will you do me a favour and go away, as fast as you can."

She picked up the money and was starting to count the notes without taking any more notice of their presence, when a shot ripped through the silence and the old man flung himself on the ground. Pistol in hand, he crawled to the well and tried to find cover there. As he did so he looked around, his head barely raised, and did not straighten up until the woman ran screaming towards him.

"Don't shoot, please, don't shoot."

Everything had happened so fast that Ludwig had not moved, and only now did he spot the boy, who must have opened the window beside the door without a sound, and was firing a toy plastic gun again and again, as his mother fell on the old man and tried to seize his arm.

"It's only the child."

The old man pushed her away and flicked the dust off his clothes. He glanced briefly at the boy, now standing at the window without his gun, pale as an albino with a shock of straw-blond hair and freckles, and then looked at the mother again. His pistol still in his hand, he stood with his arms hanging down, as though he had actually fired at the boy, and his upper body swayed back and forth like that of a man who might lose his balance at any moment, and to all appearances could find support only in the air around him.

He spoke to himself like a man in shock.

"You've got a good lad there."

After he had repeated the words several times, without seeming to register what he was saying, he wanted to know the child's name, and when his mother didn't answer he grabbed her wrist and pulled her towards him.

"I asked you a question."

For a moment he seemed to be about to break her arm, then let her go and apparently lost interest.

"It's all the same to me what his name is," he said. "But I recommend you keep a better eye on him next time."

He turned away without another word, as if a sudden horror at the pointlessness and emptiness of the whole scene had seized him, and went ahead down the path with Ludwig following him. Ludwig knew that the woman was staring after them, the man perhaps still looking at the ground as he had done ever since they appeared, and he just wanted to get away fast. The old man was nearly running too, striding on ahead, and as they reached the car Ludwig turned back and saw the couple standing outside their house, the boy between them, as if for a photo, perhaps their first photo together, he suddenly thought. It struck him for the first time that the village had died out in the decades since the war, and probably even before then was being gradually abandoned, and it gave the family something ghostly and statuesque, turning them into mute witnesses to an exodus that had happened before their time, and at the same time leaving them without anyone to bear witness to their own disappearance.

The image wouldn't leave him, and he was still thinking about it when they reached Split, telling himself that it would hardly have been worse for the family if he and the old man had in fact burned their house down, so great was their humiliation, despite their probably having had thoughts about moving themselves and, if they had to, starting again at the ends of the earth. He couldn't forgive the old man for failing at least to enquire how long they had lived there, but when he accused the old man of being heartless he just laughed and asked if Ludwig really thought it would have made things easier for them if he had dressed it all up in kitsch and sentiment and then, at the very last, begged for their understanding as to why he not only wanted the house but had to have it. At Split they checked into the Hotel Bellevue, and as darkness fell Ludwig left the old man to have dinner alone and stayed standing at the open window to stare out at the double line of palms along the seafront promenade and the harbour, where a ferry showing dim lights seemed to be putting out, despite the desk clerk's assurance that the harbour entrance was blockaded. He felt depressed at having been merely his master's faithful servant yet again, for having turned away yet again, and when he heard the old man knock and suggest he come down for a drink with him he didn't open his door, didn't bother with an excuse, just said no, and stayed at his lookout post long after the lights had gone out in the cafés and the people strolling up and down in the dark had slowly scattered and their constant murmuring had stilled in the silence of a starlit night.

Although he knew it was too late, in the end he phoned Graz, but hung up as soon as he heard his ex-wife's voice, for fear of the catalogue of sins he knew she would reopen at the first wrong thing he said, of all his failings all the way back to Adam and Eve. He wanted to talk to somebody, he had an oppressive urge to talk after his terrible day, but apart from his ex-wife he could think of no-one, and she was the last person to listen to him. He hated these moments of weakness when he felt he needed purification as much as punishment, and also because he no longer had any illusions and had known what he was doing ever since he had told his friends years before that he was dropping out of university to join the police and inevitably, one by one, they had vanished out of his life. It wasn't just that he gave off a bad smell, or had been infected by some virulent bacillus, but that with that decision he had cut himself off from the human race, and he had no need of his ex-wife to remind him that that stigma would stay with him to the Last Judgement and beyond, although nor did he have any doubt that, do what he might, there was no-one else besides her.

Afraid of not being able to sleep, he found the lens cloth he kept handy and began defiantly to clean his pistol, as he had done before when he slipped into this mood, although he had always considered the relationship many of his colleagues had with their so-called "best pieces" ridiculous, and looked at them with mingled pity and revulsion whenever they gave their weapon a girl's name or called it their sweetheart. His was the same model he had had in Argentina, which the old man had issued to him from whatever stock of weapons he had, and the butt's man-made material was warm to the touch. He ran his hand over the ribbed surface and was overcome by the old disgust he felt whenever he touched a gun that wasn't cold, an urge to vomit such as he had had on the rare occasions when his mother made him drink a glass of fresh milk, still warm from the cow, a sudden sick feeling that made him retch. He couldn't shake off the idea that the warmth was the tempera-ture of blood, and at home he had always put his service weapon in the fridge overnight, as though that might guarantee not just its sterility but a greater precision too, but there was no minibar here that he could use for that purpose. He considered whether to call down to reception for a bucket of ice, but this struck him as ridiculous, and instead he went to the bathroom, ran cold water into the washbasin, placed the pistol in the basin and felt instantly relieved, exactly as if it were part of his body, and suddenly remembered the first time he had held a gun in his hand, during his early training, and how as he stood on the shooting range a feeling of tenderness for all living things had taken hold of him, an almost religiously inspired humility in the face of his realisation of how little it would take, just one gentle pressure on the trigger, and a whole world could collapse.

At the time he had already sensed the loneliness that that feeling would bring with it, but nobody, apart from Nina, had understood it. She herself had been an example of how carrying a gun did not automatically brutalise you, and for that reason alone there was a particular irony in the fact that she had died like that, one that on some days he rebelled furiously against and on other days he resignedly accepted. It still made him dizzy every time he recalled the crucial seconds when he had run after her, and all the more so as he did not know whether another kind of memory had set in then, whether he had not already begun to think of her as though she were no longer alive. And with that idea there always came that sense of time galloping away from him and at the same time slowing down, that he could not explain to anyone, and he saw her ahead of him, stopped and her body turned to one side to offer as small a target as possible, her pistol raised and, as she called "Police!", her hands stretched out ahead of her as far as possible, it was as if he were dazzled by the light that radiated from her.

Despite these fears, he spent a quiet night, and felt no real uneasiness until the next day, which brought an encounter with two of the old man's acquaintances from the past and made him feel that everything he had experienced with him until then had been mere skirmishing. They met the two men on the Riva, and while

Ludwig tried to follow the conversation, full of allusions that he only half understood, he had a fleeting sense, no more than a presentiment, that something was wrong. It started with the way they greeted the old man, not the slightest exuberance, not the slightest show of excitement after all these years, a handshake and they sat down, and then as he saw their tattoos his hair stood on end. It was the same series of letters that the old man had on the back of his neck, except that one had it on his upper arm and the other distributed over the second joints of his fingers, and Ludwig immediately interpreted it as proof of membership of a secret sect, surrounding all three with a sinister aura. He pictured them pledging eternal loyalty as young men and had a vision of a dark act that involved an ocean of candles, a crucifix, the Bible and probably even a few drops of blood from their veins.

Otherwise the only outlandishness they provided was to seem, from the rest of their appearance, entirely harmless and apparently to both be called Mario, which was perhaps a heavy hint that it was advisable to entertain doubts about their credibility. The old man called them "the twins", though they could hardly have looked more different and came across more like a couple in a film bound together by their contrasting qualities. While one was a burly, flabby figure with a face drooping in all directions, wearing towelling slippers and jogging bottoms as though he couldn't imagine any disaster that he wouldn't survive intact, the other had the morose look of a pensioner who had lost track of his travel group and was no longer fully aware of where he was, with grey skin and dressed in grey, grey shoes, deep lines in his cheeks and a severe parting that exposed a strip of scalp nearly a centimetre wide. Like the old man, these two had gone on the run after the war and they had come back from Australia only a few months before. Their best time, as they made clear, had been serving under the Italians, which explained their fad for addressing each other as *"cavaliere"* and was probably also responsible for their ecstatic gesticulating.

The conversation went on going nowhere in particular for a long time, but it was obvious that the two Marios, perfectly attuned to each other, were intent on provoking the old man. It was all about a few weeks he had spent with them in Dalmatia during the war, and though they must have noticed how little he wanted to talk about it, they kept returning to the subject. The situation eventually became so tense that a phrase uttered by one, to which the other added a scornful laugh, was enough to make him lose his temper.

It was something about his wife, an insinuation about how lonely she must sometimes have felt in his absence, living on the coast with the child, followed by a question that for Ludwig at first seemed unconnected with the remark.

"Did you at least learn to shoot in Argentina?"

The explanation came from the one who had laughed, and there was no doubt that it was meant to give offence.

"I hope you found out how to stop it jamming, anyway," he said brusquely, and although alcohol had played its part and wine bottles were lining up on the table, it sounded belligerent coming from a man of seventy. "A bent barrel is tricky for anyone."

The other man laughed now, and the old man waited until he had stopped. He looked at him. Only when he had fallen completely silent did the old man look down at his fingertips, which he had laid together on the table.

"As for you two, I think we won't discuss your skill with guns."

He had raised his voice but now paused in mid-sentence, looked around him to see if anyone was listening, and dropped it to a whisper.

"The distance you were shooting from, it was a joke," he said, and it was clear that he meant it literally. "The world's biggest moron could hit a target set up like that."

He struck his own neck with a clenched fist, and Ludwig saw him crook his forefinger as if it were on the trigger, raise his thumb and pull it down in a smooth movement intended to mimic the cocking of a gun. He laughed, his eyes wide as if in fear, and there was something wild in his laughter. Beads of sweat stood out on his forehead, and he reached for a napkin and wiped it, then painstakingly shook the napkin out and folded it up again as he subsided into a deliberate calm.

"What was the question before you pulled the trigger?"

He was almost inaudible now.

"Do you believe in God Almighty?"

While he waited as the conversation died down at the tables around them, so that he had the silence to himself, he looked alternately at the two Marios, suddenly sitting very stiffly on their chairs. He put his hands together and the next moment spread his arms wide. Then his voice again dropped to a low murmur, supposedly to mimic that of a priest, uttering promise and threat at once.

"Then you'll go straight to heaven."

It was an exchange of words that sent a shiver down Ludwig's spine, but as he was reflecting on what he should do, the old man and both Marios leapt up at almost the same moment, the chairs went flying, and they probably only held off from setting about each other with bare fists because all eyes at the neighbouring tables were turned to them. Ludwig had stayed seated, watching them, and to his eyes they seemed to be circling each other as they stood there, the two Marios nervously looking around them, the old man breathing heavily, his hands propped on the table.

But none of them moved, and the viscosity of time became palpable, seconds that were long drawn out like drops forming on an overhead surface before they became too heavy and fell. For a few moments the three stood motionless, like actors who had forgotten their lines and were waiting for someone to prompt them so that they could bring the scene to an end. But then they seemed to reflect, and the moment the spell was broken they all started again, each saying what he had to say.

"We know what we need to think about each other."

The old man spoke first, but the two Marios echoed him, trying to outdo him in contempt.

"You're right about that," the one with the flabby face said. "You were a coward then and you're still one now."

And he spat at the old man just as the girl had done in the hotel three days before, and as the other Mario still hesitated, reddening as far as his parting, he led his friend away.

"We have no more business here."

For Ludwig the return to Zagreb couldn't happen fast enough, and the old man too was keen to go straight to the hotel, fetch their bags and get on the road. He seemed to be waiting for questions, but Ludwig asked none, he wanted no explanation, he just wanted to get back that afternoon and then get out of there, disappear once and for all. He found himself unable to console himself that the disastrous discussion had perhaps been just another of the old man's provocative attempts, begun in Buenos Aires, to allay suspicion, and at that moment he felt finally freed from him. For he knew that this was no longer the old man's strategy of brash cockiness, of telling things like they were, in the belief that no-one would take him seriously because they were so outrageous, and if a confused notion of loyalty had survived until now, a vague feeling that had always drawn him to lost causes, going any further with the old man was too much for him. The honour among thieves to which he had bound him was a pledge from which he could withdraw at any time, and if at the beginning of their relationship he had told Ludwig he had selected him because there was "something Dinaric" about him, in other words that he was the kind of person likely to exploit situations to his personal disadvantage, a phrase that had not left him since, it might have been true, but there were limits, and he had reached them.

Ludwig drove, and after a couple of unsuccessful attempts to talk away what had just happened the old man dozed off, and on arriving did not quite seem to understand when the desk clerk told him that a lady had been asking for him several times over the last two days. The description of her did not fit his daughter, nor, when Ludwig wanted to know whether it could have been the girl, did the answer seem to confirm it, and he thought no more of it simply because he was preoccupied with getting the old man to his room and making sure he was alright. Since he had made his decision that, as soon as the old man was asleep, he would disappear without a word, he had again been overcome by an indulgent concern for him. His plan was to take the car and to drive as far as he had to in order to leave all this behind him, but as if he first had to earn absolution from his own conscience, he remained close by as the old man got undressed, ran him a bath, and at his request put the towels ready beside it.

He had just helped him into the bath when there was a knock at the door. He hesitated instinctively, but the old man wearily raised a hand as if to shoo him away and looked past him.

"Go on," he said. "Open the door."

He was lying up to his chin in the water, observing Ludwig as he went across the carpeted floor. He couldn't see the door to the suite, and Ludwig paused and looked back at him once more before he reached for the handle. From behind him he heard the old man's question.

"Who is it?"

It was the girl, but he didn't recognise her immediately, and even when he did he couldn't have said how. She had cut her hair short and dyed it black, she was wearing blue workman's overalls with two yellow stripes across her bust, and her eyes looked darker than he remembered them, her pupils dull and unshining. She nodded to him, as if to say that it was all genuine and yes, he could believe his eyes, and just as he was regretting having unbuckled his holster and hung it over one of the folding chairs in the interrogation cell, he saw her hand go to her shoulder bag and felt no surprise as she brought out a pistol.

"Perhaps this comes as a surprise to you, but I have an appointment," she said, her voice toneless yet as clear as a child's. "Aren't you at least going to ask me in?"

TEN

MARIJA SPENT TWO DAYS IN HER HOTEL IN WHICH SHE DID NOT go out, two days in which she turned over and over in her mind what she ought to do before the decision was taken out of her hands, whether to wait till she was contacted again, or just to go home and forget the whole thing, and then sometimes, when anger at her own powerlessness seized her, she thought she didn't want to see her father at all, or that if she did see him she would kill him. She had continued writing, though what she wrote was turning into anything but a letter to him, it was more of a letter addressed to herself without her knowing it, as she proved to herself by her repeated astonishment when she reread the lines she had just written. Memories showered down on her, things she thought she had forgotten long ago and that she now felt unable to defend herself against. The last person to want to tease them out of her had been a doctor in Vienna, a man as finely attuned emotionally as he was solidly built, who, a few months after her first encounter with her husband, had welcomed her to his consulting room in the Eighth District, his approach so nervously tentative, with his soft warm handshake, low lighting, and somewhere in the background a muted beat of distant jungle drums, that she had felt he and she were both convalescents out on a date together. She had sought him out secretly when her husband's interrogations, his recurrent declarations that he had to get her on the right political track before she could be introduced to the comrades in his group, had made her feel that there must be something wrong with her. She didn't really believe in it, but for a few months she had lain on the couch twice a week, her monologues interrupted every so often by the soporific voice behind her head or the metallic screeching of the tram as it turned the corner, halted at the stop in front of his building, and went on again, and in the end she had found that she couldn't even trust the doctor's views, so wonderfully neatly did each thing fit together with the next for him and lead to a firm conclusion that she didn't need to be pointed out by any expert.

Fundamentally it had been hardly any different from the persistence of her husband, whose maxims about free love had not stopped him asking her questions about his predecessors, then pronouncing judgement on all eleven of them, a number she had lightly owned up to, adding even more carelessly, "A whole football team," thus downgrading him once and for all to the role of substitute. She could hardly have done anything sillier than make this throwaway remark and then make matters worse by giggling and accusing him of jealousy which was a ridiculously bourgeois attitude, though it didn't help that she sometimes made fun of his vocabulary too and the slogans he was always trotting out, sex was nothing other than permanent revolution, permanent revolution was nothing other than sex, and grandiose assertions of a similar sort. For what ensued was an exorcism, and when, at daybreak, she lay awake after a long night in which he had pumped her about her boyfriends down to the very last detail, while he slept the deep sleep of the just beside her, she had to be careful that her former lovers didn't become in her mind the horde of demons he made them into, so that of her memories only his slurs remained, to which of course there was to be added the natural connection he traced back, sometimes verbally, sometimes by implication, to her father, which was no less erroneous and no less accurate.

The doctor however had been more interested in the British officer her mother had got to know in Vienna in the autumn after the war, and Marija didn't know whether she should be surprised to find that it was he of all people, Uncle Alfred (as she used to call him) of all people, who turned up again and again in the pages and pages she filled in those two days. He was, apart from a handful of other impressions, and she couldn't say with any certainty that these were definitely her own, her earliest memory of that time, a young man who drove up to the building near Margaretenplatz where they had been housed in an apartment belonging to a teacher's family, a beanpole come to fetch her mother, who looked exactly like a character in a picture-book with his cap aslant on his head, the white holster of his revolver with its white strap and his fine leather gloves, and always brought her a bar of chocolate or something else, the first certainty in her life after weeks and weeks veiled in a murky mist. Whenever she thought back to that time, she had to acknowledge that the war had not really come to an end for her until he appeared, months after the last of the fighting, because with him beside her, her mother at last seemed to radiate a sense of security, after the half-eternity of that spring and summer under the Russians when she had been permanently afraid of being picked up on the street and dragged away. That was the time when they had never gone out, except for the absolute necessities of life, when they had nothing left to eat and they pawned the last of her jewellery in the Resselpark or at the Naschmarkt or managed to grab seats on one of the buses that took them somewhere in the surrounding countryside where there were farms, and food, and Marija found herself still amazed to think how, because of him, everything had suddenly been transformed again, and how bright and sunny the days had become. She remembered an afternoon at the Kursalon in the Stadtpark, where her mother had danced with Uncle Alfred to the strains of a military band, and another day an outing to the races in Freudenau, where she had watched her mother pressing close to him and then done the same herself, and the horses flying along the racetrack seemed to have nothing in common with animals that she had seen in the city centre in the last days of the war, corpses lying in front of the Kirche am Hof that were stripped to skeletons within hours by the passers-by. On the way home her mother, her arm through Alfred's, had been in such high spirits that she had even spoken to the two auxiliary police officers in Yugoslav partisan uniform who crossed their path, though she almost always gave any soldier a wide berth and even avoided Russians who were long dead, scurrying past the few graves with Cyrillic inscriptions in the Volksgarten and crossing herself as though an evil spirit could arise from them at any time, as well as those still living at the Hotel Imperial and at the Soviet commandant's H.Q. in the former Board of Education building on Bellariastrasse, with its portraits of Lenin and Stalin and the huge red star over the entrance.

These two days were the first time in a long time that she had thought of Uncle Alfred, yet it was still with the same gratitude and sense of protection that she had experienced in his presence. For he had not only been their saviour, enabling them to venture onto the street in safety again, but on Uncle Alfred her mother had also set her first hopes that someone might help her to look for her husband. She had heard rumours of camps in Carinthia where refugees from Yugoslavia were being held, the most tenuous prospect imaginable, but she pursued it all the same, as though she were sure she was on the right track, and was always nagging Uncle Alfred to get her some pass or other document that would allow her to cross the Soviet zone and travel to Klagenfurt. To this end she planned their walks so that they often ended at the badly damaged Südbahnhof, where she would invariably ask him whether there might be a train going over the Semmering Pass, and mightn't the Russians turn a blind eye if, with his blessing, she simply boarded it, or couldn't he just take her to the airfield at Schwechat and arrange a seat for her on one of the planes that maintained the British forces' connection with their own zone of occupation in Carinthia and Styria?

Uncle Alfred accepted it all with remarkable composure. He took her to the cinema in the Sofiensaal, and once or twice even to the Hotel Sacher to which Austrians had no access, or to Schönbrunn and the Park Hotel, which had been requisitioned by the British, and he patiently reassured her when she talked about her husband that there was as yet no reason for her to worry, only four months after the war's end. He treated her like a lady, venturing at the most to give her a gentlemanly kiss with pursed lips, or taking her hand and staring straight ahead as she granted him this privilege for a few moments before gently withdrawing it. She had seen and talked to him in the street, begged him for his personal protection, and now he was trapped in the role, wanting to prove himself more of a gentleman the more horror stories she told him about the Russians, and her laments of what Russian occupation really meant, particularly for the women who were left to wash between their legs with camomile tea or even holy water after the advancing troops had left behind the word "*provereno*" painted on a building, as a sign it had been checked. A glance from her had been enough to remind him that she was married, and he could put all suggestive ideas out of his head. But it didn't stop him being her admirer, far from it, it seemed to spur him to greater generosity, to bring her gifts of stockings and underwear that he handed over shyly along with a piece of meat or half a pound of butter, and even blushing when, one day in late September, he surprised her with an invitation to swim in the Hietzing pool, for which he had had to get her a permit because it was reserved for the occupying forces, and pressed into her hand a bright yellow bathing costume he had had specially sent from London.

Marija remembered again how sometimes, when he brought her mother home, he had stood outside the building for a while, leaning against his car and smoking a cigarette in the darkness. It was a picture she held to whenever she was frightened, the man's shadow down in the street, where the piles of rubble still hadn't been cleared away and once in a blue moon a car drove by. She had always stood at the window, looking down as she heard her mother's footsteps coming up the stairs, and now these moments seemed like pure happiness to her, the click of her mother's heels approaching and the stationary figure she could hardly make out, just his glowing cigarette in the night. She remembered vividly how she had also thought that the man down in the street could be someone different and that when the door opened it might be a Russian woman, a commissar come to take her hand and lead her away. That was what her mother had always threatened might happen if she didn't stay close to her, with the barriers and check-points only a stone's throw away at the edge of the Fourth District, where the devil's empire began that reached all the way to Siberia, and so hardly was her mother inside the apartment, unpinning her hat, kicking off her shoes, than she flew to her in a fever of agitation, jumping into her arms and crying out, "Mama, Mama!" because at the last moment she had been terrified, after all.

It made her eyes well with tears when she thought about it, when she saw herself once again standing at the window on the top floor of the building. From it she had one day seen the whole sky glittering and sparkling in the sun from the silver strips dropped by advance aircraft to disrupt the ground radar before the bombers followed, and from it after one air raid she had seen the domes burning calmly in the distance, ringed in the bright midday light by a barely visible, yellowish-green flickering corona. Then pillars of smoke had risen into the air without a sound, as she still remembered, and without a sound a few days later the first Russian soldiers and first tanks had appeared at the crossroads at the end of the street, blue-grey in front of the blue-grey phosphorus spatters left on the walls by incendiary bombs. In fact it seemed to her now as though she had experienced the last weeks of the war in near-complete silence, that she had never heard the rattle of the anti-aircraft guns or the muffled crump of the bombs, only the whoosh before they hit, which had intensified the silence and which she'd never been able to forget, a sound she might hear whenever the world suddenly fell quiet around her, exactly as if someone above the clouds had tipped heaps of sand onto a steep metal slide, sand that had been sliding and sliding ever since and making her feel that for all eternity, or at least as long as she lived, a delayed-action fuse might set off the decisive explosion whose blast wave alone would sweep her off the surface of the earth.

Twenty years later, when she told him this, the doctor had described her as a girl still waiting, and had said that it was what characterised her, a waiting that had stopped being for her father a long time ago, but a waiting for something to happen that would get her life going at last, while at the same time there was nothing she feared more strongly than being snatched out of her dreamy, absent-minded state. She had thought it was just talk, but now it seemed like that to her too, that everything in her life had been a kind of postponement, that her time at school, her university years, her husband, even her daughter had not really been necessities to her, as if she lived her life only so long as she had no other and, unchanged at fifty, still felt that she hadn't really started living. That she was in Zagreb, a city on which calamity might fall at any time, seemed the most logical thing in the world to her, and when a warning sounded and she looked out of the window, an aimless longing made her search the sky for planes until, frightened that she might actually be wishing them her way, she retreated into the room and lay on the bed again. Then she took out the crumpled pages of newspaper with the photograph of her father and her two Argentinian sisters and looked at the little girls in their white dresses until they swam together before her eyes and the young woman beside them looked more and more like her own mother.

It ended with her calling Vienna, asking her husband if he missed her, and directly afterwards ringing Lorena's number in Philadelphia, where she once again met with incomprehension when she asked the same question and then, without a pause, started to talk about Uncle Alfred.

"That's nearly fifty years ago, and it's the first time you've mentioned this person," she heard Lorena say. "Do you really have to do this long-distance?"

It was said with her daughter's usual hostility, but this time Marija was not to be put off, and saw her daughter's reaction as a challenge.

"You once asked me when I'd felt happiest as a child," she said. "You probably aren't interested in knowing now, but it was then."

For a moment there was silence, and she hoped her daughter would let it rest at that and not twist every word she said again, but she was mistaken.

"What is wrong with you?"

She hated it when Lorena took this tone, but she let it pass and instead went on telling her how they really had travelled to Carinthia with Uncle Alfred the year after the war, because her mother had stuck to her resolve to shed new light there if she could. She then asked whether Lorena could imagine what that had meant for her, and answered her own question.

"I just can't tell you how excited I was when we were driving from village to village in his car," she said. "For me there couldn't have been any clearer proof that we belonged to the victors than being chauffeured by him around that bleak countryside."

For almost three weeks they had set out every day, trusting to luck, to gather what information they could about her father's whereabouts after being unable to discover anything from official agencies, and had established only that his name wasn't listed in any of the camps run by the British. She pictured again the expeditions they had made from Klagenfurt to the prohibited zone south of the Drava, her mother in the front passenger seat in her headscarf, she in the back next to the picnic basket, a provocative extravagance in those days whenever they stopped somewhere, spread out their rug in a meadow, and ate the picnic they had brought with them. She had been just six years old, and when she thought back to those days she could hardly believe how she, as a child of the war and in spite of everything she had seen, had lived in a world of dreams, always wide-eyed and imagining that the most wonderful things were in store for her. She had spent the intervening months in Switzerland, in the Bernese Oberland, on a programme run there to feed up children from Vienna, and her face now wore a different look whenever Uncle Alfred put a hand on her mother's knee, as she watched in the certainty that the grown-ups couldn't pretend to her anymore, because she'd known all about love for a long time, ever since she'd first heard in her ears the voice of the boy she had gone tobogganing with nearly every day that winter, his repeated "Marija, Marija, hold on tight!" that he called out over his shoulder as they raced downhill, though she had already pressed herself tightly to his back and wrapped her arms around his tummy.

They were a flood of images beneath which she finally fell silent, before she added that she had lived through the search for her father as a unique adventure and wished it could go on for ever.

"Please don't get me wrong."

She had almost forgotten her daughter, but from her reaction to these words she knew that they were a gift to her.

"Oh, I'm sure I don't."

She seemed to have been waiting for her chance.

"It just sounds a little bit as if you didn't want to find him at all," she said. "Have you ever considered that possibility?"

Her sarcasm was the last thing Marija needed, even if it was the same inane kind of thing that the doctor in Vienna might have said, as he explained to her how it was between her and men. She didn't reply, and wondered, yet again, what had earned her her daughter's permanent hostility that made her want to rain on her parade at every turn. There was no getting past her directness, and Marija sensed that if she were to ask again, the way she usually did, whether everything was alright, or to ask for the hundredth time whether she knew how late it was, she might forget herself.

"What do you think I'm doing here?"

She could positively hear her daughter wait before her laugh escaped her, detached and harsh, and then she also had to put up with being called Mama.

"Mama, I'd be glad if you could tell me that," Lorena said, and her new composure had something infuriating to it. "The thing is, I'm afraid even you don't know."

The words were hanging over her head like a verdict when, later that day, she was asked to come to reception and went down, thinking there might be a message for her from her father, and instead found Angelo. He was sitting in the lobby, and despite looking straight at him she didn't recognise him until he stood up and stepped towards her because he had grown a beard, was wearing a peaked cap with the ubiquitous red-and-white-checked badge, and made a generally scruffy impression in his baggy khaki trousers and sleeveless jacket. She had given up ever expecting to see him again and was so taken aback that she stood stock-still and failed to react when he held his arms out to her. As she hesitated he put on a smile and made an effort to convert the gesture into putting his hands into his belt, leaning as far back as he could to inspect her from the greatest possible distance.

"Don't you want to say hello?"

Merely from the way he looked around as he said it, she realised that this was not meant just for her or the desk clerk, buried in his papers and pretending not to listen, but mainly for the man who had so far stayed in the background and now came over to them, and whom Angelo introduced as his captain.

"He's a gynaecologist, when he's not fighting."

Whether it was true or not, Angelo laughed in exactly the way she remembered, and when she still didn't move he grasped her upper arm and led her over to the man, who offered her his hand.

"I've heard a lot about you," he said conventionally, yet it sounded like a smutty insinuation from his lips. "It's a privilege to meet you."

He was a small, chirpy-looking fellow with an old-fashioned pencil moustache that she couldn't stop staring at, thinking that it must sprout tentacles that would fasten themselves to her skin if she stood in front of him for too long. At the same time he was as nondescript as an actor you might see playing supporting roles for years without really noticing him, still waiting for his big break, with a youthful face that would fade without ageing and the nostrils of a dead man. He was standing so close to her that she could smell the peppermint of a mouthwash or mouth spray he must have just used, and as she was starting to wonder where all this was leading, he suddenly doubled up in a sort of twisted bow to try, perfectly seriously, to kiss her hand.

As she stepped back, he then went so much further in the manner of his apology, if you could call it that, she knew then and there that she would never get its outrageous clumsiness out of her head.

"There's so little opportunity to get a pop at a lady these days."

His expression scared her but when she tried to move away Angelo increased his pressure on her arm until she felt the imprint of each individual finger and wanted to cry out with pain. At the same time he brought his face so close to hers that his beard tickled her cheek. He made a wet smacking sound, pursing his lips and drawing in air like a man with a nervous tic, before saying to her in a dry and insistent whisper, "Is that a way to treat heroes of the fatherland?"

He gave no sign that he couldn't mean it seriously as he suddenly steered her across the lobby and made it abundantly clear that there was little point in her resisting.

"Be a good girl and keep us company."

They were sitting in the hotel's café before she learnt that they had both come from Vukovar and would have to go back there. Having wedged her between them, they were practically pouring wine down her throat, but when she heard this she gave up thinking of resisting and let it happen, merely curious and at the same time glad that they said nothing more and shrugged off her questions about what it was like there with ironic accounts of an unspoilt idyll. Despite having become desensitised to the endless T.V. pictures of ruined houses riddled with bullets, she was as much at the mercy of words as ever, as though only they threatened to confront her with truly unimaginable things, that she might subsequently no longer be able to keep at a distance.

"I thought the city was surrounded days ago," she said eventually. "They say that no-one can get in or out."

She had purposely turned to Angelo, but it was the other man who answered, his lips twisted with irony.

"Do we look like ghosts to you?"

He rapped the table with his knuckles and spared her the laugh that had accompanied everything he had said so far.

"Maybe you shouldn't believe everything you hear," he said. "If it was all true we'd have been dead long ago."

He was the one setting the tone, while Angelo treated her like a stranger. She had hardly spoken a personal word to him, and whenever she tried to, he simply repeated what she had said, as though she were afraid of addressing his companion directly and had turned to him as an intermediary. Her unease increased as she realised that it didn't bother Angelo that the other man had a habit of touching her as he spoke, alternately putting his hand on her forearm then putting his arm around her shoulder again, and that he had now moved on to patting her thigh under the table. He did it in an almost business-like way, and she didn't dare push his hand away, on the contrary, having let herself be intimidated so far already she felt she would have been the one going too far if she hadn't simply accepted his behaviour, to the point where she caught herself thinking how ridiculous it would be to get angry about it after everything that he must have been through. She only had to remind herself of the pictures that she'd seen of Vukovar, the recurrent sequences of a ghost town that finished each time with helicopters taking off from the far bank of the Danube to make for what little remained standing of the city's walls, and she was helpless against his advances. Though she knew that seeing other people's point of view ahead of her own was one of her besetting sins, it seemed a very trivial offence that he was groping her after he had escaped from that inferno, he could have stripped her naked in public and she wouldn't have thought about it very much, when yesterday he had been in a situation where one false move could have cost him his life.

Doubtless the wine she had drunk was partly to blame, and by the time the man, with a meaningful look, put a packet of tobacco on the table, she was almost beyond speech and instead watched spellbound as he rolled each of them a cigarette. It took him for ever, and she was sure his dry tongue was making a rasping sound as it licked the paper and he pushed the completed cigarette with deep concentration back and forth between his lips two or three times, until it gleamed moistly. His elaborate preparations had something of the fuss people had once made (though it was twenty or more years ago now) whenever someone had good stuff to smoke and rolled their special spliffs, guaranteed to take you straight to paradise. In that alone he resembled the heroes of the past, and she wasn't surprised when, as soon as she had taken her first drags and her senses had rapidly started to lighten and swim, he took her chin in both hands and turned her face to him.

"Look at me carefully," he said, his voice effortlessly silky and warm. "Who do I remind you of?"

He made a serious face.

"Is this how the big bad wolf in the fairy tale looks?"

Then, without transition, he told her she was a spoilt child and a ludicrous romantic to defy her fate so pointlessly by coming to Zagreb now, of all times.

"What are you looking for here?"

His tone of voice had changed again.

"You seem not to know what luck you had, getting away when you did," he said harshly. "What do you think would have become of you if you'd had to stay?"

It was obvious he was talking about himself, and the last thing that she heard with any clarity was his account of an attack on his village in Slavonia and how, because he had been a child in the war, he had only survived because he was small for his age, although she didn't understand what this was supposed to have to do with her. She listened without emotion, but forced herself at least to look at him, as he told her how the armed men who had appeared at day-break had measured the villagers against a rifle stood vertically on the ground, then loaded onto trucks not just the men but every boy who was taller than the rifle, and then shot them all in a nearby wood. He explained that he had been exactly a centimetre too short, but that he still didn't know what kind of a rifle it had been, from old Yugoslavian stock or looted from the Germans or even of Russian manufacture, and because this detail made her want to laugh so much she was almost powerless to keep a straight face, she let him go on rambling, one centimetre and I wouldn't be here, one centimetre and I'd be dead now.

Later, when she found herself in bed again, trying to get her bearings, his story struck her as a wildly implausible anecdote that had no counterpart in reality. She couldn't say how much time might have passed, but the window was wide open, and she saw it was dark outside. The mild night air carried voices to her, she even thought she heard singing, scraps of a song that instantly died away again. Then everything was completely silent, and it was the same silence as in weeks gone by, a silence usually only to be found deep in the country, sometimes lasting for minutes without any traffic noise, or at most the long approach of a single car coming closer and just as distinctly fading away again, and it wouldn't have surprised her to hear the calls of animals in between, the cries and screeches from a jungle at the edge of the city. The radio alarm that stood on the bedside table was blinking eights, and the light that fell through the fractionally open bathroom door convinced her for a moment that she was not alone, so strongly did a smell of sweat and urine suddenly rise to her nostrils, alarming her.

She got out of bed and assured herself that there was no trace of Angelo or his companion. But when she tried to remember whether they had ever been in the room with her, all that occurred to her was that the companion, of all people, wearing only a dressing gown open to his navel that exposed the swelling of a small domed paunch, had been standing next to her bed and looking down at her with the gentleness of a saint. She was not sure of this vision, however, and her uncertainty was intensified by the thought that she recalled him saying to her the evening prayer familiar from childhood, *"anđele moj dragi"*, and that she had had to repeat it word for word, "dear angel mine", and that couldn't be right. Then suddenly Angelo's voice was in her ears, introducing him, and she saw him before her, snapping on surgical gloves and leaning over her, and hurriedly got back into bed, hoping that it was only her drugged brain leading her to believe all this and that in a few hours' time she would be able to dismiss it with a clear head as a bad dream.

As though she had caught a chill, she pulled the covers up to her chin and wished her mother were sitting at her bedside and stroking her forehead, while she stared out at the night and surrendered again to the idea that the whole city had been extinguished in the blackout and that far and wide there was nobody living. It soothed her to think this, and she closed her eyes with the same mingled sense of horror and protection as on other nights when there had been shots audible that had reminded her of dogs barking, a yapping that began on a hill and was continued some-where else before it was lost, a sound ricocheting away in the darkness. Yet the guilt feelings that usually came automatically when her musings had gone so far didn't come this time, and however long she waited all she could feel inside herself was the euphoria of a black flame, burning her.

The morning that came seemed all the brighter, and she felt an extraordinary lightness, like a feather, as she rang her husband, told him she was coming home, and added that she would like him not to ask any questions. There were so many things that he didn't know, and there was nothing she desired less than to jolt him out of his comfortable world, a single hint and he would be pressing and pressing her for answers, while she could perhaps persuade herself that nothing had happened at all, as long as she could keep him at a distance from everything. When he nevertheless enquired in tones of concern whether she needed anything, she shook her head as if he could see her and wondered why he was starting again.

"Is it something to do with your father?"

It was a well-ordered world where people asked such questions, and perhaps even answered them, and she knew instinctively that she would have to take new root in it before she could even start thinking about what had happened. She had gone to the window, and as she looked down at the street she felt the slightest move-ment there to be beneficial. In the last few days she hadn't paid attention to whether there had been any more air-raid warnings, she had been concentrating so much on herself, but the pedestri-ans who were walking past underneath her behaved as though there were nothing to fear, and it overwhelmed her. The tram approached, stopped, and went on in the direction of the station as if it had always been like that and always would be like that, and even the uniformed men she saw seemed to be there only to complete the tranquil picture of a garrison town from another century. Perhaps everything really was alright, perhaps it was pure make-believe that she had felt threatened, and she wouldn't have been surprised to see a propeller-driven plane with a clattering engine trailing a banner across the sky proclaiming that the war had been ended overnight.

She was unaware that she had begun describing the scene to her husband, and only realised when he wanted to know why she was telling him. Although she wished he could understand how much it all mattered to her, she knew it was asking too much. He reacted as he had to react, and it was a mistake for her to take it personally.

"Aren't you looking forward to seeing me?"

The answer was a barely audible grunt, and she regretted asking him, taking care from then on only to reach safety from both herself and her sudden fit of loquacity.

"I'll find out when the trains leave," she said, like a woman returning from an entirely normal journey. "If nothing unexpected happens, I'll be home by this evening."

The things that were still on her conscience were quickly dealt with. She called the doctor at his practice in Bauerova Street to tell him she wouldn't be coming anymore, and got a lump in her throat when he called her "daughter". Then she took the tram out to the apartment near Maksimir Park to give the key back to the neighbours. She didn't really want to go in, but in the end she unlocked the front door and walked through the rooms, and when she stood in the bedroom looking at the scrupulously tidy bed she couldn't imagine that she'd ever lain there with Angelo and listened to the staccato sound of the helicopters that had only flown in her imagination. It was quiet now, no sounds inside the building, and outside not even the voices of children playing in the street that had always made a natural backdrop, and she had to fight off the wish just to lie down and go to sleep. She found a thin, broken gold chain with a cross on it lying on one of the headrests, and she couldn't see how it had come to be there, but she pocketed it before she left and her fingers felt for it whenever she felt uneasy in the hours that followed, and she calmed down as soon as she had its metal slowly warming up in her hand.

Her train left in the afternoon, and when she arrived that evening her husband made no fuss. Although it was exactly what she wanted, not having to talk, she was astonished how easily she could put him off and make him give her time, how little he appeared to be concerned about any of it as soon as she was back under the same roof and had chased her crazy ideas away. In her absence he had acquired a wine fridge and traded in his old Mercedes for the newest model, and she was glad of the distractions of these new purchases, enjoyed hearing him talk about his fine wines and happily acquiesced to his suggestion that they go for a drive that same evening, during which he explained the new car's virtues to her and which he rounded off by telling her over a candlelit dinner at a restaurant at Klosterneuburg how much he still loved her. Back at home he knocked on her bedroom door and she allowed him to come into her bed, only mentally objecting to the word he used when he told her he just wanted to cuddle, otherwise wholly content that he had no desire to prove anything, and wound her arms around his chest from behind and pressed her face into his neck, calling him in a pretend childish voice her big strong man, the way she had so often done a hundred years before.

Apart from his having a possibly more circumspect, more restrained attitude towards her, everything seemed the same as it always had been, and she couldn't quite get over how little had changed and how much trouble he was taking to maintain at least a semblance of normality. He personally, for example, took her to a meeting with her girlfriends at the Hotel Regina, who seemed to have had been well briefed by him and all spoke to her as though she had suffered a severe loss of which she mustn't be reminded. He had also made sure she hadn't lost her job at the university and told her proudly that, thanks to his intervention with the rector, she could probably keep her Serbo-Croat course going indefinitely, even if the last crazies theoretically able to converse in the language had smashed each other's skulls to pieces and nobody else had been interested in it for years. His emphatic over-excitement puzzled her, giving her the feeling that he thought he was talking to a sick person, and when he then suggested that maybe they should just forget the last year, go to Elba again in December and celebrate her fiftieth birthday all over again as though nothing had happened, she didn't protest but silently wondered whether he mightn't be better off worrying about himself.

But she also knew that this was his usual pragmatism, to reduce everything to feasible proportions, a pragmatism that for instance provided him with a convenient linguistic convention for her months of absence, for he began referring to it as her Yugoslavian jaunt, and if it had made him feel insecure at the beginning, he now claimed full rights to interpret it, because he had finally got round to writing something about the unrest in the Balkans, as he called it. The essay in question was entitled "Babylonian Exile", which incredibly carried the standfirst "The Return of Fascism to Croatia", but even though he thrust a copy of the week-old newspaper in which it had appeared into her hand and stood next to her and waited for her to read it, she didn't. It was enough for her to skim the subheadings, "A diaspora scattered worldwide", "Revanchists gather for the last struggle", "Former officers and common soldiers from WWII", "A battlefield defeat they have never got over", and she was suddenly overcome by the same weariness that had been perhaps her most constant feeling over the years, her most constant mindset towards him. With the best will in the world she could not imagine that he had the faintest idea about what he was holding forth on so cleverly, yet despite feeling hardly able to restrain her impulse to tell him so, in no uncertain terms, her response was conciliatory.

"What does your alter ego have to say about it?"

She couldn't tell from the way he looked at her whether he hadn't understood or just didn't want to understand her, so when he said nothing, she tried again.

"What about the other side?"

She only had to think about his double-entry bookkeeping, and the Balkan clarifications of which he seemed so proud lost all meaning.

"This can't be all you have to offer on the subject," she heard herself say, although she had no desire to have an argument with him. "Don't you maybe have something else I could read?"

For a moment she had no idea why the memory suddenly surfaced of him handing out flyers at her mother's funeral. It stood right at the top of the list of the things she wished she could have made unhappen, and she was still ashamed of herself for falling for his justification of what a unique opportunity it was, to agitate in front of the mourners, and that strictly speaking anyway she had been the one who supplied him with the battle cry "Death to Fascism, Freedom for the People", with which he had then interrupted the priest standing at the graveside. They hadn't known each other for more than a few months and she had probably been blinded by love, but her mother had never deserved such a farewell, and when she thought back now she could have kissed the hands of the two pallbearers who intervened, telling him he'd better make himself scarce or they would knock his block off, before each taking an arm and frogmarching him out of the cemetery.

As he saw it, of course, that had just been further proof of the necessity for action, and where such dialectic was involved he remained on excellent form years later, as she couldn't help conceding. In any case, there was no sign of the contrition with which he might have reacted to her question. Instead he had a touch of the same inquisitor about him that he had had when he had conducted his revolutionary exorcism on her and treated every one of her utterances as suspect, so long as the business with her father had not been cleared up. But because he now no longer held any terrors for her, he reminded her at the same time of a child who had never really grown up, rediscovering his favourite toy in the attic, putting new batteries in it and, after a moment's anxiety that it might refuse to work, watching with shining eyes as it went round and round in circles with the same clattering and howling as in its heyday.

He told her, as he always had done, that her taunts were only because she resented him, but the truth was, she no longer cared. He could write for as many papers as he liked, and it would only be a problem if she had to take it seriously. She still had irony at her disposal, as he reminded her when she visited him one day at the editorial offices and saw standing on his desk the photograph she wouldn't have at home because she found it so dreadful. It showed him sitting in a huge American gas-guzzler, a drophead with imposing tail-fins, a '56 Dodge as he had cheerfully explained, outside the Hotel Inglaterra in Havana where he had been invited to an international writers' congress to mark the twenty-fifth anniversary of the Cuban revolution. When he saw her glancing at it, he waved it aside.

"Just a joke."

The staging of the scene was as absurd as the car, but she had said before, without humour, that considering the situation in the country it would have served him right if he had really gone cruising around the city in it and a Cuban had brained him with a baseball bat when he stopped at a junction, and she wasn't about to discuss it again now.

"You look good there," was all she said, feeling immediately weary again. "Do you still remember what kind of car it was?"

It must surely be her fault if such irritants existed, surely her view of him that made her react truculently when he told her a few days later that their daughter would soon be coming home. She said she was glad, and when he immediately answered that there was another secret too, a delightful secret, she already had a presentiment. With great solemnity he announced that Lorena would be bringing a girlfriend with her, and his meaningful wink as he said it told her exactly what he meant, at which she felt her old aversion reviving as she sensed that, as usual, he saw the news primarily in relation to himself. Another woman, after all, would not just mean that he was the only man in the house, but he would have another mascot too, another decorative accessory such as she herself had been with her Yugoslavian origins at the beginning of their relationship, making him now not merely a textbook literary intellectual but one of much greater calibre, a true cosmopolitan with a lesbian daughter, and so probably worth his own T.V. series at least.

"Wonderful," she said. "Wonderful."

Suddenly she had the devil in her.

"Is she Jewish?"

He was incapable of understanding why she said it, and she found herself hastily explaining that a Jewish lesbian girlfriend would be even better for Lorena, though this was naturally no less liable to be misunderstood and made her sorry she had even started on the subject as he observed her with mild curiosity. She braced herself for a long discussion, but either he hadn't noticed her sarcasm or he had decided not to react.

"I didn't enquire," he said, as though she had asked him a normal everyday question. "I don't see why it should be important."

It saddened her to find herself throwing down the gauntlet like this. She was doing him an injustice, and although the explanation the doctor in the Eighth District had given her long ago was probably correct, his almost too logical assertion that in her aggression towards her husband she was actually defending her father, she knew there was something else there. She told her girlfriends that she hated the way she was always most suspicious of him when he seemed to be doing everything right, yet that was how it was, and her hostility was also greatest then, and with it her crazy longing for her own Yugoslavia, as she casually called it, which was quite obviously doing everything wrong. Sometimes she felt like dropping everything, packing her bags and going straight back to Zagreb, and then it was only because she was afraid of looking ridiculous in front of him that she didn't, plus her weariness that often made the smallest decisions seem too much for her.

It was in one of these moods that she once mentioned the pamphlet he had given her after their first night together, but the mere way he repeated its title, sharply and derisively, "The Partisan Disease as Opportunity", and dismissed the whole thing as a youthful error silenced her again. The hysterical fits he had described in it, trance-like states in which those afflicted rushed spontaneously at an imaginary adversary and rolled on the ground, lashing out wildly, had been his favourite metaphor for the regularly invoked armed conflict, although when she read it she had only remembered how he himself had jumped on her in his little room. For there really had been something of the shock trooper about him, wrestling her to the floor with his bare hands, only for lack of a weapon, a pistol or a knife, and then at the end clinging to her neck like a drowning man and yelling as if summoning scattered comrades to his aid. It would be an exaggeration to say that she yearned for that all over again, but it did help her to tolerate the worthy citizen he had turned into, it reconciled her to him and to his respectability to think about it or about one of his other escapades at the time, ending up more often than not with the night when out of sheer devilment he had run the length of a long row of parked cars and the drumming of his feet on their metal roof panels had left her in such euphoria that it had taken her heart a long time to slow down and subside into its usual rhythm.

She had been back in Vienna for more than two weeks when she first spoke to him about her father and didn't, this time, stonewall his attempts to comment. Autumn was well advanced, the first snow had fallen and immediately melted again, and in the darkening evenings and continuous drizzle the city had the melancholy look of a future that was already past, as she said to him, a remark that earned her a displeased look. It was three days before their daughter was due back, he had asked her out to dinner and coaxed her into his choice of restaurant, and so they sat like a middle-aged couple among other middle-aged couples in a gourmet establishment and she let the evening follow his direction entirely and did not even resist when, during the dessert, he began, as if by chance, to talk about the war.

Not once allowing herself to think about Angelo's fate, she had just discovered the terrible circumstances in which Vukovar had fallen, and from that moment on had stopped following the news from Yugoslavia, which was now entirely her husband's domain. He lectured, as was his wont, she hardly listened, and after going through all the horror stories he had to hand he had fully reached the clichés-and-homilies stage, while she was doing her best to forgive him the two bottles of wine he had comfortably drunk and the pearls of conventional wisdom that had followed, culminating in his observation that they could be glad they'd never had a son and the predictable truism, "Sons die in war."

It was, as a remark, not much more intelligent than the chatter of Marija's neighbour at the next table. She had been eavesdropping on her for some time, a woman of about her own age, a boss-type and secretary-type in one, who had ordered oysters and champagne and was just saying rapturously that she could never, never get tired of bubbly and slithery shellfish, and the words shocked Marija so much that she looked across at her without concealment. Yet it wasn't just the purposely vulgar tone of the woman's voice that bemused Marija, nor its blatantly sexual note and message of insatiable appetite, but the unexpectedly soft and girlish look on her plump face that also gave her her answer.

"Daughters have to survive after a war," she said, without turning back or paying attention to whether or not she could be heard by the woman. "Maybe sometimes it's not necessarily easier for them."

It sounded bitterer than she felt, and she saw that her husband was listening. She had said what she said without thinking that he might connect it to her, but the way he suddenly took her hand left her in no doubt. He sought her gaze, and said that probably she could only come to that conclusion because she was her father's daughter. He waited, and when she offered no resistance, he pressed on.

"Be glad you never met him," he said. "You wouldn't even have wanted to read it in a novel."

He had never bothered before about whether reality obeyed some sort of poetic justice or not, but now he found it difficult to stop rhapsodising about his half-formed thought.

"We should all live in such a way that we can tell the stories of our lives afterwards, and I have my doubts about whether you could do so in those circumstances with a clear conscience."

He had already reached that happily drunk stage that mingled harsh clarity with lachrymose sentimentality and kept inspiring him to new truisms, which she only parried half-heartedly.

"Live in such a way that we can tell the story afterwards?"

Her attention was still half on the woman at the next table, who had just said to the man with her that no-one could imagine how twenty years could be wasted so easily. Dabbing the corners of her mouth with her napkin, she now looked across at Marija in a way that made her turn her face away in order not to see the ravages that such a remark might lay bare in the woman's eyes. Her gaze averted, she waited until she heard the woman go on speaking, but still lowered her voice to a whisper.

"That might sound good, but it's not right."

It was only too obvious.

"We can tell any story we want," she said after hesitating for a moment, and did not understand why it filled her with such longing. "Living is something else."

She was annoyed to have got caught up in such idle talk, yet glad too that her husband seemed satisfied with her response, and she didn't instantly fall into her old feeling of being torn in two directions when she thought about her father. Since she had come back to Vienna she had forbidden herself to think about him at all, or had thought about him in a way that seemed to let her decide how much reality seemed right to her. He was alive, if she decided he was, and if she decided differently, then her Zagreb adventure, as she called it, was a small irritation on which she didn't have to expend any more thought, and he had died fifty-four years ago. At least, that was what she believed that evening as she set off for home with her husband, and though she refused to let herself get caught up in any more of his sophistry, she was all the more surprised the following day when the news of her father's death arrived.

The letter came from the man who had followed her in Zagreb, and he began by apologising for not having been in touch again after their meeting on the street, for being late in doing so now, and unfortunately only in connection with what he had to tell her. Then he wrote about the circumstances in which her father had died, and she read the lines about the girl who had apparently shot him, still in her mood of the previous day as though it were entirely up to her whether or not to believe it. She stood there, holding the two sheets of paper covered in faintly childish handwriting, and felt liberated, until it dawned on her that this was not just one of those stories of her husband's in which everything was transformed, and it would call for greater effort if she wanted to be completely free of it at last, greater effort in any case than the small gesture of closing a book that was at an end, and then thinking no more about it.

NORBERT GSTREIN was born in 1961 in the Austrian Tyrol, and studied mathematics at Innsbruck and Stanford, California. He now lives in Hamburg and is the author of *The English Years* (2002), which won widespread critical acclaim both in its German edition and internationally. He has been awarded the coveted Alfred Döblin Prize and the Uwe Johnson Prize.

ANTHEA BELL has won the Schlegel-Tieck Prize for German translation four times, and is translator from French and German of many distinguished authors, W.G. Sebald and Stefan Zweig among them. She was awarded an O.B.E. in 2010 for her services to literature.

JULIAN EVANS wrote and presented the BBC Radio 3 series on the European novel, *The Romantic Road*, and has won the Prix du Rayonnement de la Langue Française. His most recent book is *Semi-Invisible Man: the life of Norman Lewis*.